THE HESPERIDES TREE

Nicholas Mosley was born in 1923. He is the author of fourteen novels, including the Whitbread Book of the Year *Hopeful Monsters*, and, most recently, *Children of Darkness and Light*. He lives in London.

ALSO BY NICHOLAS MOSLEY

Fiction

Spaces of the Dark
The Rainbearers
Corruption
Meeting Place
Accident
Assassins
Impossible Object
Natalie Natalia
Catastrophe Practice
Imago Bird
Serpent
Judith
Hopeful Monsters
Children of Darkness and Light

Non-Fiction

African Switchback
The Life of Raymond Raynes
Experience and Religion
The Assassination of Trotsky
Julian Grenfell
Rules of the Game
Beyond the Pale
Efforts at Truth

Nicholas Mosley

THE
HESPERIDES
TREE

Published by Vintage 2002

2 4 6 8 10 9 7 5 3 1

Copyright © Nicholas Mosley 2001

Nicholas Mosley has asserted his right under the
Copyright, Designs and Patents Act, 1988 to be
identified as the author of this work

First published in Great Britain in 2001 by
Secker & Warburg

Vintage
The Random House Group Limited
20 Vauxhall Bridge Road, London SW1V 2SA

Random House Australia (Pty) Limited
20 Alfred Street, Milsons Point, Sydney,
New South Wales 2061, Australia

Random House New Zealand Limited
18 Poland Road, Glenfield,
Auckland 10, New Zealand

Random House (Pty) Limited
Endulini, 5a Jubilee Road, Parktown 2193, South Africa

The Random House Group Limited Reg. No. 954009

www.randomhouse.co.uk

ISBN 0 09 928587 8

A CIP catalogue record for this book
is available from the British Library

Papers used by Random House are natural,
recyclable products made from wood grown in sustain-
able forests. The manufacturing processes conform to the
environmental regulations of the country of origin.

Printed and bound in Denmark by
Nørhaven Paperback A/S, Viborg

To Marius and Verity

In Greek mythology the Hesperides were guardians of the Tree of Life with its golden apples that grew beyond the river-ocean at the extreme western limits of the world. They were part human and part god, and sometimes had the appearance of clouds gilded by the setting sun.

I

When I was a child I used to think that I could learn from my parents; even that this was what they were there for. My father used to talk; I liked to hear him talk; my mother seemed half to listen and half to be ready to tease him or divert him if he got too carried away by words. I had the idea that this was how families worked.

It was only gradually that I came to realise that other children did not see their parents like this. They were apt to look on their fathers as something of a joke or a threat; and their mothers, though perhaps somewhat sacred, had to be challenged even if guiltily. And when my school friends came to visit me it was evident in spite of their good manners that they saw my parents in this way – my father as an authority figure to be subtly thwarted or evaded, and my mother to be charmed perhaps but as a matter of themselves showing off. Everyone except special friends was likely to be seen as a potential enemy.

One of the things my father liked to talk about was this characteristic of humans who, in order to stay alive, had had to learn to distrust and to fight other creatures, often even those closest to them. But now this sort of programming had become too dangerous (my father would begin to orate) – the attitudes of distrust and aggression which in humans had evolved for their preservation were in this technological age working to their destruction. But how could what had become programmed, built-in, decide to change itself? Did it not have to wait for something outside to change it?

My mother would say 'But you don't believe that. You believe that if we recognise the situation then the programming can change.'

'Yes I do believe that.'

'Then why don't you say it?'

'Perhaps if we get smug then things don't change.'

When I went to school I found myself involved in the usual hostilities and alliances; but by that time I had learned that there was something odd about me – at birth there had been something fragile about my skull and this had never quite corrected itself. As a consequence I was kept from playing some games and was warned to keep out of trouble. I had sometimes been taunted about this, but once I had fought back with such ferocity that it had seemed I might die and my tormentors had become alarmed. After this I was for the most part left alone and could get on with my own devices.

I did not mind my solitariness: I was able to read a lot, and wanted to find out how things worked. I had got hold of the idea (I suppose picked up from my father) that things evolved when some individuals stood out from the crowd; and thus I could imagine some virtue in my vulnerability, while the likelihood that I would die young was a counterweight to being smug.

My father was a maker of documentary films for television. He specialised in scientific subjects which should be of more than academic interest. A year or two before the time about which I will be writing he had made a series of programmes about the science of the first half of the twentieth century; these had brought him a certain acclaim and he was now being encouraged to do a similar series on the second half of the century that was coming towards its end. But he maintained that this was much more difficult to do, because although the science of the first half had been intellectually puzzling – what with quantum physics, conundrums about genes, and so on – it had been strikingly dramatic, with the splitting of the atom leading to the release of nuclear energy and in biology the lead-up to discoveries about DNA. The science of the second half however was largely taken up with trying to know how to handle or even to understand what had been uncovered in the first – there seeming to be some incapacity in the mind concerning this. Physicists for instance had coined the phrase – Anyone who thinks he understands quantum physics doesn't understand it. And with regard to genes – well, were humans helplessly in thrall to them or were they not?

I had said to my father 'But can't you make a series of programmes about that?'

'About going along in the dark?'

'Couldn't that be exciting?'

My father had recently bought a motor caravan in which to go on reconnaissance trips for his work. I had been on one of these journeys with him and there had then been opportunities to talk – we had floated off into speculation without being brought down to earth by my mother. We had ruminated on what life was all about; whether it had any meaning. But after a time it seemed that such words became too cloudy even for us; and my father would break off and say – 'But the important things anyway can't really be said. Words can take you so far then you have to go on a journey.'

I said 'But aren't these exciting discoveries being made in biology now? That's what the master says at school.'

'Yes but for every puzzle solved there's always another.'

'What about the mutants without which there wouldn't be any evolution – that are usually, but not always, snuffed out.'

'Well yes, but if they're not, that depends on extraordinary coincidences.'

I wondered if my father thought I might be talking about myself.

I used to spend my holidays with my parents, but then when I was seventeen and working for my A-level exams my parents went off in the caravan on their own on a tour of restaurants in Europe, of which I was both scornful and jealous. But I thought – All right, I'll be going off on journeys on my own.

Then in the summer of 1998 when I had taken my exams and was due to go to a university in the autumn there was talk of going in the caravan to the west coast of Ireland. My mother had inherited a cottage there; her family had originally come from Ireland but the family house had been burned down at the time of the troubles in the twenties; this cottage however with a small patch of land remained, and my mother had to decide what to do with it.

Also my father planned to visit a wildlife station in the vicinity. There was a bird sanctuary on a rocky island just off the coast where it had been noted that the habits and physical features of certain varieties of birds had been changing with unusual rapidity. My father's interest in making a film about this was rekindled. He explained –

'Well yes, new varieties do seem to be developing perhaps due to pollution in the sea or in the fish they eat or to changes in the climate – or whatever – I mean varieties which seem able to deal with the new conditions. The changes in the birds are not very striking, but statistically they do seem relevant to one of the puzzles about evolution. I mean how small changes

4

in the environment can lead quite quickly to new varieties of organism or even conceivably eventually a new species. This goes against the orthodox Darwinian view that genetic mutation results in adaptation only slowly.'

I said 'So these birds learn to survive.'

'Well in a sense, but it's not exactly learning, the idea is that stress caused by a changing environment speeds up the occurrence of random mutations so that amongst such birds there are quite naturally likely to be one or two fitted to dealing with the changing environment. And so these instead of being wiped out would flourish and proliferate. And so it might seem that organisms might not only adapt to circumstances but pass on their adaptability, but it's more a matter just of who lives and who dies.'

I said 'And that's what's happening on this island?'

'If I make a film it'll probably end up being about a lot of academics quarrelling with one another.'

My mother said 'Your father will love that.'

My father said 'What.'

'What you really want to make a film about is the way people love bashing one another about.'

'Well, yes, and how they might change.'

My mother said 'What your father can't understand is how the benighted Irish, who seem to live permanently under conditions of stress, never seem to produce any variation at all.'

My father said 'I've got the explanation for that.'

'I'm sure you have.'

'Bashing one another about is to the Irish a perfectly normal condition. So it's not stress.'

'You see?'

'But I mean, how miraculously have they adapted to stress!' He put an arm round my mother.

When my father and mother went on like this it seemed that they knew what they were doing. My mother was by profession a psychotherapist: she believed I suppose that all relationships contained stress, but these could be guided to work themselves out.

I said 'Do you think it's all right for people to blow each other up?'

My father said 'No, but people may only learn by things getting worse before they get better.'

When my parents had been planning the trip to Ireland there had been some talk about my perhaps not going with them. I had been wondering about this myself; but as soon as it was put into words I felt disconcerted – so in this I was no different from everyone else? But we had not travelled as a family in the caravan before, and it might just be too crowded, and were they not offering me my chance of freedom? But it would be a sad moment for us as a family when I took off on my own. It seemed we were getting into one of the predicaments that my father talked about in which for quite good reasons people were pulled in two ways at once. He said 'But do you or don't you want to come?' I said 'I don't know.' My mother said 'Of course he wants to come.'

My father said 'I thought we might be giving you a chance to get away.'

My mother said 'Well we've done that.'

I said 'Yes thank you, I'd like to come.'

The motor caravan was high and wide but not all that spacious inside. It had two narrow double bunks – one on a platform crossways above the front seats, and the other made up from the settee-type seats at the back. I said that I would not mind sleeping on the floor if my mother and father each wanted a bed to themselves – when they were both working late at home they sometimes slept in different rooms. But here again we seemed to be approaching a ludicrous situation in which I, by thinking I was being considerate, seemed to be suggesting that my parents could not bear sleeping together,

6

or that I could not bear the thought of this. I had read somewhere that children were supposed to be horrified at the idea of their parents making love. This had seemed to me ludicrous, but how could I explain?

My father said 'No you must have the top bunk. And perhaps something miraculous will come from the stress of your mother and I being squashed together at the back.'

My mother said 'Actually we rather like being in a small bed.'

So we set off across England and Wales and my father was once more in a situation in which he could orate. (My mother said – 'I thought you were going to get the radio mended.' My father said – 'I've lost the code that gets it started. Ah, couldn't I have lost my own code!') So with my father driving and my mother sitting beside him and myself reclining in the back, he said as if over his shoulder –

'How much do you know about Ireland? I mean the history, the politics, the oppression, the famines, the violence. All this for centuries blamed on the ghastly English invaders but then when the English wanted to get out and there might at last have been peace then it was as if the Irish had got so used to outrage that they had to carry it on between themselves; and indeed Catholics and Protestants could just as easily blow each other up.'

I said 'I thought something had been settled this Easter.'

My father said 'There are signs that that won't last.'

My mother said 'You really think people don't want to change?'

'Not unless there's something more exciting.'

'There's getting rich. That's a change.'

'Yes, that could be a stage.'

We spent the first night somewhere off the road in Wales. I lay in the top bunk screened by a curtain, and I could hear my father and mother giggling in the back. I thought – Well, they must know that I'm in no way horrified at the idea of their making love. Might not a cosmic ray have come down at the time of my conception – to give me my vulnerable skull, my mark of being a possible mutation? At least I have no interest in bashing people about.

The next day we crossed the sea and trundled through the central Irish plain. There were peat bogs on either side: I wondered how anything so soft and damp could burn. My father seemed to want to counteract the impression he had given about the Irish the previous day, because he talked now about the paradox of the Irish being so humorous, so imaginative, so creative – about their legends, their poetry; about how before the coming of the English Ireland had been a country not only of warriors but of scholars and holy men and shrines.

'This island for instance where nowadays seabirds breed was for centuries a home for hermits and monks; they came to find refuge from the butchery of the Dark Ages, in which every activity seemed to be a provocation for hatred and revenge. The monks wanted to break out of this, to break the cycle, and perhaps they did for themselves. They fasted and prayed, practised terrible austerities, copied and illustrated amazingly beautiful manuscripts. They adapted to paradoxes but they didn't transform society.'

My mother said 'In the end they did.'

'What survived was the Church.'

I said 'And that didn't work?'

'It got hooked on power.'

My mother said 'The other thing works secretly.'

I said 'What is the other thing?'

My father said 'Well, holiness. But that's what you can't quite say.'

I thought – You mean, it's like cosmic rays whizzing about?

My mother said 'It's not God's job to make things easy.'

I said 'What is God's job?'

My father said 'To make things possible.'

When we got to the fishing village somewhere in the vicinity of which was the cottage that now belonged to my mother we could not at first find it, and we were at the end of a long day. My mother said she was sorry, but she had been there for only one holiday as a child: my father said 'No one's blaming you.' We enquired at a farm and a woman directed us up a track and there was a white-painted cottage with a tiled roof and my mother said she remembered it as being made of crumbling stone and thatch. We turned back to the farm and the woman seemed to have become hostile: she said she had told us correctly and retreated into the house. My father said 'Perhaps they burned the old cottage down to get the insurance.' My mother said 'I don't think I can stand your jokes.' We went back to the cottage and stared at it and my mother said 'Well if this is it I don't want it.' My father said 'Didn't you notice all the nice new cottages along the coast? I expect people are making fortunes smuggling explosives.' My mother got out of the caravan and went through a small garden to the door of the cottage and found the key which had been left by the local agent under a stone; this fitted and she went in. My father followed. I stayed in the caravan: I thought – Perhaps I won't find it so difficult after all in this place to get away from my parents; this is a place where there have been those monks, those birds.

After a while I thought that I would get out of the caravan and walk towards the sea. I tried to imagine the holy men who had come here to live on rocks like birds; they had hoped, imagined themselves to be mutations? But they had not wanted to alter the world? They had dreamed of another world?

The track along which we had come ended at the cottage,

but there was a footpath going on directly into the setting sun so it seemed this must be the direction to the sea. But the sun was in my eyes so that I could hardly see: I thought – Well this is what we have been talking about, isn't it? The journey to where one wants to go without exactly knowing where one is going; moving in darkness towards the light and the sea.

By shielding my eyes I could see that I was coming to the edge of a cliff; the path led to where there seemed to be steps going down. The steps were narrow and cut into the cliff face; there was no railing. The steps led, so far as I could see, to a narrow beach of shingle and a promontory of black rock; to the right of this there was the long curve of a bay where waves came in ceaselessly; on the left beyond the shingle there was what looked like a narrow concrete landing stage. In the setting sun the dark sea gleamed; the rocks appeared suffused with blood; the whole scene was like a mythical scene in a painting.

Just off the landing stage there was a small boat and the figure of a man or boy leaning over the side with his hands in the water. This might be the miraculous draft of fishes: the dipping of whoever-it-was by his heel into the sea? Myths seem to have meaning without having to say what the meaning might be. Or might it be that the boat was simply that of a smuggler or gun-runner such as my father had hinted at – his arms in the water to drag up a sunken cache of weapons, or even to hold down the head of an enemy condemned to be drowned. My father had said this was a favourite part of the coast for terrorists to land weapons: in which case shouldn't I turn back? But if one was on some mythical journey, should one turn back? And the man or boy was more likely to be a fisherman. I had begun to grope my way down the steps with the sun against my eyes like varnish on a painting; the man or boy was struggling with something in the water; someone not yet quite drowned? some great fish being dragged to the land? As I went on down the crumbling steps I could see that the figure in the boat was manoeuvring it in towards the landing stage with one hand while with the other he hung on to whatever it was in the water. This seemed to be alive because it reared up suddenly as if with the arm or neck of some strange monster; it did not seem to be a fish because it was too splayed out and craggy: perhaps indeed it was a mutant: but then – a bird? It was a wing rather than an arm that was waving up out of the water. I had arrived at the bottom of the steps; I had to set off – unless I turned back now – across the shingle to the landing stage. An explanation of the scene if not the meaning seemed to become clear: the boy – for the figure in the boat was that of a boy, perhaps even one of much the same age as myself – the boy was trying to rescue a bird that had become trapped or injured in the water; probably it had become contaminated by oil; that was why the sea had seemed to glisten like a painting. And so of course I was right to come and help the boy. I crossed the shingle. The boy had now got the boat up to the landing stage and was holding it there while at the same time trying to lift out of the water the large bird by its seemingly infinitely extensible wing; but he could not do this without using two hands, which would unbalance the boat and might upset it. However if I knelt on the landing stage and put my arms in the water under the bird we might together lift it, the boy and I, on to the landing stage or into the boat or whatever. This I found myself doing. The bird was like something taboo to the touch; clasping it was like getting a hold on its tendons, guts, lungs; we struggled with it, the boy and I, dabbling our hands in the oily water that was like blood. We did not speak; it was as if for what we were doing it was not necessary to speak. We got the bird up on to the landing stage; it was the size of a large goose or swan, but I did not think it was a goose or swan, it had too short a neck and a curved beak; its colouring was obscured by the oil. It looked at us, the boy and I, with a dark bright eye. Then I saw that as well as any contamination by oil there was entwined round its feet a mess of wires and plastic that might have been part of a fisherman's tackle or net; the bird would not have been able to take off and fly or even probably to swim; before long it would have drowned. The boy began to pull at the wires but they were too tight, they were cutting into the bird's legs. Also the light was now fading so that we could not see what we were doing. I thought – You must take the bird home and disentangle it carefully: it would be easier for you to do this than me. Then I heard my mother calling from the top of the cliff.

I helped the boy to get the bird from the landing stage into the boat. He smiled at me as if to thank me but he seemed to be hurrying to get away, as if he felt that it was important for him not to be seen by anyone but me. He pushed off with an oar and used it like a paddle to go silently out to sea. He went into a mist that was now rising from the water; the sky above it was like the roof of a cavern. I did not want to call out to my mother to tell her that I was all right because I thought that any sound might shatter the odd fragility of this scene. The boat disappeared in the mist. Then there was the sound of an outboard motor starting up. I had not noticed the outboard motor; perhaps now the mythical spell of the scene could be broken. And what indeed had been mythical about it, except that there was still the feel in my nerves, my mind, of the odd roughness combined with softness that had seemed taboo – of the bird's feathers and bones that had been so uncanny in my hands. And the boy, what had it been about the boy, that he was like myself in some other existence? I had crossed the shingle and begun to climb up the steps. I thought I should not tell my mother of what had happened – how could I describe it? You would have to experience such a scene for it to have meaning. The boy and I had not spoken. I thought I should tell my mother that I had just gone to look at the sea.

My mother and father and I spent that night in the caravan. My mother had found traces of rats in the cottage, and we did not anyway want to move after dark into a strange environment. In the morning we set about cleaning and sorting out the cottage: there was little furniture except a rusty bed and some hard chairs in the front room. We swept the floors and threw out rubbish. There was an ancient kitchen range in the front room in which we lit a fire. I thought – I would like to come and live here one day, like those holy hermits.

But I felt awkward about not having said anything to my parents about my adventure of the night before – my father had come here after all to find out about strange birds, and the story might be useful to him. So when we were sitting out in the sun in the small front garden taking a break from cleaning I said 'You know, when I went down to the beach last night, there was a boy in a boat and he was rescuing a bird which seemed to have got its feet caught in some wire, or fishing tackle, or an oil slick, or whatever.' But the words did not come out quite right, and it sounded as if I were either not telling them everything or making up some story.

My father said 'What sort of bird?'

'Well it looked like a goose or a swan, but I don't think it could have been, because it had a curved beak and not a long neck. I couldn't see much of its feathers because of the oil.'

My mother said 'I didn't see any oil.'

'I thought it might be an albatross.'

My father said 'An albatross!'

'But I suppose there aren't any albatrosses here.'

'No.' Then – 'I'll ask about it at the wildlife station.'

13

My mother said 'I expect it was one of your smugglers salvaging a stash of guns.'

When we had been cleaning out the scullery at the back of the cottage there had been some straw and cigarette ends in a corner, so that it looked as if someone might have been sleeping there – some tramp, or someone in hiding. I had noticed this and I think my father had noticed it, but we neither of us said anything to my mother: I supposed we did not want to make her anxious. I thought – But it's the grown-ups who insist on mythical worlds of guns and smugglers.

My mother wanted to throw out the old bed and take it to a rubbish dump, but I said 'Oh do keep it, someone might want to stay here one day.'

'Who might want to stay here?'

'I might.'

'You? Of course you can't!'

'Why not. Do you think it would be dangerous?'

In the afternoon my father set off to visit the wildlife station and he dropped off my mother and me in the local fishing village to do some shopping. We said we would either walk back the two or three miles to the cottage, or hire some bicycles. My mother seemed to think there were always bicycles for hire in Ireland.

The village consisted of a row of neat painted houses facing the small harbour with a few paths straggling up towards the hills at the back. The road ran between the houses and the quayside. My mother and I went and sat on the rocks at the back of the pier or breakwater that protected the harbour. There were boats moored along the pier and at the quayside in front of the houses; the sun was bright and the scene was like that of a stage set. I was looking out for my friend of the night before. For the first time, so far as I could remember, I felt somewhat irritated about being with my mother.

She said 'I suppose you'll be going away from us soon.'

I said 'Oh I don't suppose I'll get far.'

'I sometimes worry that you're with us too much: I mean with Dad and me. You used to have friends at school. What's happened to them?'

'They're all right.'

'I suppose we've been a bit protective of you because of your illness. But perhaps you should get out more now. Perhaps one day you could come here without us.'

I thought – Why, what would you be doing if I was here?

A group of girls, schoolgirls, had appeared from round a corner at the far end of the quayside. They looked along the road cautiously, or half as if they were play-acting; then they disappeared back round the corner suddenly like a shoal of fishes.

My mother said 'You know, when I was pregnant with you, I – we – were nearly blown up by a bomb. I haven't told you this before. I'd gone for a walk in the park, and a bomb went off by a bandstand. I wasn't much hurt, but I worried about you, I always wondered if it might have affected you. Affected what you were born with, I mean. Your poor skull. I felt guilty.'

'Why did you feel guilty?'

'I thought I shouldn't have exposed you. Then there was the idea, that if you had been damaged, I might have had a termination.'

I thought – What an odd word. I said 'You thought of getting rid of me.'

'No. Never really.'

'But you were told it might be sensible.'

One of the girls who had appeared for a moment from round the corner had been very pretty. She had seemed to be the leader of the group. She had short fair hair and wore jeans and a white T-shirt. I felt that if I were not with my mother, I might go wandering after her.

I said 'I've never minded the stuff about my skull, if that's what you mean.'

'Of course I don't know if the bomb had anything to do with it.'

'It might have been much worse. I might have been normal.'

I hadn't paid much attention to girls before; this had been another thing that in my last years at school had distanced me from my schoolfellows. Now this girl who had poked her head round the corner seemed to have imprinted herself on my mind as if she emanated some cosmic ray, and I were a setting prepared for it.

I said to my mother 'Why haven't you told me this before?'

'I don't know. You were such an odd little boy. I didn't know what effect it would have on you.'

'You thought it might make me even more insufferable.'

'Yes.'

'I might even think myself special.'

The girl who had put her head round the corner now reappeared, coming out into the open and stepping carefully along the quayside. The village otherwise seemed curiously deserted. The girl was moving in an exaggeratedly tiptoeing manner like someone in a ballet. She was followed at some distance by her chorus of schoolgirls crowding together as if for protection. I thought – And somewhere by a bandstand there might be a man with a bow and arrow, or a bomb.

My mother said 'We never talk about your poor skull much.'

'It hasn't stopped me doing what I wanted.'

'Do you still feel that?'

'Yes. I used to think it might enable me to receive messages from outer space.'

'You see what I mean!'

'Did they tell you I might die at any moment?'

'No. But I suppose you might have done.'

'Well I don't mind feeling that.'

The girls had come to the edge of the quayside just across the water from where my mother and I sat on the breakwater. The one who was their leader had stopped and was looking down at a boat. I thought it might be the boat in which the boy had been the night before. Then the girl looked up and across the water straight at me, and it was indeed as if I had been hit by one of those particles of light.

My mother said 'But you see why I'm a bit funny about bombs and Ireland.'

I said 'I wondered if I might come across in the village that boy I was telling you about. The one I met last night on the rocks.'

My mother said 'That girl's very pretty.'

The girl had left the boat and was tiptoeing further along the quayside. Her entourage were now staying behind and were gesticulating to her as if to tell her to stop, to come back. I was trying to remember – Well what does happen in that ballet: a swan flutters about, then is shot? When the girl came to the point where the pier or breakwater joined the quayside there was a hut, a rectangular building of a kind in which fishermen's equipment might be stored; she stood on tiptoe facing it and put her fingers on the sill of a window to look through. She was like something poised, an arrow: but also the bird: I thought – But I am the one who has been shot. The girls who had been clustering on the quayside had turned and fled; it was indeed as if they were frightened. Then the girl by the hut turned and looked at me again briefly and then beyond me out to sea. Then she stepped

17

back and moved quickly beyond and behind the hut like someone going off-stage.

My mother said 'Don't you think she was pretty?'

I said 'Yes I think she was very pretty.'

I thought – Of course these events, performances, mean something; what does it matter if one doesn't know what.

It was getting cold. It was time we were going.

My mother and I found a shop from which we could hire bicycles; we rode them home along a switchback road sometimes pushing them up steep slopes and then freewheeling down with our legs stretched out like children. I thought – Perhaps this is the last time that my mother and I will be together like this; will she have anyone to play with when I have gone? We went down one long hill too fast and it was almost as if she might be wanting to come to grief at the bottom. I thought – But you were quite wanting me, weren't you, to come across some girl like that one in the harbour? Or perhaps not quite so pretty as that.

We were pushing our bicycles along the rutted track to the cottage when we saw that there were three men standing outside the broken-down gate to the small front garden. One was tall, one short, and one medium-sized; they were like characters in some comic cartoon about gangsters. They watched us as we approached but showed no sign of acknowledgment or emotion. I thought – Is this another scene about to become mythical? When we were close to them my mother said 'Hullo, can I help you?'

The medium-sized man who was in the middle spoke to the others in a language or dialect that I did not understand.

My mother said 'I am now the owner of this cottage. Perhaps you knew my grandmother, Mrs Ferguson.'

The medium-sized man who had reddish curly hair said 'Are you moving in then?'

'I'm not sure. We've just come for a visit. We've got a caravan.'

The tall man said 'Where's the caravan then?'

'My husband has gone in it to the wildlife station. He's doing research there. He'll be back shortly.'

The short man said 'Have you been into the house then?'

I thought – Now is the time, if they are people who smuggle guns and explosives, for me to do a great kung-fu leap and lay them all out with my legs and arms like a catherine wheel.

I said 'Why do you want to know?'

My mother put her hand on my arm. I thought – You mean, people who do kung fu simply get shot by people who have guns?

The short man said 'Who's this then?'

My mother said 'My son.'

The curly-haired man put a hand on the short man's arm. His eyes moved to and fro like an arrow on a computer screen. Then he said 'I was just wondering, my dear, how such a young lady as yourself could be having such a grown-up son.'

My mother said 'As I told you, my family comes from around here.'

I thought – So he and my mother are going to charm one another.

The tall man and the short man were waiting to take their cue from the curly-haired man. He laughed, and then the others laughed. My mother began to push her bicycle towards the gate to the cottage garden. The curly-haired man said quickly 'We've come to ask you a favour.'

My mother stopped and said 'Oh what is that?'

'One of our friends has been taking liberties here, you see. He saw the empty house, and I regret he's been taking the advantage of a little free accommodation.'

I thought – They really do talk like that!

My mother said 'I see. We did notice there were some things lying about.'

'What things?'

'Cigarette ends.'

I thought – I didn't think you'd noticed. Then – The man could have been talking about guns.

He said 'You have sharp eyes my dear.'

'Do you want to go in and tidy up then?'

'If you wouldn't mind my dear.'

'While we wait outside?'

'That would be very considerate my dear. We wouldn't like you to be troubled.'

I thought – It's because she's Irish that my mother knows how to deal with this. Or it's because she and the curly-haired man think each other attractive.

The men went up the garden path and into the cottage. My mother and I sat on the bank of the lane opposite the garden gate. I thought – They're looking under the floorboards for the guns, or explosives that they've been smuggling in from the sea: they store them in the cottage. My mother and I did not talk. I thought – But how extraordinary that my mother knows how to handle this!

When the men emerged they did not seem to be carrying anything. But they were wearing long loose coats, so they might have had weapons underneath.

The curly-haired man said 'Thank you my dear. Our friend does not seem to have left anything there after all.'

My mother said 'I'm so glad.'

'It's our pleasure, my dear. And anything we can do for you.'

I thought – And now they go and blow each other up off-stage?

After the three of them had gone off up the track keeping

20

side by side like people in a Western film my mother and I went into the cottage. We looked around at the walls, the floor, but there did not seem to be any signs of loose bricks or floorboards. I thought – We are like people who have stumbled or been charmed into other people's myths.

I said to my mother 'I think you did that brilliantly.'

'I was quite glad your father wasn't here.'

'Why, would he have got angry?'

'It would have been much harder for a man.'

I thought – You mean you do find the curly-haired man attractive?

When my father came back from the wildlife station we told him about the three men and we all went round the cottage again poking about on the floor, and my father seemed amused, as if he were thinking of something else, and he said 'Oh well, perhaps it's all for the best I wasn't here.' My mother said 'Why?' My father said 'Now they'll all be a bit in love with you.' My mother said 'They might have murdered us!'

I thought – My mother doesn't really like my father having been away at the wildlife station.

We eventually found some loose bricks beneath the sink in the scullery and my father did the trick of putting his hand in the opening and then screaming and pretending that it had been seized or bitten by something from the back. My mother said 'I don't think that's funny!' My father said 'You do, but for some reason you don't want to.'

I thought – My father may have found someone he likes at the wildlife station?

– But he and my mother are all right really?

When we were in the caravan and having supper I said 'Did you find out anything at the wildlife station?'

My father said 'Oh yes, it's all very interesting, but still a matter of how you interpret the statistics. On the one hand there are the recorded changes in the environment, and on the other the tiny changes in the birds' anatomy and habits. You feed all these into a computer and the computer comes up with correlations and patterns, but it's you who've set up what the computer is to do, and you still have to see meaning. And the island's not isolated enough for controlled experiments like those islands in the Galapagos. But it does seem, yes, that under environmental stress a species can adapt more quickly that has been supposed.'

I said 'But enormous numbers still have to die.'

'Oh yes.'

My mother said 'I want to get out of Ireland.'

My father said 'But humans have other ways of learning.'

I said 'Such as —'

'Well, if you can see your conditioning, there's no reason why you shouldn't try to get the environment which will let it change.'

'Change the genes? Or change the conditioning?'

'Perhaps change the mental environment as well as the physical. Either way you give different genes a chance to emerge.'

'But what if people don't want to change. If they don't mind things being violent and difficult.'

'Then I suppose, yes, numbers will go on dying.'

My mother said 'Will you listen! I've said I don't want to stay in Ireland!'

'All right we'll move on tomorrow. I can come back to the wildlife people later.'

'I didn't mean that.'

'Then what did you mean?'

'Why do you want to come back to the wildlife people?'

'I'm making a film.'

'I thought you said it wouldn't work.'

I said 'But what if it simply becomes boring? I mean if

22

the liking of things being painful and difficult becomes boring.'

My father said 'Oh yes, there's always a chance of things changing if they simply become boring.'

My mother said 'I can't think of anything more boring than this conversation.'

We seemed to be talking of too many things at once – the Irish, my mother's confused ancestry, the tyranny of genes, the birds; even whatever it was on a personal level that was niggling at my father and my mother – had he some instinct about the man with curly hair? And I was thinking – Supposing one met someone special, like that girl, or like oneself, and mingled one's genes, then might not something extraordinary occur?

I said to my father 'Did you find out about my bird?'

For a moment he did not seem to know what I was talking about. Then he said 'Oh the albatross, yes. No it couldn't have been an albatross. But birds do quite often get caught up with fishing tackle and nets. It's quite a problem.'

My mother said 'An albatross is a symbol of death.'

I said 'Only if you kill it.'

My father said 'That's a good point.'

My mother said 'I don't want to kill anything.'

My father said to me 'It seems it might have been a gannet.'

I thought – Perhaps my mother has remembered something about when she came to the cottage as a child or teenager.

While the others were preparing for bed I thought I would walk again to the top of the cliff and if not go down it at least sit at the top and observe from beneath the huge vault of the sky the beach, the promontory, the landing stage: try to imagine how I might come across again not only the boy but the girl whom I had seen by the harbour. It struck me suddenly – They were very alike: they might be brother and

23

sister. And were not such coincidences those which altered the conditioning of the universe? Were there choices one could make that would make effective the coincidences? My father seemed to imply that this was possible if one was in a state of readiness to take advantage of what turned up. Those hermits for instance who had come to this coast in their small boats – they had come to the ends of the world; but how much had they changed it?

I sat under the stars. There was no moon, but there was reflected light from the sun that had set and I could see the waves on the long curved beach crawling up and fading and falling back ceaselessly. They were like armies flowing into no-man's-land and being shot down; sea creatures struggling to get on to earth. Millions would die before one or two got through; but then would these be the start of a new species? The stars were like peepholes through which the gods looked down: but for experiment; not just amusement?

The next day my mother and father were going to visit a lawyer in the local town to find out more about my mother's inheritance. I said I would take the bicycles back to the village because there was no point in my coming to see the lawyer. My mother said that I could not ride both bicycles to the village and we could take them on the roof of the caravan. My father said 'Perhaps he wants to go on his own to the village.' My mother said 'Why should he?' Then – 'Oh I see.' I thought – But how striking that it is my father who sees that I want to go on my own to the village: though he'll be thinking that I want to meet just that boy who rescued the bird with its feet entangled in a net.

When I was on my way pushing the bicycles to the village the sky got very dark and it began to rain; there were huge drops like pellets. I began to have an almost physical sense of having no idea what I was doing; I was surrounded by curtains of water; I was like someone in a magician's magic

24

box about to be made to disappear. This was a trick: but where on earth might the persons or objects be supposed to have disappeared to? to some other dimension? oblivion? Of course I had wanted to go to the village so that I might have a chance of seeing the girl with fair hair again or indeed the boy with the bird; they seemed to have been like creatures from another dimension, where things happened mysteriously or what was called at random, but was not this 'random' the force that ordered the universe? If I came across the boy or the girl I might not have anything to say to them but there might be something to do, that might occur; as there had been with the bird; also with the girl who had seemed to dance and then had seemed to recognise me.

When I got to the village the rain was coming down in swirls; it was like the waving of banners; there was again no one about by the harbour. Boats bobbed up and down on the water as if they had a life of their own, as if they were animals anxious about thunder. I took the bicycles back to the shop and then thought I would go and sit on the rocks of the breakwater further along from where my mother and I had sat the previous day; I would perch there like a hermit half hidden and would hope – what – for something to come through from some other dimension? Did not visions come more easily to people who were wet and cold – some protection having been stripped off them like dirt and varnish from a painting?

I had been sitting for some time on the rocks trying to accustom myself to the rain that was like something scrubbing at my surface; my mind becoming blank but my eyes peering out for whatever vision might be available. The figure of a man had stepped out from the hut at the end of the pier where it joined the quayside; this was the hut through the window of which the girl had been peering. The man – I could not see clearly – had a hood or cowl pulled down over his face: well why should he not in the driving rain? but he was like one of those pictures that one had so often seen in papers and magazines and indeed in comic cartoons – pictures of men in balaclava helmets with guns; of men trying to look like apes or villains from another dimension. He was facing up the breakwater towards where I sat; I was half way between the hut and where it ended at a marker by the open sea. Then the man stepped back into the shelter of the hut again as if he did not want to be seen. But why should he not want to be seen by me?

So what had the girl been looking for when she had stood on tiptoe to peer into the hut?

There was a boat coming round the end of the pier into the harbour. I could see this clearly because there was a momentary break in the rain; even a shaft of lurid sunlight like a stage effect. The boat had a small cabin in the centre so that it was not the boat in which the boy had struggled with the bird. There was a man in a yellow oilskin standing at the back holding the tiller. I looked back towards the hut and the man in the balaclava helmet had reappeared from behind it; he was gesticulating violently in my direction up the pier. I thought – But dear God, he cannot be signalling to me. It seemed that perhaps I should get down at the far side of the breakwater on the rocks by the sea; there I might be out of any line of fire. It had struck me before how odd it was that even in the rain there were no people in the roadway in front of the houses; it was as if they might be watching from behind the protection of drawn curtains. I clambered over the rocks and lay on my stomach at the far side of the breakwater so that I might be out of sight but could, if I raised my head, see what was happening in the harbour. The boat with the man in the oilskin in it was heading towards a place in the pier somewhere in front of where I was lying; there were bollards there to which the boat might be tied.

Then I became aware that there was someone lying on the rocks close to me and parallel to me; he had been out of sight from where I had been sitting before. He too was facing the harbour but keeping his head down and he was still; he was the boy who had been in the boat and with the bird and myself two evenings before. I was sure it was the boy; he had his cheek pressed against a rock but his head was turned towards me and it was as if he knew me but needed to make no sign of recognising me because we knew each other too well. I looked back in the direction of the hut and I saw the man in the balaclava helmet coming towards us fast, clambering over the rocks of the breakwater that were on the side by the sea; he was crouching as if he too were trying to keep out of sight of the harbour. He was carrying a gun. I thought – Dear God, that really is a gun. The engine of the boat that I had been hearing as it came into the harbour was now cut; the boat would be arriving at the edge of the pier. The man in the helmet ran right up to me and past me; I had wondered if he might shoot me but he did not; he seemed hardly to see me; he went and stood over the boy and pointed his gun at him and fired a shot at his leg. The boy had raised his head to look at him; he jerked almost silently and rolled over on his back; bits of rock, or cloth, or whatever, seemed to ricochet. I had jerked too as if I might have been hit; but it was still as if the man in the helmet was not noticing me. The boy was clutching his leg but was making no sound. The man in the helmet scrambled to the top of the rocks where he could see over into the harbour; there he stood upright as if he no longer minded about being seen; he fired another shot in the direction of the harbour but almost at the same time there was another shot, or might it be an echo, and the man seemed to be hit himself, and came tumbling back down the rocks and fell just beyond the boy, flopping and twisting. It was like one of those video films in which you think you have missed something and you want to run it again to see what happened; but it never does become clear, and what does it matter, you accept what is there. The man in the helmet had become still: he seemed to be dead or at least dying. I did not know what had happened to the man in the oilskin in the boat: presumably the man in the helmet had fired at him and the man in the oilskin had fired back and hit him: perhaps it had been one of those ludicrous films where two people point guns at each other and bang! with what seems like one shot they both are dead. I found myself shaking as if in response to the rain that was bouncing off me.

The boy who had been shot in the leg was pulling at his trousers as if to get at his wound; it seemed that this might not be too bad because he was quite composed. He was reaching for something in his trouser pocket and after a time managed to pull out not something to deal with his wound as I had thought, but a gun of his own; this he now held out to me not as if he wanted to shoot me but with the butt of it towards me, as if he wanted me to take it. So was he asking me to shoot him like one of those people strung up on wire in the First World War? But I worked out – The man in the helmet is dead, perhaps the man in the harbour is dead, you don't seem to be doing too badly; you want me to take the gun? So I took it. Then he was making insistent gestures for me to get away. In my mind things began to become clear: I thought – I see, you do not want to be found with a gun because if you are you could be taken to be an accomplice of one or other of the men who did the shootings; whereas if you have no gun you will simply seem a victim. And the reason why the man with the helmet shot you was because you had been designated to shoot the man in the boat and if you would not do this then the man in the helmet had been appointed to deal with you and then he would do it himself. I did not put this into words, but it seemed to make sense. I took the gun from the boy and put it in my pocket. It seemed important that I should do what he wanted and should not stay in any other way to help him; it might be useful just to see what had happened to the man in the boat. I looked cautiously over the top of the rocks of the breakwater. The boat that had had the man in an oilskin in it was drifting in the harbour apparently empty. With any luck (this was how it struck me) that man too was dead. The boy was still making gestures for me to get away.

There was now the problem of how to manage this without being seen. I could go along the rocks on the ocean side of the breakwater continuing to keep out of sight of the houses facing the harbour; go along the coastline for some distance until it would be safe for me to emerge and rejoin the road some way from the village. The rain was coming down hard again so this would be an added protection; but people had seemed to be keeping themselves behind closed doors anyway as if they might have had some forewarning of the shooting. And so they would continue to want to know nothing of it? And the boy could then make up his own story.

I scrambled along the rocks and this did not seem too difficult. I was still trembling a bit but it seemed clear what I had to do. I got to the place where the pier-breakwater joined the land: this was where the girl had come tiptoeing like someone in a ballet and had looked into the hut; she had had some knowledge of the possibility of the shooting? And she had seen me?

I did not think that when I got home I should tell my mother and father anything of this encounter: it would sound too improbable; and was not the point now that as much of it as possible should remain secret? Then we might get away with it, the boy and I: he did not seem to have been hurt too badly; he might be able to say that he had been wounded by the man in the boat. There was no reason why anyone should have seen me except the boy and the man who was now dead; or anyway, why would anyone want to say that they had seen me? The boy would know he and I were in league; he had wanted me to take the gun rather than just throwing it into the sea.

I was climbing up a low sort of headland towards the road. It seemed that what I should do now was keep the gun and hide it: if it was found, I could make out that it was a gun that had anyway been hidden in the cottage by the men who had come for it but had overlooked it; I could even put it in the place underneath the sink in the scullery where indeed it might once have been. I was by this time so wet from the rain that I might have been swimming: I was running along the road towards the cottage. I thought – Oh I am one of those strange creatures that have been waiting for a chance to come up out of the sea.

I I

During my last two years at school I had been working for my A-level exams in biology and physics and chemistry; these were the subjects I had planned to study at university. But at school we seemed involved with none of the interesting things that I talked about with my father. In biology we were taught that living organisms should be considered like machines: the DNA from which organisms were constructed also contained precise instructions for their functioning; the processes were unalterable. The machinery was programmed to replicate itself until some chance mistake in copying caused a variation; but nothing more could be said about 'chance'; this was by definition beyond the bounds of science. There was also some puzzle about how, although every cell of an organism was formed from precisely similar strands of DNA, yet some cells went to form this part of a body and others that. My father suggested that this showed there was some organising activity beyond that of the mechanism of DNA. My biology teacher said – Not so: all shape, functioning, evolution, comes through replication and chance variation, and then natural selection by trial and error for what fits into the environment.

I said to my father 'But if it's just chance that might allow one cell to live while enormous numbers of others die –'

My father said 'Yes?'

'Shouldn't we be finding out more about this chance, if it's that by which we live or die?'

'It's only science that says we can't find out anything about it.'

'Then what's the point of my doing science at university?'

'What else would you do?'

'What about philosophy?'

'Philosophers used to try to be scientists. Now they're saying philosophy's a form of literature.'

'Then what about literature? That must be talking about what's chance, what's determined, what human beings might have some hold over.'

This conversation took place in Ireland some time after the shootings on the breakwater. I had got back to the cottage that evening and found that my father and mother were still away. I had hidden the gun in the cavity behind the loose bricks under the sink – from which I had imagined it might even have been taken by the three men who had come looking for it. I wiped the gun clear of fingerprints as I had seen people do in films: if it was found, it should seem reasonable to say that neither myself nor my father nor my mother knew anything about it. We only stayed in the caravan by the cottage one more night: my mother had wanted to get away after our meeting with the three men: she said she would decide later whether or not to keep the cottage. My father said it would suit him to come back to the wildlife station when he knew more about the possibilities of filming: and of course it suited me to get away. To make our trip worthwhile we went on a short tour of Northern Ireland. For a few days I avoided looking in newspapers for any report of the shootings; then I made myself look but found nothing. I thought – Perhaps everyone in this weird country wishes to keep such things secret.

I felt that for myself however something decisive had happened, though I could not exactly describe what. I had been given a gun: it had seemed important to keep quiet about the gun; if I was to help the boy I should not burden my parents with a story which they might feel they had to do something about. But why had I assumed so unquestioningly that I was in some special relationship with the boy? This was one of those impressions beyond the bounds of rational enquiry?

I said to my father 'But I mean, if there is some organising activity beyond that of chance and DNA, then wouldn't it be to do with an attitude of mind? I mean can't humans make for themselves a sort of environment in which one thing, one chance, rather than another, might be likely to turn up?'

My father said 'You mean depending on how you see things?'

'Isn't that what literature's saying?'

'Oh well, it's always easier I suppose to be saying how things go wrong rather than how they go right. Language seems a bit out of its depth when it tries to say how things might be right.'

During my last years at school I had been caught up in some of the fashionable enthusiasms of my contemporaries; and there had been moments to do with music, films, the watching of sport, when things seemed to be right in a way that words could not explain. But then in everyday life there was often a reversion to idiocy or malignancy so that I felt myself aloof again, if I was not to be scornful of myself as well as others.

I had imagined that when I got to the university I would find more people like myself who wanted to challenge prevailing fashions; but then I wondered – Do I want not to be aloof?

At the university I went to the Director of Science Studies to try to arrange my transfer from the biology course for which I had been accepted to that of English literature. He said 'You think that by doing literature you can find out how human beings work?'

I said 'Well, I suppose it shows how people behave.'

'Literature's a matter of personal interpretations.'

'Well, I suppose you can find out about those.'

'Indeed.'

'I mean, why do we see things the way we do –'

'But that's what you learn from biology or physics.'

'Is it?'

'The way we see things depends on our make-up; our conditioning.'

'But that's an interpretation itself put out by our conditioning –'

'Indeed.'

'But we can alter that.'

'Can we?'

'If we can see it, can't we?'

'You think we can alter our genetic make-up?'

I thought I might say – Well something can. But I thought I should stay on the right side of this man or I would be stuck with him doing biology or physics.

I said 'Well with literature I suppose one learns about one's prejudices.'

He said 'You have made my point exactly.'

And so he allowed me to transfer from science to English literature.

Then after I had been a few days at the university it did not seem so very different from the world of the school that I had left: there was the same curious need to assert oneself without

34

standing out from a crowd. For this it was now necessary to become a vociferous member of a group – a political group, a protest group, a feminist group, a gay group: these were people who got their identity from being part of a special crowd. And those who wished to remain individuals seemed simply to disappear.

There was a pub that I took to going to in the evenings because although I liked the idea of being alone I still perhaps needed to feel identified as such by being cut off within a crowd. The pub consisted of a huge vaulted beer cellar in which I could prop myself in a corner beside a pillar and watch what seemed like a Shakespearean crowd going through its routine of everyone talking at once and saying 'Rhubarb rhubarb.' I wondered – But on a stage 'Rhubarb rhubarb' is supposed to sound as if people are talking of other things; but what if their script or conditioning just requires them to talk about rhubarb?

The man who was designated to be my English tutor I liked better than the man with whom I had had to arrange my change of studies. The English tutor was thin and grey-haired and ascetic-looking; he had a way of fiddling with an empty tobacco pipe throughout the session. He said 'So you want to do literature not to look at texts and interpretations, but to find out what might be true.'

'I suppose so yes.'

'Then you won't get far in this place. Not unless you recognise that as an interpretation.'

'Well, I can look at my own interpretations, I suppose, and ask what's true?'

'I don't know. Can you?'

'I mean as I go along.'

'A university isn't a place where you go along on your own. You're here to learn about what other people have done and are doing. Tradition.'

'Well I suppose I can look at tradition.'

'So you can say where it's wrong?'

'Well that's the point, isn't it?'

'What?'

'Well I mean if you can say what's wrong, then you might see what survives.'

'So you want to be part of what survives?'

'I suppose so. Yes.'

Towards the end of this first session my tutor suddenly broke the stem of his pipe.

Then one evening some time after the beginning of term I was in the beer cellar and I was trying to sort out what I thought wrong about the people in the crowd – opening and shutting their mouths and accepting that anyone should be able to make of this what they liked – something profound or hostile or catty or witty but hardly anything that might alter the world – and a profound lethargy came over me as if I was a freak on a rocky island with no environmental niche; I would be frozen, snuffed out, and then would it not simply be I who had been wrong.

Then also propped against a pillar that evening was a young man who seemed in much the same situation as myself, though in appearance he was not much like me – he was tall and gaunt and sandy-haired with a high forehead and beaky nose and on his face a look of immense disdain; he wore student-type clothes from another age – grey flannel trousers ending above the ankles and a pullover with a pattern of diamonds such as golfers might wear. He had steel-rimmed spectacles that were mended with tape and rested on his nose crookedly; it seemed that he had gone to some trouble to look out of place. I immediately wanted to get to know him. I thought – He might not be a kindred spirit but he is surely someone from whom I could learn.

I thought I should move closer to him and see what

occurred: any more obvious approach might propel us apart. Then someone happened to nudge me and some beer spilled from the glass I was holding; some drops might have splashed him but I did not think they had. I said 'Sorry.' He said 'Well I'm not going to buy you another if that's what you think.'

I said 'No I was thinking of having something different.'

'Such as?'

'Well what about red wine.'

'I don't think they have any decent red wine in this place.'

'Well anything will do.'

'No anything will not do.'

'Right.'

He was like some sort of tattered eagle on its rock. I thought – Or Prometheus: but was not Prometheus having his insides torn out by a bird?

Without raising his head to look round the room he said 'What are you doing with this *canaille*?'

I said 'Probably the same as you.'

'Which is what.'

'Hoping to feel superior.'

'And do you succeed?'

'Not always.'

'Why not. Don't you get pleasure?'

'From what?'

'From seeing everyone rushing to the edge of a cliff.'

'Sometimes. But I don't like that.'

'Why not?'

'Do you?'

'Yes. It passes the time.'

'Before what –'

'Curtains.'

He remained solemn. Then he said 'And for you I suppose carpets; and all the trappings of a bourgeois life.' Then he smiled sweetly.

37

I thought this witty. It was certainly better than rhubarb rhubarb. I laughed and said 'Oh something usually turns up.'

'Such as me?'

'Yes.'

'Will you have dinner with me?'

'Yes.'

'Now?'

'All right.'

'Then maybe we can get a decent bottle of claret.' He did his sweet smile again. Then he said 'You prima donna!'

I supposed he was gay. He might just be trying to pick me up. This did not seem to matter.

As we went out of the pub he said 'I've only one stipulation, that I must pay. Otherwise I feel insecure. Do you have any trouble with that?'

'None.'

'Some people do. You've no idea what problems rich people have.'

'How rich are you?'

'Very.'

We made our way to a restaurant which was the sort of place I had sometimes been to with my mother and father: it had cut-glass chandeliers and tables with linen napkins and vases with a single red rose. My new friend had no difficulty in getting a table: it seemed people might know him. I thought – I will learn things from him, yes.

When we had settled and been given menus like magazines he said 'I can't see why most people shouldn't be wiped out.'

'The people in the cellar?'

'What good do ninety per cent of the human race do?'

'Ninety!'

'All right seventy.'

'Why not ninety-nine? Nearly all the cells that come into existence are wiped out. But you can't have anything worthwhile without enormous waste, so in fact there isn't any waste, everything's worthwhile.'

'What are you, a God freak?'

'Yes, a biologist.'

'Things become extinct.'

'After they've done their job.'

'Which is what.'

'Of being at some sort of stage. What's yours?'

'Ordering a meal.'

He was staring at the menu. A waiter had come up and was standing by us. My friend said 'My friend wants a really good claret. What do you recommend?' The waiter pointed to something on the wine list. I said 'Not too expensive.'

My friend said 'My friend's a moralist.'

The waiter pointed out another bottle on the list.

My friend leaned across the table and said to me 'There are too many people. You know that. If you were God, what would you do?'

'Mind my own business.'

'Which is what?'

'Leave it to chance.'

'Why.'

'Only chance takes into account all the facts.'

'What facts?'

'About what should live and what should die.'

'Then shouldn't chance be God? Why shouldn't God be chance?'

'Indeed, that's what I think.'

The waiter said 'I'll come back later.'

My friend said 'No, we've decided. We'll have that very expensive bottle.'

I said 'No.'

He smiled and said 'You'd rather not take the responsibility.'

I said 'That's right.'

When the waiter had gone and we had ordered food, a silence came down between us. It was as if we were tennis players taking a break with our towels and sips of water.

When the wine arrived and I had taken a gulp and it was like nothing I had ever tasted before, I said 'You like to play God?'

'That's what we're supposed to do isn't it?'

'You think now we might be able to?'

'Well we can, can't we?'

'How? Tell humanity what to do and threaten to wipe it out if it doesn't?'

'You think we're better than God?'

'There was always something to stop him.'

'Such as?'

'One or two people who were all right.'

'And you'd put yourself among them –'

'I suppose I'd hope to.'

'Then you're even more arrogant than I am.'

I had begun to feel sleepy. The wine was very powerful and I had not known about taking only small sips. I hoped I would not drop off before the food arrived.

My friend said 'Where do you get all your God-and-science stuff from?'

'From my father.'

'Good God, you listen to your father?'

'Yes.'

'Do you know who my father is?'

'No.'

'You mean to say you picked me up without knowing who my father is?'

When the food arrived it was such that it seemed necessary

to eat it not only in tiny mouthfuls but in silence. I think it was scallops done in thin white wine sauce. When we had finished and were sitting as if back by the umpire's chair again, I said 'Do you get your money from your father?'

He said '*Touché!*'

I said 'Oh why shouldn't you, but I mean, who is your father?'

'My father thinks he's God. He thinks he can play the information systems of the world. Don't you think that's playing God?'

'I don't know. I don't know much about it.'

'He makes computers. Software. He's made possible the setting up of the Net. He thinks that by this anyone can be like God, so he's a sort of super-God.'

I tried to consider this. I said 'Like the Tower of Babel.'

He said 'Yes like the Tower of Babel.'

The second course had come, which was some small bird stuffed with foie gras. I said 'God encourages humans to build a tower, but when they get close to heaven, he confuses their language and it falls down. So what's the moral of that – Don't use language?' But my friend was concentrating on his food, and I do not think he heard me.

Then when we came to rest again, he said 'He thinks he's got me, but he hasn't. Any moment I could bring him down.'

'Who, your father?'

'Yes. Who do you think? God?'

'Why do you want to bring him down?'

'Why do I want to bring him down? What a question!'

He had begun to drink heavily, as if he wanted to get drunk. I thought – Well that is his way of not getting up to heaven.

I said 'You mean your father thinks that if anyone can talk to anyone on the Net, that would be heaven? But that's what humans thought, and God knocked them down, so it's you, yes, who are playing God.'

'Has anyone ever told you what an insufferable prig you are?'

'Yes often.'

'Who?'

'My mother.'

The bottle was empty. He was looking around as if to order another. I had managed to fill up my own glass in time, and so I was happy.

He said 'Will you come home with me?'

I said 'I'll see you home.'

'But you're not gay, if that's what I mean.'

'Yes that's what I mean.'

'You'll see me home. What sort of an offer is that? Like a fucking footman.'

I wondered if he were one of those homosexuals who got their kicks by provoking people into beating them up. Or might he be a complete fraud and this was a ploy for him to stagger out and leave me with the bill. But when the bill arrived he pulled out a silver and gold card and tottered only slightly when we got up to go. And then when I put out a hand to steady him and I felt his thin bony arm through the rough covering of his jumper it seemed for a moment that he was like that bird which I had hoped to rescue from the sea, and I pulled my arm away as if it had received a shock. Then I made myself take hold of him again. I thought – Dear God, perhaps this evening will involve more than I can guess.

Out in the street it had begun to rain and we stood on the pavement and waited for a taxi. When one arrived it was a small battered minicab and there seemed hardly room to get my friend in at the back; his arms and legs floundered like a neck and wings. He gave the driver an address and then sat crouching forwards with his hands on his knees as if he were about to make a dash for freedom or flight. After a time he said 'I'm sorry.'

I said 'Oh that's all right.'

'Would it make a difference if I said I was buggered by my uncle at the age of twelve?'

'I don't think so, would it?'

'As a matter of fact I wasn't.'

We travelled on for a time. He was staring closely at the back of the driver's head, who was a thickset man with almost no neck. Then he said 'Shall I leave you something in my will?'

The driver said 'Fucking hell, is he talking to me?'

My friend sat back in his seat. He had that upside-down sort of smile that long-legged birds sometimes seem to have – ostriches? flamingos? Then he said in a polite refined voice as if he were quite sober – 'I'd like to tell you how much I've enjoyed this evening, and I hope we can meet again.'

I said 'Yes I enjoyed it too.'

'Of course I'd like to go to bed with you but that's not the point.'

'No. And it wasn't just the food and wine for me either.'

Then he said as if it were a quotation '– And then she reflected for the last time in her little long life and she made up all her myriads of drifting minds in one –'

I thought – That's supposed to ring some bells in the unconscious?

He opened the door at the far side of the car, and at first I did not try to stop him because I thought he was just going to be sick. But then he was trying to throw himself out, head-first, and the car was travelling quite fast; but he was too large, he was getting stuck in the door again, and I could hang on to him by his jersey although the material seemed to be crumbling like old sacking. I shouted to the driver 'Pull over! Stop! He's going to be sick!' The driver pulled into the kerb and my friend was flopping out at the far side and I was easing him out so that he was face down on the road; then he began to crawl around the back of the car towards the pavement and I walked behind him. The driver called out after us – 'You're both fucking sick!'

On the far side of the pavement there was a shop entrance and in the recess were two small boys with the cardboard cut-out of a dummy collecting money for Guy Fawkes Day. My friend crawled towards these boys and propped himself against a shop window and said 'Hullo boys, I'll make a much better dummy.' He pulled a bundle of money out of his pocket and handed a note to me and said 'That's for the taxi'. Then he handed a note to each of the boys and said 'That's for letting me hang out here for a while, I'm being pursued by furies.' He settled himself against the window and appeared to go to sleep. The boys put the notes in their pockets and watched him cautiously. Then he opened his eyes again briefly and said to me 'It's all right, I don't fancy children, but I've always fancied myself as Guy Fawkes, as you know.' Then he seemed to go to sleep again.

I said 'Are you sure?'

He said 'Yes.'

Then as I was going I heard him saying to the children 'Guy Fawkes had his insides pulled out like a string of sausages, you know.'

My relationship with my friend who was called Edward (as I found out later, as I found out so much about him: it seemed that I wanted my knowledge of him to grow naturally and not to be forced into a mould by asking unnecessary questions) my friendship with Edward that had begun with us both feeling arrogantly that we were getting identity by cutting ourselves off from a crowd, had gone by the end of the evening into farce: it was Edward's accomplishment that he seemed to see the necessity of this – if you are tempted to see yourself as a superman, then remember also that you are likely to end up hung drawn and quartered like Guy Fawkes. In the beer cellar where I had seen people as extras auditioning for parts I had seen Edward more as Don Quixote but thus still tinged with farce: and then did I see myself as Sancho Panza on his donkey? I had ended by feeling that I should perhaps in some way look after Edward – a bird entangled in the traps or trappings of his world.

In my sessions with my English literature tutor, after we had been through my formal essays, I would chat with him for a few minutes while he seemed to be trying to make up his mind what to do with his pipe. I said 'But so much of literature portrays humans as characters, types, who are stuck in what has made them what they are and have no autonomy except to be clowns, comic or tragic. And readers like this, because then they don't feel they have to do anything about anything themselves: they don't have to think, they feel satisfied because everyone and everything appears as helpless as they are, and they can even feel superior to clowns.'

My tutor said 'Are you making a statement or a complaint?'

'I suppose a complaint.'

'But it's the role of literature to portray people and things as they are.'

'Why not as they might be?'

'You can have sermons I suppose. But what's more depressing than that? Or there's science fiction, yes, about other worlds in which people and things are what they might be, but then characters are not recognisable as humans at all.'

'But why aren't there novels, stories, about people trying to learn, to understand, to set themselves or the world to rights?'

'But there are. Like Hamlet. But such people don't succeed. And then they are likely to be comic or tragic clowns.'

'Then what is it that keeps the world on course?'

'Is it kept on course? It just happens.'

'You think people are just spectators.'

'People are what they are. Writers, artists are spectators.'

I talked about this with Edward, but he was scornful of most academic studies. He said 'Of course human beings can alter the world, but they don't do this by talking about it. They have to be cunning.'

I said 'Are you cunning?'

'If I were, I would be too cunning to talk about it.'

I found out about Edward's father by coming across an article about him in a magazine. He was a hugely rich media tycoon called Connie Constantine; he had made his money in the early days of computers and computer games and software; he had for a time owned a national newspaper and then had gone into satellite television and was now said to be getting into films – he was negotiating to become a major shareholder in an ailing Hollywood company. He was written about, as Edward had said, in terms of wishing to control a global information and media 'empire'. He had once been known as a playboy, but nowadays had the reputation of being reclusive and mysterious – he had a wife and a mistress or mistresses whom no one knew much about, and homes in France and London and New York. There was no mention of children.

Edward and I used to meet in the beer cellar in the evenings and then go out to supper. We did not always go to a grand restaurant; I took him to eat Chinese or Indian food. He would pick at this and say 'Locusts and wild honey.' Then – 'Do you think ascetics can alter the world?'

'As much as anyone I suppose.'

'A tasteful loincloth and a few deftly placed arrows.'

Edward was doing a course in business studies but his obsession was for computers: he spent much of his day working or playing with his computer in his room. I did not know much about this: I had used a computer for writing essays during my last year at school and occasionally for finding information on the Net; but for the most part the school computer room had been used for watching pornography. One could choose a time when one knew that a master would not be there and then embark on a laborious journey past advertisements and warnings and promotional lures until one reached a site where bums and breasts bloomed like exotic flowers and vegetables, the latter blown up to the size of prize marrows. Some of my schoolfellows had the use of credit-cards and by giving their numbers one could go deeper into the haunted forest with strange images of animals and ghouls and torture-chambers and children. But then it began to seem that the tendrils and roots of the forest were stretching down, round, up, to entrap one; and I would wonder – But what is it in the mind that welcomes these images? And then a master would come back into the room and we would click our buttons and there would reappear on our screens austere and respectable information to do with trigonometry, or entropy, or the French Second Republic.

I became somewhat perturbed by the temptation of this. I thought – Perhaps after all it's best to have a pre-emptive wank twice a week before a bath and after some beers.

I said to Edward 'What do you do with your computer? At school we just used them for pornography.'

Edward said 'I don't think nearly enough people use them for pornography. There are too many babies being conceived.'

'Don't you think there'll be a puritan backlash?'

'My dear, half the fucking porn is backlash.'

'I feed you your best lines.'

'I told you, what would I do without you!'

Edward had been at a school in Switzerland where he

had been one of a group making themselves experts at manipulating the Net. Their aim was, so Edward said, to break into, break up, establishment networks which manipulated power as if they were functions of God. But if the networks were closer to Babel, then might it not indeed be a more realistic God-like function to break them up.

I said 'But can you do that?'

'You prepare some software and you e-mail it to whoever you want to bugger up, and you say – Click on this and it will give you access to the most fascinating trips in the world – and so they take it on, nasty buggers, and with luck it infects their system in more ways than one.'

'Can't there be safeguards?'

'Not if they're tempted.'

'Like Adam and Eve.'

'More like AIDS.'

I did not quite know what to say about this. I said 'So you're the puritan.'

'I told you. It's I who wants to save the world. You can't save it without getting rid of what's destroying it.'

'Which you think is your father.'

'He's the great pornographer.'

'By giving people what they want.'

'Yes.'

We got quickly into the area where words go round and round. I said 'But if he's giving people what they want, and that's destroying them, and you think they should be destroyed, why get rid of him? Perhaps they'll learn.'

'What does he learn?'

'Does he need to?'

'Doesn't he? All right I'm like Mephistopheles, I make people learn.'

'But you can't say that.'

'Can't I?'

'Better go to the mountains. Become a freedom fighter.'

'I've thought about that.'

Edward looked sad. I thought – But I'm not supposed to be fighting Edward.

There was a walk that I sometimes went on by the river when I felt there was too much going on in my head, when things were tripping over each other, and I wanted to be moving in a space outside myself. Edward believed, as his father did, that the Net that he had access to on his computer was a space outside in which he could wander and explore and use for good or ill. But it seemed to me to exist as an extension of an inner world of desires, hardly to represent an outside world at all. I had been trying to say to Edward, to my English tutor – But there is a world, a network even, out there, which has nothing to do with manipulation nor indeed with what one might think one wants, because one does not know what one really wants, though through this scarcely known network one might find this. It is to do with what happens to one rather than with what one makes happen; though by being aware of this one thing rather than another might happen. It is a world beyond appearances that occasionally seem to become apparent; a network that tells one not where to go, but how to see that where one is going might be all right.

When I walked by the river I toyed with all this; not as if I were trying forcibly to sort things out (which did not seem possible) nor wishing to wander by some babbling stream of consciousness or unconsciousness, but rather as if it might be possible to go hand in hand – if one were attentive enough, respectful enough – with whatever just beyond consciousness might be 'there': somewhat like being with a loved one whom one might long to possess, but if one simply grabbed or willed this then love would disappear; love has to have its own autonomy. The images I had in such ruminations were often those of the girl and the boy I had come across in Ireland: they seemed to me to be figures whom I had met in legend.

At this time I was still in some limbo about sex; perhaps using my presumed physical vulnerability as an excuse not to think I had to go in pursuit of it. I still liked to dream about, rather than to have much contact with, girls. At school I had had the choice of a few sexual encounters, but I had felt happier and safer in dreams. I had not bothered to justify or feel anxious about this: the reality of such an area seemed to waste a lot of time in turmoil and pain.

When I had in some sense fallen in love with the fair-haired girl in Ireland this had largely remained a dream: in legend, was not romantic love separated from sex? Nevertheless a physical need had grown: my daydreams were becoming more incessant and even more redolent of the sad stuff glimpsed on the Net. To deal with this there did seem to be some need of reality.

My walk by the river went close to some playing fields where girls played hockey. My daydreams had not previously much featured girls playing hockey; but now such images seemed to be reaching to me like roots beneath the earth; burrowing animals to be grappled with and rolled around with in the mud. Was there not healthiness in mud? Was a root not clean and beautiful as it travelled whitely through the dark earth?

There was a Sunday in late November towards the end of this my first term when the weather returned to an Indian summer and the sun shone on the few leaves clinging to the trees. There were few people in boats or on the towpath; willows hung over the river like animals drinking but keeping clear of the entanglement of weeds. It was as if there was something trying to break out of the thin skull of my head and out of my groin; some bird pecking as if at the shell of an egg. There was an island in the river just ahead of where I was walking which was said to be the location for wild parties in summer – a sort of Hell Fire Club for New Ravers. There had once been a bridge to the island but it had been dismantled to deter intruders or protect revellers; the island now could be reached only by boat or by swimming. I had thought that in the summer I would go to one of these parties and there perhaps lose my allegiance to romanticism: there might be mud, nettles, brambles to roll in; the pleasures of being torn by bacchantes.

The island was a long strip parallel to the bank of the river. There was a wooded end across the water from where I was walking; then at the far end a stretch of open ground with long or trampled grass. Here there were now figures seated quite motionless all facing the same way into the watery sun; they were like those statues on Easter Island; some wore white smocks and some, both men and women, were naked to the waist. They were I supposed some sect of nature worshippers come to catch the last of the autumn sun: eco-freaks were quite plentiful at universities; people turned to gods where they could find them. I thought – Good luck to them; they may see visions like those monks on their rocks off the coast of Ireland.

Then there were some boats, canoes, coming on the river behind me being paddled upstream towards the wooded end of the island. The paddlers, all men, were wearing funny hats with feathers; some even had slightly blackened or camouflaged faces. I thought – They are jokers, yobs, pretending to be Red Indians or savages. They arrived at the wooded end of the island and tied up their boats: they set off through the trees silently. I thought – But they are also some form of latter-day marauders; they are intent, like a lot of self-obsessed people, on wreaking revenge on people who are different from them. They came up behind the seated figures quietly and began to push them, knock them over; the figures seemed to be allowing this to happen quite passively as if they were skittles; as if this might all be part of their exercise, their meditation. I was watching from the far bank and did not see what I could do; I raised my arms as if I might shoo away vultures. One or two figures were briefly punched, but in the end it did not seem that this was much more than a game. When one of the attackers saw me watching he faced me and stood to attention and did a mock nazi salute. Then the attackers set off back to their boats.

There was something crawling or slithering in the reeds at the edge of the island near where the fallen figures were beginning to pick themselves up; the figure that emerged from the reeds was that of a young boy; he was on the other side of the water from where I was standing beneath a willow. The boy, naked to the waist, was plunging into the river as if to cross it. I thought – But why does he need to get away when the raid is over? Is it the sun-worshippers he needs to get away from as well as from the raiders who might in fact have freed him? But the river was muddy and the boy was soon up to his neck and struggling: I thought – The mud and weeds will drag him down: he may not even get a chance to swim. The sun-worshippers were returning to their poses of meditation; they did not seem to have noticed the boy. He was getting into obvious difficulties half way across the river; I stepped down into the water to help him. The water was cold; I was up to my waist quickly. I thought – Well, I am getting into some mud after all; not quite what I had intended. I held with one hand on to the willow and held my other hand out to the boy; he got hold of it; I could pull him in towards the bank quite easily; at this point the river was quite narrow. When the boy was on dry land he lay there gasping and spitting: he was wearing nothing but white shorts and trainers; he was smeared with mud; he looked like

52

a large baby. I had the impression I was looking down at some earlier representation of myself. The boy looked up at me and seemed to be trying to say something, but then it was as if there was too much mud and water in his throat. I wondered if I should slap him on the back as one does with a new-born child. But after a time he stood and ran off across the meadow. He ran towards some playing fields in the distance where there were the girls playing hockey. Some of the people on the island had now come to their river bank and were facing in my direction as if to see what was happening; they looked beyond me to where the boy had run up to a group of women who were watching the hockey. The women spoke to him; the players paused in their game. I thought – Well all right, I will become involved with those girls: it does not seem too difficult.

I I I

When I went to our home outside London for the Christmas holidays, my father was away on a filming assignment, and my mother was involved with reading for a Master's degree. I tried to read, but was waylaid by images of girls in short flared skirts and brown legs. I made an expedition to Soho and bought a porn video but then I had to find somewhere to hide it and this seemed more tiresome than the hiding of my gun.

One of the groups I had been aware of in the beer cellar were the feminists. I did not know how many of the women who played hockey were these. There was talk in newspapers and magazines at this time of men becoming emasculated by feminist women, but it seemed to me that men were using this image in order not to have to worry too much about their own responsibility in relationships.

And there was one group at the university who were devotees of an American feminist academic who pointed out the absurdity of the fashionable view of most feminists who saw women as victims and yet derided men as insignificant. She claimed that there was a subtle power-game going on which at the moment men were still winning because they adapted to whatever was the fashion while women got stuck in entrenched positions. If women had the confidence of their femininity, she claimed, then they would not have to adopt attitudes of aggressive feminism; in most areas their rootedness in basic requirements would give them a natural superiority over men if only they could accept responsibility for this. She was attacked by old-fashioned feminists who seemed to need to cling to their images of themselves as victims and of men as both savages and babies.

At the university the leader of a group of the new confident non-victim feminists was a dark-haired flashing-eyed young woman called Christina. I quite often saw Christina in the beer cellar or in the street: she seemed to pop up here and there as if projected from my unconscious. I did not fall in love with her as I had done with the fair-haired girl in Ireland: but that girl had seemed romantically unobtainable (was that part of love?) and what I felt about Christina was that her very toughness might make her attainable. I wondered if she might be a hockey player; but she seemed more likely to be one of the women who watched from the touchline and whom the boy from the reeds had run up to. I thought I might meet Christina on equal terms and engage in some contest with her; this might begin with words but then would go on into sexuality – was not this the sort of practical process she advocated for men and women? She was two or three years older than me; but then would it not be up to me to show her I was neither a brute nor a baby?

But how could I get into a situation in which I might confront her with my wit, my boldness; my sudden heartfelt tenderness?

Not long after the beginning of the winter term she wrote an article for the university magazine in which she set out her ideas. She outlined her quarrels with the old-fashioned feminists; then said that there was one subject on which she and they were in full agreement, which was on the subject of abortion – it was imperative that women should have the right of choice to have abortions. This freedom took precedence over an outmoded sense of maternal responsibility.

I thought – But surely it's the fact of maternal responsibility that gives, or should give, women their power?

I was surprised by my feelings. I suppose that they must be to do with the pressure my mother had been under to have me what she called terminated.

Some way into the winter term Christina announced a meeting at which the speaker would be the notorious American academic; the public were encouraged to come and to take part in questions and answers afterwards. There were rumours that the meeting might be attended by hostile orthodox feminists; also by men who might wish to relish their reputation as thuggish babies. And so the meeting got a certain amount of advance publicity; but then at the last minute the American academic was not coming: it was said she was ill, or she had got tired of her appearances being taken as an occasion for a circus. So interest in the meeting fell away. But Christina announced that some gathering would still be held: there would be a debate between the various feminist factions in one of the colleges, and men would still be welcome. I had intended to go to the original meeting and had hoped there for a chance to make contact with Christina; now in the lower-key circumstances it seemed that it might be easier to make myself known; to stand up for her if she were attacked, or throw in my own subtle challenge.

Then when I got to the meeting it seemed that I was the only man in the room. In fact not many people had turned up, the chance of there being a fracas having receded. There were women who from the style of their clothes seemed to be orthodox feminists; but any differences between them and other women present seemed insignificant in contrast to the difference between all the rest of the gathering and me. Christina herself was an amazon in black tights and a short black leather skirt; it was as if she might have a few shrunken heads or a bull's pizzle hanging from her belt. She stood on a platform and said how sorry the American academic was that she was not able to come: she, Christina, would give a short account of what she understood the American academic had been planning to say, then she would throw the meeting open to anyone who wished to speak.

It was time, she said, for women to have the confidence of the natural superiority that they must surely feel in any relationship with men. They should be able to feel this because they were the ones less plagued by questions of security and status; they were more in contact with the deep undercurrents of life.

While Christina was talking she looked at me from time to time: I told myself I should not be surprised, being the only man in the room. But then I began to have a fantasy (this was what men did?) about how she must have seen that if I was the only man bold enough to come to the meeting, then I must surely be someone worth getting to know: someone worthy in fact of joining her in an adventure into the deep undercurrents of life.

Then a woman in a large padded jacket stood up and asked Christina about her attitude towards abortion.

Christina said that her attitude was well known: she was in favour of the freedom of women to have choice.

The woman in the padded jacket said that this wasn't good enough. What sort of choice would Christina recommend women to make?

Christina said that choice meant that it should be left to the individual woman according to the circumstances.

The woman in the padded jacket said –

But I had stopped listening. The woman in the jacket

seemed a mythical beast trying not to have an argument nor even to provoke a battle but to lay an ambush, a trap. And I thought – Perhaps this is what Christina would really like to be talking about: the lack of respect, courtesy, in which style women seemed to be emulating men. And then I heard Christina saying 'But shouldn't we be hearing from the only man in the room?'

I thought – You mean me? Just because I happened to be dreaming of such a thing?

Christina was looking at me with her black hair framing black eyes like the face of Medusa on a shield.

I said 'What do you want to hear from me?'

'Whatever you like.'

I said 'Well I suppose if you want to be in touch with the deep undercurrents of life, you can't say abortion is nothing but a matter of choice.'

The woman in the padded jacket had turned to look at me and she said 'Jesus, a weeper!'

Christina said 'Let him speak.'

I said 'I only speak because you asked me to. Of course men should take their responsibility, should be in touch with the deep undercurrents of life, which I agree they're usually not.'

'And you think you are?' This was the woman in the padded jacket.

'I don't know.'

'Well get ready for the plug to be pulled.'

Christina said quickly 'You don't think women should contemplate abortion?'

'Oh of course contemplate it, and men should contemplate being responsible for looking after children.'

'You would?'

'Yes.'

'God help the children!' This was the woman in the jacket.

People had begun to laugh. Someone was chanting 'Sit down, sit down.'

I said 'Also it's a biological problem. You may make the wrong choice, get rid of the wrong thing, if you let anything other than nature do the selecting.'

Christina said 'Humans shouldn't select?'

I said 'Sorry, I got that wrong. Humans of course have to select, but they should do it with some sort of attentiveness to nature.'

Some women began chanting 'He got it wrong! He got it wrong!'

I thought – This is no proper contest. What's that Greek myth about a man being torn to pieces for intruding on women's rituals?

Christina was bending down to talk to a woman who had come up to the edge of the platform. The two of them were glancing towards me. I said 'I'm sorry, this is silly, I'd better go.' I had been careful when I had come in to get a seat near the door.

I made my exit from the hall. I had to find my way back through the purlieus of the college. I thought – But why might not Christina be that person, what was her name, who needed to be rescued from a monster in a labyrinth?

When I reached the garden on the way to the gate there was the sound of someone running behind me. I did not imagine it could be Christina. I stopped and I saw that it was the woman whom Christina had been talking to on the platform; she was a tall thin girl with boyish close-cut hair. She reminded me of someone, I could not think who. She came up to me and stood awkwardly and kept her eyes lowered and did an odd placating gesture with her hands. I thought – She is one of the women who play hockey? She said 'Christina asked me to come after you and say she's sorry.'

I said 'Oh that's all right.'

'She should probably have announced that the meeting would be for women only but she didn't want to.'

'I probably shouldn't have come.'

'Oh no, Christina's glad that you came. She'd like to see you again.'

'She would?'

'Yes.'

The woman glanced up at me quickly, and then away again. I thought – You mean, all this has actually worked?

The woman said 'She'll get in touch with you.'

'She knows how?'

'Yes.'

I thought – There is a poem, somewhere, about a meeting like this in a garden; a man comes across someone whom he imagines is himself.

My encounter with Christina had taken place some way through the winter term. I did not know if she would get in touch with me: I did not think that I should get in touch with her. It seemed necessary that whatever process (if any) we were involved in, it should not seem that I was pursuing her.

But my dreams, my fantasies, became concentrated on Christina – still more in the way of lust rather than love – but if one made no pretence about this, she would not have contempt for lust? I would like to grapple, wrestle with her; manoeuvre with holds, locks, grips; were these not rituals that animals did on dusty plains? And was not this the practical part of love – the pouncing, mounting, lurching, clinging; the dominance and submission coming together so that at the end both were enhanced and none diminished? I sometimes wondered whether Christina might be a lesbian – her special friend being the woman who had followed me out into the garden. But then might there not be an added challenge in complexities?

I was having trouble with my English literature course. My tutor had told me to write an essay in the Christmas holidays to say what I found unsatisfying about it. I tried to be coherent about what I had said before – that literature seemed to treat humans no differently than science did; as characters predestined to behave in the way they did, very occasionally happening by chance to change, but with no awareness of any autonomy. Their brains produced no more than a stream of consciousness or rather unconsciousness because they contained no feel of how humans might be creative. Thus literature became a chronicle of humanity's oddities and crimes and follies, peopled by characters with no virtue except that of being quaint. This was decked out indeed often enough in glorious or subtle language which gave the impression of empowerment; but there was little feel of this in the characters portrayed.

My tutor said 'But we've been through all this. If this is the human condition, then it's the job of literature to record it. And why not make it palatable?'

'But it's literature that allows it to be the human condition – by not providing models of anything different.'

'Good heavens, what would these be models of?'

'Of our actual experience.'

'What is our actual experience?'

'Well, that we do have some autonomy. Though we can't easily put this into words.'

'Then can't literature portray it? But of course it does. The mark of literature, as distinct from ordinary writing, is the sense of something conveyed beyond the scope of words.'

'Who for instance?'

'Jane Austen, Henry James, D.H. Lawrence.'

'All right, for the reader there's a feel of something going on behind the words; but there's not much of a feel of the characters themselves being aware of this – I mean living with the awareness that by what they do, or by what they are, they may be able to affect whether things or they themselves go this way or that.'

'You think one has this ability?'

'One has the experience of it.'

'You think you make rational choices?'

'Oh well, not rational.'

'What then?'

'You watch. You listen. You observe what happens as if it were an experiment. Perhaps I should have stuck to science.'

'What sort of freedom of choice does science talk about?'

'Well, if you observe, and if you do one experiment rather than another, you do apparently effect things.'

'Oh dear, you've been listening to those totally irrational scientists.'

Some time in the winter term my father sent a message to say that he was coming down to the university to do one of his interviews with a physics professor: it seemed that he had come round to the idea of doing a series of programmes on the science of the second half of the twentieth century. He suggested that I come and watch the interview and then we could have a drink or dinner afterwards. I had not seen much of my father during the Christmas holidays, and I had sensed that he was not getting on well with my mother. I did not know why this was, and I had wondered if there was anything I could do about it. I knew that in the autumn he had been back to the wildlife station in Ireland.

When I went to see him doing the interview with the Professor the scene in the laboratory was already set. The Professor sat on a high stool in front of a bench on which there was electronic equipment – monitors with screens and keyboards and boxes with switches and dials. He had his legs crossed and his hands clasped round one knee; he was perched like a parrot. I thought – He wants to give the impression of being on a knife edge between certainty and uncertainty.

My father sat facing him to one side of the camera which was on an elaborate tripod and was attended by two men. A woman and a man were with the sound equipment; the man held a long pole like a fishing rod at the end of which a woolly-covered microphone dangled like a bait above the Professor. There was also a woman with a clipboard who was good-looking with reddish hair and orange lips and heavy eye make-up. I wondered if she might be one of the women whom my father from time to time carried on with.

Bright lights came on. It was as if the laboratory were an operating theatre and there was about to be a demonstration of surgery.

My father said 'Professor, it has been said that the main task of science in the second half of the twentieth century has been not so much to make new discoveries as to try to give explanations of what has been discovered. Can you comment on that?'

The Professor said 'Many scientists don't believe it is their job to give explanations. They make observations and predictions, and if a prediction is sufficiently validated, then it is said to be the case.'

'But you yourself in your special field have been driven to hazard explanations. You have written that physics cannot go further fruitfully – cannot in fact know in what direction to go – until it can be understood to be making sense.'

'You're referring to what I've written about that old chestnut, the two-slit experiment.'

'Can you describe it for us please.'

The producer murmured 'Cut.' Then – 'We've got a film of that?'

The woman with the clipboard said 'Yes.'

'Do we want a description then?'

My father said 'The point is whether or not the explanation makes sense.'

The producer looked impatient. He said 'Right.'

The Professor said 'A light source is placed in front of a screen which has two slits. At the far side of the screen is placed a photographic plate. The intensity of the light beam can be made so low that the light passing through the slits is in individual particles or photons. If we close one or other of the slits the effect of the particles shows up on the plate behind the open slit in the form of a narrow band of hits. But if we leave both slits open, then what shows up on the plate is not, as might be expected, two narrow bands of hits, but a whole array of bands, a stretch of them, indicating that the photons have not been acting as particles but as waves, forming an interference pattern. Thus the experiment shows that light is composed neither of particles nor of waves but of both, or of one or the other according to the nature of the experiment.' The Professor paused. He said 'Are you filming this?'

The cameraman said 'Yes.'

'Of course I'm oversimplifying grossly.'

My father said 'So what do you deduce from that?'

'That when both slits are open there is a superimposition of states. That when only one slit is open what goes through is either a wave or particles, but when any observation or measurement is made then the wave function collapses and what is manifest is particles.'

My father waited for a moment and then said 'And how do you arrive at that?'

'As an explanation?'

'Yes.'

'To me, there's only one rational explanation for the ramifications that follow from the two-slit experiment. The wave-state is a superimposition, an amalgam, of photons and shadow photons from actual parallel universes. When the wave-state collapses as a result of a particular observation or experiment, then both the observer and what he observes branch into one particular universe rather than another, though evidence for the others exists through the existence of the wave-patterns.'

After a pause my father said 'But why different universes?'

'Because they have affected one another, however weakly, through interference phenomena.'

'But why not just potentialities? I mean – in just one universe, that which exists as a range of potentialities becomes, by the action of an observer, one actuality or another.'

'Potentialities are hypotheses. Hypotheses cannot have a physical effect.'

'And parallel universes are not hypotheses? They can be assumed as a result of a physical effect?'

'I don't see any explanation for the interference phenomena, or for the collapse of the wave function, unless it is accepted that they are affected by unseen presences.'

My father became silent again for such a long time that the producer said 'Cut!'

My father said 'And that makes sense?'

The Professor said with a smile 'As the great Niels Bohr said, anyone who thinks he has understood quantum physics hasn't understood quantum physics.'

My father said 'But can we really get no more comprehensible connection between interference patterns on a screen, and the existence of multiple invisible universes?'

The Professor said nothing. He seemed to preen slightly like a bird on its perch.

The cameraman said 'A quantum jump!'

The producer said 'Perhaps we can do it with just the pictures of the experiment.'

My father said 'No this is fine! What I want to show is how the words don't make sense.'

The Professor said 'It's not that our consciousness, our choice, directly affects things, but we can be aware that we are part of infinitely complex interactions.'

My mind drifted away. What my father was wanting to show (I imagined I understood him) was that although the words did not make sense, this was not necessarily an indictment of science; it might rather show that science was an indication, a metaphor, for the idea that there was a world beyond the scope of words or indeed the senses – a world of possibilities, potentialities, from which this or that was made actual in some way and to some degree by the activity of humans. And if scientists talked about alternative universes, and this did not make rational sense, then what did this matter, if it was the result of experiment and observation?

There was a pause in the filming. The producer and the Professor were having cups of coffee; the woman with the clipboard was leaning over my father with her head down close to his. I wondered – Did she go with him when he went to do research at the wildlife station in Ireland? Had they come across the girl or the boy – those denizens of that strange world of unseen or indeed seen presences?

The bright lights for the interview came on again. The Professor talked, but I was not listening: I was thinking that perhaps I would not go through my allotted years at the university but should leave at the end of this academic year and go and live like a hermit in the cottage in Ireland. Hermits did not try to make sense, but seemed to put themselves in the way of experiencing alternative worlds; of breakdown of wave functions, of emanations of shadow particles giving intimations of unseen presences.

The film people were packing up. My father suggested that we all go to a bar; but the Professor excused himself, and the producer and the film crew said they had to get back to London. My father asked me to suggest where he and I might go for a drink.

I thought I would take him to the beer cellar because there we had a chance of bumping into Christina and I thought this might impress my father, since he and my mother seemed to be becoming anxious about what they saw as my lack of women friends. It might not impress my father if we were to meet Edward, but I knew Edward was away that weekend.

We sat in the cellar with our glasses of beer and I expected my father to ask me about myself, how my work was going. But instead he said 'I'm not getting anywhere with these programmes.'

'Why not?'

'If it's become a business of not being able to put things into words, then what's the point of going on saying this?'

I said 'I've been feeling much the same about my work. Writers don't seem able to put what life's like into words; they have to be saying how sad or awful or silly it is.'

'And you don't think it is.'

'I suppose it is if one wants to think it is.'

'But if you say life's all right there's a danger that your saying this exposes you and things go wrong.'

'But there must be some trick.'

'Some trick to do what.'

'To feel life can be OK without becoming arrogant.'

'I don't think that's a trick.'

'What is it then?'

'I think life does it for you.'

There was a woman at the bar with long blonde hair and bare legs; my father was watching her.

He said 'Those programmes I did about the first half of the century were about politics as well as science. They were comparatively straightforward. There were passions, wars, causes and effects, victors and vanquished. But in the second half things have been much more obscure: the collapse of communism, for instance, was almost as mysterious as that collapse of a wave function – as if it were affected, effected – well by what? – by unseen presences.'

I said 'But then if you're aware of them –'

'What –'

'That's the trick? All right reality, not trick.'

There was a woman with short-cut dark hair coming down the stairs into the cellar. I recognised her as the friend of Christina's who had come running after me in the garden of the college. When she saw me she paused, as if she did not know whether or not to recognise me. I thought – Is it possible she has some message from Christina?

My father was saying 'I went back to the wildlife station, did you know?'

'Yes, Mum told me.'

'They're trying to find out about the unexplained instincts of birds – about homing, timing, finding their way. These must have some bearing on the business of survival. But they can't find a proper way of talking about it.'

'Did you meet any of the people in the village?'

'I didn't stay at the cottage. But apparently one or two of the people in the village were asking after you.'

'They were?'

'Yes. You seem to have made quite a name in the village.'

'I helped that boy with that bird. I told you.'

'Oh yes.'

I thought – My father feels he can't say much more about this?

Christina's friend was hovering about at the bar as if trying to make up her mind about whether to come over. I thought – But how extraordinary all this is! What a superimposition of universes!

68

My father said 'It seems to be an instinct with the birds, yes, but in tune with outside forces' Then – 'That girl seems to know you.'

'What girl? Oh yes. The one at the bar.'

'She's very good-looking.'

I thought – You don't mean the one with long blonde hair?

Then – Not so good looking as Christina.

My father said 'Mum's been trying to sell the cottage, but there haven't been any offers. I think those men that came must be frightening people off.'

'I was thinking I'd like to go back to the cottage.'

'They may be using it again.'

Christina's friend was coming over towards us. She stood in front of me and smiled. She said 'How are you.'

I said 'All right.'

'Christina's been trying to get in touch with you.'

'Well here I am.'

'But she's so hopeless. She can't make up her mind.'

I thought – For God's sake, make up her mind about what?

My father said 'Who's that girl with blonde hair at the bar? I think I know her.'

Christina's friend said 'I don't know.'

I was thinking – But what could people have been talking about in the village? About the scene on the breakwater?

When Christina's friend had gone, my father said 'Who's Christina?'

I wanted to find out from Edward more about computers. The one clear thing, my father suggested, that could be said about science and indeed almost everything in the second half of the twentieth century was that it was dominated by computers – and by the so-called information explosion on the Net.

I would visit Edward in his room where he sat hunched over his keyboard like a witch with a crystal ball. He pushed and clicked and images came up on the screen and he transposed them so fast that I could not gather where they came from or what they referred to. I said 'You must slow down: explain.'

He said 'It won't be any good if I explain. You've got to learn it for yourself. You make your own reality nowadays, haven't you heard?'

'But I want something that isn't my own reality.'

'All right. Find it.'

Edward clicked and fiddled and brought up on his screen pictures of dead bodies in a morgue with men and women leaning over them. I said 'Is this pornography or reality?'

'What's the difference.'

'But isn't that what your father says? You're supposed to be trying to subvert him.'

'He wants to impose what he thinks on people and make them think it's reality. I want to make people think everything's up to them: reality's nonsense.'

Edward was carrying on an e-mail correspondence with people who said they were a business tycoon in America and a schoolmaster in Australia. To the former he gave the information that he was a defector from the Central Intelligence Agency; to the latter that he was a ten-year-old delinquent boy. To me he explained 'Reality's in the mind. Why shouldn't these things be true?'

I said 'And at some moment you masturbate.'

He said 'Don't you?'

He was in league with some so-called hackers or crackers whom he stayed with when he was in London. They were the people trying to break into the networks and systems of businesses and governmental agencies. They could introduce viruses into their networks by tempting them to download pornographic images.

I said 'You just want to cause chaos?'

'I suppose I want people to know their limitations.'

'To know their weaknesses?'

'Not to be so sure they know what reality is.'

Recently however there had been reports that some hackers or crackers in America had succeeded in inserting a worm or a virus into a military system and had been arrested and had subsequently disappeared. I said 'But is it worth it? Isn't it dangerous?'

He said 'But isn't the other thing dangerous too?' Then – 'You know these bombing raids on Iraq?'

'Yes?'

'How do you know whether they're real?'

'People on the ground presumably know whether they're real.'

'What people on the ground? How would you know?'

'You think they might not be happening?'

'I think if one made them seem silly enough, they might stop.'

I said 'But with luck, may not all this all this computer stuff be cracking up anyway?'

This was the time when there was beginning to be serious concern (though no one as usual knew what was true) about the so-called millennium bug, which was the supposed inability of computers to handle the change of date to the year two thousand: this might lead to large-scale breakdowns in society. There was alarm amongst not only cranks and catastrophe freaks but people responsible for running the world – company directors, ecological pundits, and so on – who were said to be laying in stores, cash, weapons, and retiring to remote parts of the country to await or outwit Armageddon. And this was in parallel to the plans of religious freaks who were said to be intending to congregate in swarms on the Mount of Olives in Jerusalem to await the Second Coming; and if it did not come, to carry out mass suicides.

Edward said 'But that's nonsense about the bug.'

'How do you know?'

'Unless we manage to insert it ourselves.'

Edward took me out to lunch at another expensive restaurant. We ate oysters. He said 'But anyway, why shouldn't we be approaching a state of grace – eat drink and be merry, for tomorrow we may die, or on the other hand we can act as if we might.'

I said 'I've always thought I was going to die.'

'Why?'

'Apparently there was something wrong with me when I was born.'

'Ah they spotted that did they?'

'So I can take advantage of it, yes.'

'My father wants to make a film about apocalypse at the millennium. Some sort of dreadful warning. No meteors or spaceships, but people rushing to Jerusalem wanting to die.'

'He thinks that will happen?'

'He's picked up something on the Net. He's got an idea about a new biological weapon.'

'My father once wrote a film script about a bomb in Jerusalem.'

'This biological weapon is supposed to be genetically engineered to distinguish between ethnic groups, so that it will kill only whom one wants. So the last restraint on using a biological weapon will have gone, which was that it would wipe out the users as well as their enemies.'

'That's possible? I mean, it's true they might get a virus that would distinguish between groups?'

'As I keep on telling you, who knows what's true?'

'But who's supposed to be doing this?'

'Since it won't work as planned anyway, what does it matter who?'

'You mean they may try it, and we'll all be wiped out? That's what your people are saying on the Net?'

'That's what my father's saying.'

'That's what you say he's saying?'

'Oh shut up.'

After lunch I wanted to go to an art gallery where there was an exhibition of paintings on loan from a local country house, including a famous Madonna and Child by Giovanni Bellini. Edward said he would come with me. I said 'It's important to be able to say goodbye to loved ones.' Edward said 'It's all right for you who are supposed to be dying anyway.'

When we got to the gallery I felt I might cry. I am never quite sure what to do in front of a great painting: you stand facing it, look at it, and then from time to time it is, yes, as if they are waves from another universe coming in and forming particles in your brain; and yes, for a moment your and their worlds become superimposed: there has been an earthquake which reaches you as a wingbeat. After I had been for some time in front of the Bellini Madonna and Child I did find that I was crying. Edward said 'Are you all right?'

I said 'It's so awful.'

'The picture?'

'No. Us.'

'Oh well, so long as it's not the picture.'

I thought about this. I said 'Yes I see.' I stopped crying. I said 'So that's all right.'

The image that I had had of a joust with Christina was one which I felt now had led me to make something of a fool of myself; but still she had as it were thrown me a bouquet for my effort. But this was as far as such a feminist went? The feelings that I had towards her were still sexual; but not so much now in the style of grappling, of contest, but rather of being at the command of some dark goddess, as men in story-books are supposed to be nobly and romantically, but on the Net squalidly.

I did not hear from Christina until almost the end of term, in spite of the message that had been given to me by her friend when I had been in the pub with my father. Then one day there was a note for me in my pigeon-hole in the college: Christina was inviting me to the private showing of a film; we could meet in a pub, and then go to the film together.

The pub was not one I had been in before. I wondered – It is propitious or unpropitious that she apparently does not want to be seen with me by her friends in the cellar?

I was determined to try to make something sexual happen at this meeting; it seemed pathetic that I had not yet had a full sexual encounter. I did not think I need worry about being irresponsible here; one of the virtues of Christina was that surely she would take responsibility for herself. I worried, of course, that I might make a fool of myself. But she had shown that she liked me, had she not?

On my way to the pub I was full of imaginings about how Christina and I would not even get as far as the film; we would go without much preamble to an upstairs room; there it would be like – well, not like anything on the Net, nor even those urgent clothes-tearings such as one saw in films. Just something, I continued to think, rather business-like and sensible. But what of the stories of first-time impotence – the more you wanted it the more you failed; and so was there any trick by which you could make out to yourself that you did not really want what you so much wanted? Why did books talk about failures or rapturous successes but never about skill or application to get from one to the other?

The pub was an old-fashioned one with middle-aged drinkers amongst whom Christina in her black tights and short leather skirt stood out like a glamorous executioner. She said 'I'm sorry about this place.' I said 'I thought perhaps you were trying to be incognito.'

I do not think I felt nervous. I was so pleased to be with Christina, it seemed that most of my desire had gone.

She said 'I wanted to ask you something about what you said about biology.'

'About biology.'

'Yes. You said it was necessary to let nature do selecting for survival, or else the wrong things were likely to be picked.'

'Oh yes, well, because nature's the environment, and the environment is what judges what's fitted to it and what is not.'

'You don't think we can judge.'

'But I said I was wrong about that, because of course we're part of nature, and in so far as we can see that, then perhaps we can be a bit more than nature; part of the deciding, yes.'

We had sat down at a table. I thought – We are like people who have five minutes' visiting time to plan an escape from prison. There had been no question of getting any drinks.

She said 'What does it mean, being more than just part of nature?'

'Well, we feel we're in some way responsible for it, don't we? Have you seen that Bellini Madonna and Child?'

She looked away from me dreamily. I thought – She is being touched by some alternative world?

She said 'Why did you come to that meeting?'

'I wanted to get to know you.'

'Why?'

'Why do you think?'

'I don't know.' She looked at me; and then it was as if her question had not been rhetorical, but one to which it was vital she should know the answer.

I said 'Well I don't know either.'

'You can do better than that.'

'All right, I wanted to make love to you.'

'By coming to the meeting?'

'Yes.'

She did a short raucous laugh. She looked round the room as if she was expecting people to have noticed. Then she said 'All right let's have a drink.'

I went to the bar and ordered. When you are at a bar, and the person who you are with has stayed at a table, it is like having a short holiday from care.

When I came back to her she said 'You expect a lot don't you.'

I said 'No I don't think so. I don't think expecting things pays off.'

She laughed again. Then – 'You said men should take responsibility.'

'Yes.'

'For what –'

'For what turns up.'

'What if women don't need them to take responsibility?'

'Then that's all right, isn't it?'

I thought – But she is nervous! Then – For all the feminist business perhaps it's harder for her than it is for me.

She finished her drink. She said 'Come along then.'

I said 'To the film?'

She said 'Oh for God's sake, don't be funny!'

When we were out in the street I did not know whether to take her arm; this might seem proprietorial. I walked rather cautiously with my head down and my arms by my side like people are told to do when they think they might be mugged. I thought – But this is funny.

She said 'I sometimes wondered if you were gay. I've seen you with that Edward Constantine.'

I thought – So you had noticed me!

I said 'I don't think I know what I am.'

'And what does that mean?'

'Well we'll find out, won't we.'

She seemed to know where we were going. The pub was quite close to the college where there had been the meeting. I wondered if we might be going up to her room there, but she stopped short of the college at the door of what looked like a lodging house. She said 'Look, you don't have to do this if you don't want to.'

I said 'Of course I want to. Of course I have to do this.'

'All right then.'

She had a key for the door; she led me across the hall and up some stairs. She did not put a light on. Following her I thought – This is like going up a ladder into a new universe.

In a room on the second floor she put a bright light on. I thought – So now there's going to be the testing; the interrogation.

Christina took her skirt and tights off and suddenly it was like nothing that you see in films: it was as if she were a huge baby and she was watching me with black eyes that did not want to trust anyone, that had never before trusted anyone; why on earth should anyone trust anyone? I took my clothes off and knelt over her and stroked her as I had read in books that one should do, and I thought – But isn't it prostitutes who don't take their tops off? She said 'You don't have to do all that.' I said 'Can you take your top off?'

After a moment she sat up and did so.

I thought – But there is something miraculous after all about this body when you are over it, on it: it is like a Chinese garden, with its landscape of smooth stones and soft rocks, its pathways and bridges, its sudden intimation of the sacred that wishes to take you in; but can it; can you? Then I thought – Oh God I am so grateful: I'm going to be able to do this, and to adore this, after all! She tolerated me for a time: there was a moment when she said 'There's some grease on the table' and I thought of saying – There's perfectly good grease here. Then she was beginning to change: she became like one of those magic pellets that you drop into water and what has been like a hard seed blossoms, explodes into an exotic flower. This was happening to both of us. There was a moment when she murmured 'Oh God I'm going to like this!' and it was after all not so difficult – that strange conjunction of the mechanical and spiritual, the collapse of particles into a tidal-wave function.

When it was over I lay on top of her like a jellyfish when the tide had gone out, my arms and legs feeling as if they were iridescent, my body not so much myself as a colony of all the beautiful bits and pieces that have lain on a beach after making love.

After a time she said 'You're squashing me.' Then – 'No, I don't mean that, please go on.' Then – 'I've got to learn.' Then – 'Where did you learn?'

I said 'I didn't. I've just learned.'

'You mean it's your first time too?'

'It's your first time?'

'In a way.'

'Yes, in a way.'

She moved her head away from mine so that she could see me and she said 'That's why you didn't take any precautions?'

'Oh I'm sorry, but I didn't think that was the point.'

'What did you think was the point?'

'I thought you were so wonderful!'

'You trusted me?'

'Yes I trusted you.'

She was searching as if for something just beyond my eyes. I wondered – But what is it that she has trusted?

78

Then after a time she said 'I mean, that I didn't have AIDS.'
She gave another of her short raucous laughs.

I said 'But if it was the first time, you couldn't have AIDS.'

'But you didn't know it was my first time.'

'Oh no, that's true.'

Then we were both laughing. I thought – But there is something quite different happening here; not so much what we didn't expect, as what we still don't quite know about.

She said 'And why didn't you think I was gay?'

I said 'Well you don't seem to be gay.'

'Well I am, actually. Do you mind?'

'Why on earth should I mind?'

'That I made use of you? I just wanted to see what it was like?'

'Well I made use of you too. And if that's what it's like –'

'What?'

'Very nice, thank you.'

Then we both seemed to be quite carried away with laughing. I thought – We are like particles of dust being shaken out from a carpet and being carried off round the universe.

I V

I did not see Christina again before the end of term. It seemed that this was what we both wanted. I tried to explain to myself – There are turning points in one's life that are this just because they have their own momentum.

During that Easter holidays of 1999 there seemed also to be some turning point in the outside world though this was not immediately apparent. It was the time when the Western Allies began to bomb Serbia on account of the Serbian persecution of Albanians in Kosovo: it was said that the bombing was being done on moral grounds to prevent ethnic cleansing. But the area was of little strategic or economic importance to the West, and the bombing itself could be seen as a form of persecution. What forced itself on to Western moral consciousness was the portrayal of Albanian victims on television: it seemed that there had to be some response to the visual witnessing of atrocities, even if the only ones that were noted were those that happened to be convenient, and the outcome of responses to them was dubious. Technology, that is, under its blanketing cover of triviality, seemed to be creating a sense of global responsibility: and this was a sense in which an instinct about means took precedence over an evaluation of ends. And it probably prospered just because it was enabled to remain somewhat secret.

In my work I was trying to look at the origins of European literature: why had Homer's Iliad for instance been so much honoured and loved – a story of young men spilling one another's guts out on the sand outside Troy; offering entrails in honour of the gods. This had set a style of revenge and rhetoric which humans had revered for three thousand years: not much had changed, except perhaps there was a growing reluctance on the part of nations or groups to glorify themselves. Moral precepts had once been flaunted for the justification of one's own cause and the doing down of one's enemies; now the style was rather to ridicule and drag down almost everything. But here too under cover of the bombardment of cynicism and denigration the forces of orderliness were perhaps enabled to creep forwards unmolested. With such massive displays of entropy, pockets of energy might have a chance to spread.

That seemed to me to be a hope at least, for which every now and then there broke through scraps of evidence. But was there any evidence for connections between public and private worlds?

I sat upstairs in our house outside London where I had the use of my father's computer when he was away. I fiddled on the Net, and it was as if I had the run of a sluggish and meaningless universal mind; there was so much information coming in and so little with which to sort it; nothing except the wayward and puzzled and puzzling human mind. But in front of the Net the human mind was worn down, benumbed: how could one have the means to make any judgment about what was relevant, what was true? There was a certain amount of hate on the Net which seemed representative of what went on in the outside world – the bloodstained earth outside Troy; in the back yards of Kosovo.

Or could it be that the Net was a sort of exercise ground on which hatred could wear itself out.

In the course of wandering on my father's computer I came across some letters from my father to someone called Anna; they had been written quite recently; one was dated the previous autumn. I could work out that Anna must be someone at the wildlife station. The letters were sad and rather beautiful; they were not love letters in the way of expressing needs and longings; they were rueful about what might have been rather than what was. I thought – But how bold of my father not to have wanted to wipe these off his computer: is this a sort of trust that if things are acknowledged, they will sort themselves out?

But this might explain why I had felt some awkwardness between my father and my mother – even some distancing between them and me. Neither would wish to involve me in any trouble between them: but had we not all agreed that I should now be distancing myself somewhat from them?

When I went back to the university for the summer term I did go looking for Christina. In the lodging house where she had taken me I found her friend who I had learned was called Emily; she said that Christina was not coming back this term; she was spending the spring and summer doing fieldwork in Turkey. I had not, until then, paid much attention to the fact of Christina's subject being archaeology: I now wondered – What on earth is there to dig up in Turkey? Emily did not seem hostile to me: I did not feel hostile to her. I had worked out – Emily must be, yes, the special friend with whom Christina is gay. This almost seemed to make a bond between me and Emily now that Christina was away.

I went to find Edward. He had spent some of the holidays with his father in his house outside Paris. Edward said 'My father's wondering whether he's missed the bus with his film about the millennium. He thinks the balloon may go up before the Second Coming.'

I said 'What balloon?'

'That ethnic biological weapon does seem to be true. And you can buy second-hand Russian rockets to deliver it, or you don't even need a rocket at all.'

'But as you say, it won't work as planned.'

'And doesn't that cheer you up?'

I became depressed that summer term. I minded Christina being away, and that she had not been in touch with me.

I said to Edward 'There's always a race between the people, or the forces, who on purpose or inadvertently want to blow up the world, and the half-dozen or so who keep the whole show on the road.'

'What half-dozen people?'

'That's a legend.'

'You can tell that to my father. He wants us both to come and stay at the end of term.'

'You've told your father about me?'

'Oh yes, he knows about you.' Edward laughed.

I thought – He's being mysterious: well I'm not going to fall for being curious, though of course I'm flattered.

Part of my depression was due to my interest in my work seeming to reach a dead end. I had wanted to understand how humanity worked; how it might be changed; but people in the humanities at the university did not seem interested in change, and even scientists, though tinkering with engineering, seemed to insist that there was no need to look where they were going. I found it difficult to write acceptable essays; difficult now to argue either with my tutor or with Edward. I began to think of giving up the English literature course, even of leaving the university at the end of term. I daydreamed more than ever of those hermits who, confronted by an apparently mad and self-destructive world, had retreated to the west coast of Ireland. Stories of present-day atrocities persisted: together with stories of stories of atrocities being made up, to satisfy people's craving for such stories.

My dreams of Ireland revolved around my going to stay in the cottage and there coming across, perhaps even giving shelter to, the girl with fair hair: might not she, as well as the boy, be in some danger from terrorists? We would lie together, the girl and I, with our arms round one another; we need not make love; we would wait for the flood of violence and hatred to go down, every now and then sending a bird out from our Ark.

I went for walks by the river. The hockey players had gone; there were no more sun-worshippers although it was summer. On the island there were sometimes at night parties with fiery lights and screaming music. I went to one of these and went through the motions of shaking my fists and fingers at the dark sky.

Then one day towards the end of term my mother telephoned to say that she was coming to see me and would I book a table to have lunch. I thought – She wants to talk about my father? She has found those letters on his computer?

I took her to lunch in the restaurant where I had first had dinner with Edward. Sitting across the table from her I was struck, as I often was, by how young and pretty she looked; but she had also always seemed vulnerable. For as long as I could remember I had felt that as well as being dependent on my mother I should be protective of her: but now, when she might need some protection, I found myself curiously aloof. Sons are supposed to be in love with their mothers? I had felt nothing odd about this. But now – was it just that I was in love with someone else?

I was prepared to be wise and reassuring about my father – Oh yes, but haven't we always known that he's silly about women? Then when we had ordered food and beer my mother said 'I hear you're a friend of Eddie Constantine's.'

I said 'Yes, he took me to dinner here as a matter of fact the first time we met. Have you heard of him?'

'Why haven't you talked about him?'

'I don't know. Perhaps I thought it would be showing off.'

'Showing off!' Then – 'How did you get to know him?'

'I bumped into him,'

'And you like him –'

'Yes.'

'I was once a friend of his father's. Did you know?'

I thought – Well this is more interesting than a conversation about my father. Then – You mean, you had some carry-on with Edward's father?

I said 'No.'

'I suppose I should have told you. But it was a long time ago.'

'Why should you have told me?'

'It didn't crop up.'

'No.'

I wondered – But why didn't Edward tell me? Or he didn't know?

– Or it might have been why he was being so mysterious about his father wanting me to come to Paris?

My mother said 'Things became a bit dramatic.'

'How?'

'I'll tell you one day.'

I thought – Why not tell me now?

I felt irritated with my mother. She was playing a game. She and I did not usually play games. I thought – You mean, it's because we are sitting like grown-ups across a table.

I said 'Edward wants me to go over to Paris with him one weekend.'

'Yes, so I hear.'

'What's it like there.'

'I don't know, I haven't been.'

I thought – So what did you mean by 'So I hear'? This is ridiculous. This is, yes, how grown-ups seem to behave.

I said 'I don't think I'm doing much good at this place. I mean the university. I'd like to get away in the summer. Are you keeping the cottage?'

'I don't know. Would you like me to?'

'Has Dad been back to the wildlife station?'

'He was there in the autumn. Did he talk about it to you?'

'He didn't think it was much good for filming.'

'No.'

My mother was trying to eat her food quickly as if she was hurrying past whatever it was between us, but the excellence of the food kept slowing her down. I thought – But how does one get out of, through, this sort of thing? My mother and father usually seem to manage to.

I said 'I mean, I sometimes think I'm the only sane person at this place.'

'Perhaps you are.'

'I don't suppose so.'

'Eat up your food.'

'I am.'

I thought – The reason why my mother has come down to talk to me is because she is anxious about what I might find out in Paris.

She said 'You're angry because I've told you about me and Eddie's father.'

'You've told me nothing about you and Edward's father.'

'Do you want me to?'

'Not if you don't want to.'

'Why are you being so horrid.'

'I'm not.'

'Are you worried about me and Dad?'

'No.'

'Well you might be.'

'Why.'

'All right let's change the subject.'

We ate our food. I thought – This is another symptom of the grown-up world – the way people love pushing and pulling at each other like knobs in a computer game, rather than finding out what's actually happening.

I said 'I've often wondered about that story you told me about a bomb going off by a bandstand before I was born. Why did you tell me? I mean what do you think it meant?'

'What do you mean, what do I think it meant?'

'You didn't make it up did you?'

'Good heavens, why should I?'

'To explain why I'm a freak.'

'But you're not a freak! You're perfect!'

I thought – Oh yes, that was what I was pushing and pulling to hear.

After lunch we walked, my mother and I, along the path by the river past the island where in the winter there had been the people sitting with their faces turned to the sun: where in the summer people shrieked and shook as if the fire was underneath them. This was the Sunday when there was the news of the bombing of the Chinese embassy in Belgrade, and the chance of escalation into a full-scale war.

My mother said 'Look, I'm sorry I sprung it on you about Eddie's father. It's just that Connie's a difficult man and he might make trouble.'

'You had an affair with him?'

'Yes. But that was before your father.'

'How could he make trouble –'

'He was jealous of your father.'

'Jealous of Dad?'

'Yes.'

'So what.'

She put her arm through mine and her head on my shoulder. She said 'And then you were born.'

We were coming to the place by the river where I had helped the boy to struggle out of the reeds. I thought – You mean, are you really trying to say something about the possibility that Connie Constantine might be my father?

She said 'Connie was difficult about you. He's supposed to have sometimes hinted that you might be his son.'

'And I wasn't?'

'Absolutely not. Good heavens. No.'

'How do you know?'

'Connie couldn't have children. I knew it. He knew it. He didn't want other people to know it.'

'He had Edward.'

'Edward was adopted.'

'Oh. Does Edward know?'

I suddenly felt even more enormously depressed. This, yes, was the grown-up world with its intrigues and deceits, its aggressions and claims of possession, its trivialities coming after you like the ghastly witches and ghosts in *Macbeth* or *Hamlet*; or those men in canoes on the river with their painted faces and funny hats.

I said 'There was a boy here who got stuck in the reeds. I helped to pull him out.'

She said 'It was Connie who minded my being pregnant. He said I should think about having an abortion. Yes, that's what I feel guilty and resentful about.'

'You were still seeing him?'

'We were trying to work something out.'

'What?'

'About ourselves. About what people are like.' Then –
'I'm still trying to work that out.'

'But you didn't. You didn't have an abortion.'

'No. But it was so awful. So awful.'

My mother was making a face as if she might cry. I thought
– All right, it was so awful. But none of this matters now.

I said 'And you're telling me this now because you're
afraid of what he, Mr Constantine might say if I go to Paris?
Did Dad know about this? Are you having a difficult time
with Dad?'

'Dad was wonderful! I'll always be grateful to your father.'

'Well then.'

'I seem to be having a difficult time with you.'

'Now stop it!'

She had started to cry properly. I faced her and put my
arm around her. In the distance, beyond the reed-like strands
of her hair, I could see a group of girls standing by the field
where in the winter they played hockey. The field now had
bright sunlight on it so that it was like a painting. I thought
– I'm sure that one of the girls that the boy I helped from
the reeds ran to was Emily.

My mother said 'I shouldn't have said any of this. I'm
sorry.'

I said 'Why are you sorry? Why not say it? What does it
matter.'

'You're right about the bandstand. I've no idea what
happened.'

'This is like the stuff that's poured out on television.'

'What stuff?'

'Everyone having a whale of a time with their faults and
guilts. They go round on a merry-go-round of them.'

'But you are upset. I knew it!'

'I'm not. It's convention. I'm pretending to be upset. None
of this matters. Get rid of it.'

'How?'

'You press a button. It's over. Gone. Wiped out. Forgiven.'

'There may have been someone killed.'

'Oh there may have been someone killed! How many millions of people a day are killed!'

'Who's going to forgive me?'

'What for? I forgive you. Your children can forgive you.'

We were walking on. I was keeping my arm round my mother. I was thinking – What on earth did she mean that there might have been someone killed? Something more than an abortion?

I said 'I don't know if I'm even going to Paris.'

'Oh aren't you?'

'I don't give a fig for Mr Constantine. But I do want to get away at the end of term. Can I go to Ireland?'

'You're not really thinking of packing up here?'

'I don't know. I'll see. One doesn't know what will happen.'

'You want to get away from us.'

'I want to get away full stop. Edward's got some computer friends who think they can blow the whole thing up.'

'Blow up what?'

'Start a war. Start mayhem. Armageddon.'

'Can they do that?'

'I don't know.'

We walked on. My mother was calmer. She seemed to come to some resolution.

She said 'Look, I'll show you something that I wrote about that time when I was with Connie. I was fond of Connie.'

I thought – You lived with Connie?

I said 'I'd like to see it.'

'Dad wanted me to write it. You have to learn. Don't you think you learn from your mistakes?'

'So then are they mistakes? Yes.'

'Dad said you had a girlfriend who he met in the pub when he was here.'

'She wasn't my girlfriend.'

'So you have got a girlfriend?'

'Oh yes, yes, I suppose things do work themselves out, one way or another, if you let them.'

The weekend that I was to spend with Edward's father was due to take place at the end of term. I could not imagine much what it would be like: it would take place in some unknown area – both in what presumably would be a style of super-richness, and because I would be in a world once inhabited by my mother and apparently even visited by my father, about which they had told me nothing until now. I had a vision of myself entering this world like a lonely gunfighter, but I had got rid of my gun! People without guns however might be free to take advantage of whatever turned up?

I arrived in Edward's room after lunch on the Saturday. I had made some formal protestations to Edward about this weekend: I had said – I haven't got any clothes, I haven't got any money. Edward had said – My father would be most put out if you had either clothes or money. So I carried a plastic bag with a toothbrush and a book and a change of shirt. Edward was wearing a striped blazer like a cricketer in a thirties musical. I thought – For this weekend he plans to be more like Bertie Wooster than Don Quixote; does he expect me to be Jeeves?

I had understood we were going to France for just one night; there had been no talk of trains, planes, buses, so I assumed we were going to be picked up and to travel as the super-rich do – by private plane or helicopter. I had decided to ask no questions so as not to appear to be impressed;

thought this of course might be taken as a sign that I was impressed.

Edward and I set off on foot to where a car was to be waiting for us. I tried to work out — We can't be picked up at the college because Edward would be ashamed of too grand a car? Anything to do with his father has to be kept secret because of — what — risk of kidnap? Assassination?

Edward said 'Have you told your parents you're coming on this weekend?'

I said 'My mother seemed to know about it already.'

'She did?' Edward seemed put out. I wondered — Does this mean that you did or didn't know about your father and my mother?

He said 'I didn't think you knew about my father and your mother.'

In a side lane over a bridge there was a large black Mercedes with a black man in a black leather jacket standing by it. The man said 'Hi.' Edward said 'Hi.' The man opened the back door of the car. I thought — We are going to be strapped into one of those machines in which you are launched into virtual reality.

Edward and I sat in the back of the car and stretched our legs out as if we were sunbathing. There was a glass partition between us and the chauffeur. When we had driven some way Edward put his head close to a small grille in a side pillar of the car and said 'Is this thing working?' The man beyond the glass partition showed no sign of having heard him. Edward said 'The trouble with you lot is that your brains are much bigger than your penises.' There was a faint wheezing noise coming from some hidden speaker which might be the black man laughing. Edward said 'Testing testing.' Then he lay back and said 'Mister Buster listens to everything and then reports back to my father.' A voice said 'I can still hear you Mister Edward.' Edward said 'I'm working on a self-activating programme that will so upset Mister Buster that he will stop listening.' The voice over the speaker said 'I can live with a small penis Mister Edward.' Edward said 'The trouble is with the other thing.'

We drove on in silence. I thought – Perhaps the point of being bugged is that one needn't talk at all.

We arrived at a primitive-looking airfield with huts and a few small planes. The car stopped at a barrier and the black man got out and Edward said 'Let's have a pee.' I was going to say that I didn't need to pee but then in this virtual world nothing need mean what it said, so I got out and Edward and I stood at the edge of the road and he said quietly 'If we don't get another chance to talk, I must tell you that the point of this visit for me is that I want to get hold of a bit of my father's equipment, so if I seem to be doing something odd, you'll know what it is, right?' I said 'Right.' I thought – In a virtual world there's not much to say except 'Right'.

We drove on to the airstrip and up to a small jet plane. Sitting on the steps leading up to the cabin was a short neat man in riding breeches and an old-fashioned leather flying helmet: he greeted Edward with a kiss on both cheeks. He had a thin film-star face with a small moustache. Edward did not introduce me. We waved goodbye to the black man and strapped ourselves into seats. There had been no passport or customs formalities.

When we were in the air and the noise had settled Edward leaned forward and said loudly by the pilot's ear 'Did you do anything more about Puy-de-Dôme?'

The pilot said 'No I'll think of something.'

Edward said to me – 'My father thinks there's an alien base in an extinct volcano in the Massif Central.'

The pilot said 'He doesn't think it, he wants other people to think it.'

We flew on. Watching the back of the pilot's neck, I thought – Edward is in love with this man.

Edward leaned forward again and said 'How's operation Noah's Ark?'

The pilot said 'They're too well guarded.'

'Do you want more guns?'

'We've got guns.'

I wasn't sure if I was hearing correctly. Edward leaned back and said to me 'Stanislaus is a Kurd.'

I tried to work out – The Kurds are in Turkey? Turkey is where Noah's Ark came down? The Kurds are fighting for their freedom, or autonomy, like people in the Balkans?

The pilot said 'We're too scattered.'

Edward said 'That means you can have influence.'

'That's not what we want.'

'No.'

'You'll come with me?'

'If I can.'

The noise of the engine made hearing difficult. We were not in the air for very long. We crossed the Channel then there was another small airstrip in a clearing between woods. I thought I could see Paris in the distance.

The pilot said 'Let me know then.'

Edward said 'I will.'

When the pilot said goodbye to Edward he put on an actor's voice and said 'Here's looking at you kid.'

I thought – They really are lovers?

There was another car and another chauffeur, to whom Edward spoke briefly in French. We drove along a twisting route through wooded suburbs. I wondered – In virtual reality, who sets up the programmes? Who does the dialogue, the scenery? I said to Edward 'Is there anything more you should tell me before we arrive?' He said 'About what?' We came to tall iron gates on either side of which were pillars with heraldic lions on top with security cameras between their paws like prey. The lions stared into space; the cameras pointed down; the gates opened mysteriously. We went up a drive and came to a house in the style of a French château with cone-like turrets and a somewhat blank façade with rows of windows. A servant opened the door of the car for us; the house had a peculiar orange glow in the evening sun. I thought – It is a gingerbread house, with lighting as if for a fashion show.

There was a hall with a floor of large black and white marble tiles. Along one wall there was scaffolding as if part of the house was being rebuilt; or like the back of a stage set. A woman was by a table arranging flowers in a vase; she had pale brown hair and when she turned there was something strange about her face; she was pretty, but her skin was rounded and smooth like a computer simulation. She watched us come in as if she did not quite know who we were; then she murmured 'Oh Edward!' and came forward and offered her cheek to be kissed. Edward pecked at her and said loudly 'The cavalry's here!' then he turned to me and said 'You have to shout, she's deaf.' The woman said 'You don't have to shout, I'm not deaf.' I shook hands with her; I suddenly wished I had not come to this place. The woman said 'I'm so glad you could come.' I said 'It's very good of you.' I thought – But this isn't Edward's mother, it's his stepmother, or one of his father's mistresses. Then – She's like a computer simulation of my mother.

The servant had followed us and tried to take my plastic bag. I hung on to it. Edward said 'Better let him have it, he won't give up.' The woman said 'Oh why shouldn't he keep it?' I thought – I can run, but where can I run to?

We went through to a drawing room where there was antique furniture and tall windows looking out on to a lawn at the back like parkland. The woman stood in front of a wood fire in an open grate and she rubbed her hands up and down at the back of her skirt. It seemed that bits of her might melt if she got too close to the fire.

She said 'Did you have a good flight?'

Edward said 'Stanislaus was adorable.'

'Did he get up to any of his tricks?'

'No unfortunately.'

The woman said to me. 'He sometimes flies upside down just for fun.'

Edward said 'Stanislaus sometimes does a lot of things upside down for fun.'

Edward sprawled on a sofa. I had perched myself on the edge of a hard upright chair as if I was being interviewed. The woman said 'Are you sure you're comfortable?'

I said 'Oh yes I'm fine.'

Edward said 'What Phyllis means is that chair's a very valuable bit of Louis the something-or-other, and she's afraid you might smash it.'

She said 'Oh Edward, I didn't!'

We sat in silence for a time. I thought – Perhaps I might learn how to levitate. Phyllis had raised the back of her skirt by the fire. I thought – She may want to burn.

Edward said 'And how are the plans for world domination?'

She said 'Oh Edward, you are silly!'

Edward said to me 'My father's making a takeover bid for the world. He's been through God's accounts and finds they don't add up. So he thinks he might get a bargain.'

It seemed that what one had to do in this environment was to think of something witty. Witticisms would keep you afloat in this thin atmosphere like blasts of hot air into a balloon.

Edward was saying 'He thinks the shareholders will agree if the money's right.'

I said 'How much is he offering?'

'How much is he offering, Mother?'

'You must ask him.'

'Comfort, ease, titillation. Poor old God doesn't stand a chance!'

I said 'He's not offering choice?'

'Choice? Good heavens, no, not choice!'

'I thought you said he wanted to give people what they want.'

'Oh and so he does. But that's not choice.'

I was thinking – When Edward said 'Mother' he was being ironic. But then everything in this simulated world is ironic; and I am still not being witty.

I became aware that someone else had come into the room – a thickset bald man who was standing by a table in a far corner where there was an array of drinks. He was now coming towards us carrying a glass. Neither Edward nor the woman called Phyllis were paying attention to him. I did not think he was Edward's father, of whom I had seen photographs.

The man said 'No, not comfort and ease. What people want is excitement, danger. Whether or not from their armchairs. Everything on the edge of catastrophe.'

Edward and Phyllis still ignored him. I thought – Perhaps he is a simulation; one not yet programmed to respond to any attention.

He said 'Danger from the enemy without and the threat from the traitor within. Who was it who said that?' He paused, then answered himself; 'Sartre I think.'

Edward said to no one in particular 'Stanislaus says there's been massive activity around the Puy-de-Dôme. American defence shuttles coming and going like flies.'

The man said 'Really?'

Edward said 'No of course not really.'

Phyllis said 'Edward, your father's not been well.'

The thickset man said 'Human beings don't want happiness. Who said that?'

I said 'Bernard Shaw I think.'

Edward sat up and held his head. He said 'No no no, you can't say that! No straight answers to straight questions!'

I thought – They are all play-acting as if for someone watching through a two-way mirror in the next room.

Another man had appeared through the door by the drinks table. This did appear to be Connie Constantine. He was a rather fragile-looking man with a high forehead and swept-back hair; he had prominent lips, rather lizard-like. I thought – The thickset man comes into the room first like someone with a red flag; a sort of food-taster.

The thickset man had come up and was standing close to me. He said 'People love the threat of aliens: they both give a thrill and hold a hand out to us like Jesus. When we can get them into people's drawing rooms it will be peace on earth and good will for all shareholders.'

I said 'You think you'll be able to do that?'

The man said 'And provide a fuck if they want it.'

Edward said 'He's not even here!' He came up to the thickset man and put an arm round him and made as if to lift him off the ground. He said 'Look! He's chips! No fish!' The thickset man stared down into his glass. I thought – One day he may kill Edward.

Connie Constantine was coming towards us. He was being followed by a servant who was carrying a tray with glasses and a bottle of champagne. As Connie came up to me the others moved slightly away. He stood in front of me smiling. He was paying no attention to the others. I thought – This is the style of these people: they choose who shall be here and who shall not.

Connie had pale eyes like small whirlpools. I thought – One doesn't usually notice that eyes are there to suck light in.

I had stood up. I had begun to feel slightly faint. I thought – So what do you do to prevent yourself being sucked in? Put out claws? Recite a multiplication table?

The woman called Phyllis said 'Edward's here.' Then – 'Have you said hullo to your father yet?'

Edward was saying to the thickset man 'And who would you keep in your drawing room? Corpses? Under-age teddies?'

The thickset man said 'A joystick up the arse for you, Edward.'

I said to no one in particular – 'Is it true that you'll soon be able to get this sort of thing plugged straight into the nervous system?'

Connie Constantine smiled at me. Then he turned away and moved towards Edward. Edward left the thickset man, but as soon as Connie held out his arms to him Edward moved away; and when Edward seemed to be waiting for Connie to follow him, Connie went up to the woman who was in front of the fire and took from her the glass of champagne she had been holding and put it on the mantelpiece and took hold of her with his hands on her forearms, smiling.

I thought – These are pre-set moves in this game.

I had stopped trying to listen to what anyone was saying. I thought – They are in orbit round Connie; they have to keep performing: Connie is a burnt-out sun, but burnt-out suns are black holes, and things that are sucked in can never get out.

My hearing suddenly came on again as if I had inadvertently sat on a remote control. Phyllis was saying 'You haven't said hullo to Edward's friend.' Connie was saying 'I have.' Then to me 'Haven't I.'

I said 'Oh yes you have.'

Connie stood close to me again. I wondered if he might be going blind. Or perhaps he really did think I might be his son.

He said 'You have a particularly low view of the human race.'

I said 'Have I?'

'I hear you think we are irredeemable.'

'No I don't think so. Who told you that?'

'Or that things can only be redeemed by dying and starting again.'

I thought – He's been talking to my mother. I said 'But are you talking about people or ideas?'

'Genes seem most inefficient. They simply replicate.'

'Yes.'

'But with ideas one can construct an orderly society. People can be given what they want.'

'That may not be what they want.'

'They need to fight? Then they can be given games. Monty is taking care of that.'

I had finished my glass of champagne. I was looking over Connie's shoulder to where the servant was by the table with the drinks. I was thinking – The game here is for me not to drink too little, or I will become inarticulate and desperate, nor too much, or I will pass out.

The thickset man, who was presumably Monty, was saying 'We were thinking of calling the new company Nero.'

Phyllis said 'What a good name.'

Monty said 'I've got a soft spot for Nero. He was an artist.'

Edward said 'He was a scientist. He killed people who he thought were not biologically correct.'

Connie said 'There's no evidence for that.'

I said 'It's all right to get rid of ideas that are not biologically correct.'

The servant was coming round with more champagne. I held out my glass. I said 'Just a little more. Thanks.' I wondered – Why does every word that I say sound not only not witty but half-witted?

Connie said 'I knew your mother.'

'Yes I know.'

'She told you?'

'Yes.'

When he smiled he had teeth that were like those of a crocodile that might have been modelled for this effect.

I said 'It's not me, it's my father who thinks things can only be redeemed by dying and starting again.'

Connie said 'And so what do you think.'

'About what?'

'You think people should be taught new ideas?'

'Not taught.'

'What then.'

'People have to discover them. Learn from their mistakes.'

'Isn't that what your mother says?'

'Yes.'

This time when he smiled it was as if porcelain might come loose and tumble out of his mouth.

Edward said 'Watch out he doesn't bite.'

I thought – Both he and my mother are insistent that I should know that they have been seeing one another again.

The servant was murmuring something to Phyllis. Phyllis was saying 'Dinner's ready.' Edward said 'Do you want to wash?' I said 'No I'm all right.' I thought – But he might be wanting to say something to me secretly in this world of games; and I might have got hold of another glass of champagne.

We trooped across the hall and into a dining room a wall of which was the one that in the hall was supported by scaffolding. On this side too there were signs of construction – large squares of shiny tiles or panes of glass criss-crossed by strips of tape. It was like the unfinished wall of a war room on which there would be a huge map on which bombers would crawl to and fro like flies. On a daïs by a bow window there was a small round table laid with four places. I thought – So they weren't expecting me after all. Or is it Monty that they really don't think is here. Phyllis said 'I do hope you'll forgive this terrible muddle!' I said 'Oh it doesn't matter.' Connie said 'He doesn't think anything matters.' I thought – Oh all right, we've all got the message that you've been talking to my mother. Then – But indeed, what does that matter. Phyllis was saying 'Connie wants that whole wall to be something on which you can bring up anything you like.' Edward said 'You make it sound like something on which you can indeed be sick.' I thought – Yes, that's witty.

Phyllis was pulling out a chair for me to sit by her. Connie said 'No I want him by me.'

Phyllis said 'We need an extra place.'

Edward and the man called Monty were standing at the back of the same chair. Edward said 'When the music stops, Monty, turn and fire.'

Connie was settling down and saying to me 'Does your father still write scripts?'

I said 'No, he makes documentaries for television.'

'Yes I know that. Years ago he wrote one very good script.'

'Yes.'

'About Jerusalem.'

'Yes. People took it up but then wouldn't do it. It seemed impossible to get people to see what was happening.'

'Well what was happening?'

'Well there were all these absurd things going on on the surface, but what mattered was what was going on underneath.'

'I thought it was about a plot to blow up the Mosque.'

'Yes, but what happens then?'

'Well what did happen then?'

'I don't think anything much happened, actually. But if it had, would that or would that not have been a bad thing. But that's what you can't say.'

'Then what can you say.'

'Make the best of what happens.'

An extra place was being laid for the man called Monty. It had begun to seem that I should know who he was. His face had been in the papers? Wasn't he, perhaps, a junior cabinet minister?

Connie said 'I'm making a film about Jerusalem.'

I said 'My father said he wanted his film to be from a God's-eye view. But God doesn't seem to be all that much interested in who's wiped out, he keeps an eye open for who's saved.'

'And that's what you can't say?'

'I suppose you can say people wipe themselves out. God sets up the possibilities for who's saved.'

'That was in your father's script?'

'I can't remember. I think I'm just making it up.'

'Go on.'

'It's like the wave function. Do you know about the wave function?'

'Tell me about the wave function.'

Connie was smiling. He was keeping his mouth closed. I thought – But I am drunk! I have got my timing wrong, sat on the wrong button, and am going into meltdown.

I said 'The wave function is light when it exists as potentialities. Then when you give it your attention it becomes one thing rather than another.'

'And God is the wave function?'

'Yes! That's right!'

'And we are –'

'What makes one thing rather than another. Of course we can't do anything without the set-up. Like a butterfly's wingbeat. Do you know about a butterfly's wingbeat?

103

'Yes I know about a butterfly's wingbeat.'

'Wham, bang, and Jerusalem's hit the fan!' I thought – Oh God, surely that's quite witty?

Connie's smile had become almost seraphic. I thought – Perhaps he will leave my mother and me all his money.

Phyllis was saying 'Aren't you going to eat your food?'

Edward said 'Oh crap, crap, crap!' He banged on the table.

Monty man said 'For once Master Edward, I think it's you who've hit the fan.'

Connie said 'If you want a crap, go and have one.'

Phyllis said 'Oh Connie!'

Edward pushed his chair back and stood up unsteadily. He said 'I'm feeling rather ill.' He stumbled down from the daïs and set off across the room. I wondered if I should go after him. Connie said 'Leave him.' Monty said 'He's been cooking up for this all evening.'

I tried to remember what Edward had said at the airport – Don't be surprised at anything I do? He had wanted to get hold of a bit of his father's computer equipment?

Connie was saying to me 'You'd be interested in a film about Jerusalem?'

I said 'I don't know about Jerusalem.'

'How would you get any of your stuff in a film.'

'You'd want a story about people who watched the uproar but were interested in what might come out of it.'

'And they'd be survivors?'

'Well, I suppose, that's what they'd be interested to find out.'

'But you think so?'

'You'd have to leave it open. You wouldn't be able to say.'

'To say what –'

'It would have to seem to be chance.'

'But it wouldn't be?'

'Oh, yes, yes, of course it would be.'

'But you might see what you can't say?'

'Oh, you might see a pattern looking back.'

'You think your father might be interested in this film?'

I could not make out how drunk I was. A footman had been coming round with wine like a man baling out a boat. I was excited because I seemed suddenly to have seen the answer to all the philosophical and aesthetic problems of the universe. Of course it was possible that this could be drunkenness.

And might not Connie's attention to me just be due to a desire to keep in touch with my mother?

Edward had reappeared in the shadows by a door at the far end of the room: he was like a ghost summoning off-stage some paralytic Shakespearean actor. It seemed that I might have undertaken to provide some cover for Edward, so I said 'I think I'd better just see how Edward is.' Connie said 'I should like to continue this conversation in London.' I said 'Yes I'd like to.' I got down from the daïs treading with care. I thought – But I am really drunk! I will not even have to pretend, like Edward.

Out in the hall there was the scaffolding and Edward was sheltering behind one of the props: it was as if he were both hiding and wanting to be found as in a children's game. He whispered fiercely 'Well now you know why you're here!' I said 'Why?' He said 'He's after your mother.' I said 'Oh is he.'

I thought – Then you mean, he hasn't got her?

Edward said 'Will you watch out for me? Tell me if anyone's coming.'

I said 'All right.'

'I'm going into his study.'

'What are you going to do there.'

Edward ducked underneath the scaffolding and tried to open a door that appeared to be locked. He said 'Bugger.' Then – 'They made home movies, did you know?'

I thought – And that's the bit of software with which you think you might blow up the world?

Edward heaved at the door and it seemed it was not locked, there was something propped against it from inside. Edward put his hand round the door and removed a piece of scaffolding. He said 'They're supposed to have bumped a man off, did you know?'

I thought – Oh dear oh dear, yes I heard about that one, you mean they made snuff videos?

The room that the door opened on to was like a library but most of the books were still on the floor. There was a huge desk in the centre on which there was computer equipment with a monitor from which wires went trailing away: it was like the body of an octopus with long thin tentacles that flowed over the encrusted ridges of books and files. The windows were shuttered so that the room was mostly in darkness, but light filtered through from the slats and from the door. I thought – We are under water but can breathe. Most of the wires led to the wall by the door which like the wall in the dining room was still being constructed for some system of display; it gleamed furtively with semi-opaque glass squares. I thought – The whole house is being wired for fantasies, for dreams: is he trying to get back to my mother for reality?

Edward had gone to the far side of the desk and was pulling at the drawers. He got one or two opened and was rummaging though them. He was swearing and nodding his head. I said 'Who was bumped off? What sort of movies?'

He said 'But that's not what I'm looking for.'

I was moving towards the unfinished wall which was being built to house the screens; I wanted to touch it: it might be like that special effect in films when your hand goes through as if through water. I thought – Well what are you looking for: you think there is really some software that might give you power? I came to strands of wire that were like weeds and hard edges like coral; then something soft like a sea anemone. I had been thinking – Or you mean Connie and my mother just liked watching videos of themselves: in which case – Good luck to them! But I jerked my hand away when I had come across what had felt like a sea anemone or an eye and then the whole texture of the room suddenly changed; a splintered light came in like arrows; it was coming through the gaps and cracks in the closed shutters from what seemed to be a very bright light outside. Then a loud disembodied voice was saying first in French and then in English – 'Do not move. This house is surrounded. Stay exactly where you are.' Edward said 'Oh fucking hell.' I thought – We will become victims in a snuff movie?

Edward, holding something like the container of a disc in his hand, was moving towards the door. He said 'Say we saw someone from outside breaking in.' I said 'What's that in your hand?' He went out into the hall.

What happened next was obscure because there was too much going on all at once, there was not enough time for it to be sorted. I followed Edward into the hall by the scaffolding. There were sounds of footsteps running on the driveway outside. Edward and I stood like people who have been told to put their hands above their heads. I said 'Edward give that to me.' He said 'It's nothing to do with you.' I said 'What is it then.' He said 'It's for Stanislaus.' I thought – Oh good, I needn't do anything about it then.

The door from the dining room behind us opened and from it someone came running and at the same time the front door opened and the bright light from the driveway came flooding in. Edward's face was towards me and in the pale light he was like some striking medieval figure on the doorway of a cathedral. He said 'Sorry.' Then someone came up behind him and put an arm round his neck as if to strangle him. I thought – It is Monty, the thickset man; and he does have reason to want to kill Edward. Then I was trying to say – Oh well, never mind, we both might be able to use this to our advantage. But then something hit me on the side of my head and I fell down; and I thought – Oh well, so long as I am not dying.

V

When I had been kneeling on the floor of Connie Constantine's house near Paris it had seemed that I could take advantage of appearing to be for a while half-unconscious because like this I need not struggle with convoluted explanations about what I was doing with Edward under the scaffolding in the hall and with the door open into Connie's study. To make sense of this I would have to get my story to tally with Edward's, and Edward seemed to have disappeared. But when you are knocked out you are supposed not to remember what happened just before and of course just after; so when it seemed that I might take note of what was going on I could plausibly look round half-wittedly and mutter as if I hardly knew where I was or what I had been doing. But then it struck me that because of my absurd fragile skull I might really be dying, and how on earth might that be an advantage to me?

It seemed that what had happened in the hall was that after myself or Edward had set off the burglar alarm some security men had come running in from outside at the same time as the man called Monty had run in from the dining room and got his arm round Edward's throat thinking he was a burglar (or not? he had reason to feel hostile to Edward) and in the general mêlée of who might or might not be an intruder someone had bumped against a prop that held up the scaffolding and a cross-beam had become dislodged and had fallen against my head. That at least was what was likely; though I could make out that I imagined I had been bashed by one of the security men, and this would give me some hold over the situation, because people would surely be anxious to allay the effects of my having been gratuitously injured. Anyway there I was on my hands and knees and blood was dripping on to the floor and I was thinking – Oh good, this must look quite dramatic; so long as I am not dying.

The rest of the evening seemed to carry on in this style: there were people standing round me talking, pulling at my shoulder, feeling my hair; voices were saying 'Get a bandage' 'We must get him to hospital' 'Get Stanislaus' 'No you stay here.' I wondered why Edward was not there: had he already gone to join Stanislaus? They had been planning to make some getaway. I was being lain on my back, was being sat up, someone was sponging and holding a cloth to my head. Connie was saying 'He needs stitches.' I was saying 'No I'm all right.' Connie said 'Phyllis you go with him to the hospital.' I was saying 'No I must get home.' I was thinking – As a victim you have some sort of power; people want to get rid of you; they feel guilty.

In my determination that in order to protect myself I had to get away from Connie's house and get home – by home I meant no more than back to England – I suppose in fact I was suffering from some form of concussion. Phyllis came with me to the hospital; perhaps she wanted a respite from manoeuvres and explanations. After I had been given injections and the wound on my head had been stitched Phyllis was saying I must come back to Connie's house, but I was still insisting that I must get away. I had my head bandaged like an Indian fakir and I felt that like this I did have some mad authority. It was arranged that I would stay for the night under observation in the hospital and in the morning Stanislaus would fly me back to England. In the event it was not Stanislaus who flew me; there was a message from Edward at the airport to say he was glad I was all right and he would be in touch.

When I got home – I realised with some surprise that all this time I had been thinking of my room in college as 'home' – I settled in and thought I might sit cross-legged on the floor with my bandages like a turban and await, as fakirs do, the return of my moment of illumination I had experienced when talking to Connie. This had become lost in some corner of my brain as such things do; but I thought if I was patient it might return. It was officially the end of term but I got permission to stay on in the college: I explained that I had work to catch up with; also in a few days I would be going to the local hospital to have my stitches removed. I did not want to make contact with Edward or Connie and his entourage nor indeed with my parents: what hints I had picked up about my mother in the past had not affected me in that I believed they were necessarily true; but the whole experience at Connie's house seemed to exemplify the atmosphere of intrigue from which I wished to get away; and so I felt myself justified in feeling driven into some sort of hiding. But what was the flash of possibly quite spurious illumination that I might coax out of the recesses of my brain like a shy animal?

When my father had spoken of the science of the second half of the twentieth century being not so much to do with discoveries as with trying to understand the discoveries that had been made, it was not clear what form such an 'under-standing' might take. What had been discovered seemed irrational, so understanding could hardly be expected to be rational; and at the university I had learned what little weight philosophers and literary people gave to the chance of getting hold of any objective 'meaning': the word was held to be valid only if it referred to the interpretation that a reader or critic might give to it. There was no 'truth' or 'authenticity' to be discovered 'out there'.

To people of my father's generation this situation seemed often to be one of disintegration and doom: with no moral or religious precepts generally accepted as guidelines, civilisation was felt to have lost its way. However the people who spoke like this for the most part lived in and looked out on a world that seemed to be getting along quite nicely; and indeed my father, who spoke of the likelihood of catastrophe before there could be regeneration, did this with an excited and hopeful gleam in his eye.

So it seemed to me that the very lack of certainties – this was what I tried to drag up from the depths as I sat like an Indian fakir in my room – it was as if the very lack of certainties might provide opportunities more lively than certainties; and it was words that, like bodyguards, might protect one against being too foolhardy. Humans were in the business of creation – of themselves, of the outside world – and this was of a more exciting if risky nature than that of obedience to laws and 'truths' that had been accepted at one time as useful. But with this sort of understanding there did nevertheless seem to exist an 'out there' – not unalterable, but one to be worked upon, searched within – and this could be experienced, because otherwise humans would be flailing in a vacuum, which they did not always feel themselves to be. However one could not talk about this much or one would be pinning down as a captive what one should be in relationship with as it were as a friend. There could be a partnership, that is, between oneself and a world 'out there'; and if the experience of this could be accepted, then in time it might come to be trusted. This might be appreciated in the form of moral or religious understanding: it was just the attempt to set this fast in words that made it so often ridiculous. Words were good at saying what things are not, not for saying what things are. A telling legend for humans was, yes, the story of the Tower of Babel.

I tried during this time to take more than passing note of what was being written up in the newspapers. I had once thought that people's satisfaction in reading about famines in Africa, floods and hurricanes in Central America, massacres and mayhem in the Middle East, was simply perverse – demonstrating enjoyment of accounts of cruelty and suffering, or a scarcely less grim pleasure in feeling oneself aloof from the agonies of others. But now I wondered – Might not this sort of interest be that of a blundering people trying to find their way in the dark; trying to make out their responsibilities in a world in which there no longer seems to be a responsible God, groping to come to terms with the realisation that it is they who have to do something about savagery and suffering but bewildered by how little they can do: but then what little after all had the old God seemed willing or able to do? But by bumping through the puzzling and dangerous hazards of a maze might not humans be learning what sort of creators, experimenters, discoverers (not dictators) they, standing in as it were for gods, might be able to be; even that there did exist for them something of what had been imagined as the power of the old God, since there was still available the conditions by which they might learn.

In particular at this time there was news of the war in the Balkans that seemed to have begun without much forethought or planning: atrocities were reported and shown on television; there had been the reaction 'something must be done'. And so bombs had showered down like rain; atrocities had grown and flourished; and the question ceased to be one of who would win a war and who would lose it, but of how long horror and absurdity would have to go on before people

113

became fed up and saw that it might be something new that had to be learned. But what might this be? Not just the horror of atrocity nor that it would be better if it stopped: so much had been evident. But rather – what should humans do about what seemed their entrapment in absurdity: should they renounce efforts at responsibility for others and withdraw within their separate containments; or might they learn that, in spite of lack of immediate or obvious success, there might be trust in the evolving long-term effects of trying to sort things out.

Edward had told me of a computer game that some of his friends had been trying to develop during the winter; this was to do with traditional politics and antagonisms concerning nationality, race, religious convictions. Settings would be, for instance, a cabinet room in Jerusalem; an underground bunker in Baghdad: figures on the screen and players would have limited choices – to carry out a pre-emptive or reactive strike, make this or that bluff, carry out executions or reprisals here or there – but the programming, the imagery, of the game would be set. There would be scenes on the steps of planes of triumphant or exhausted diplomats moulded into smiles by cameras; crowds of wild-eyed men in white or black cloaks, with white or black beards, scurrying and prostrating themselves or shaking their fists at the sky. And coming into close-up at regular intervals the scenes that are the favourites in this sort of presentation – those of weeping women and mutilated children and bodies discarded on the ground like oily rags. And above it all perhaps the sound of laughter, which would be the sound of players enjoying the game – the chief player having once been thought to be that old God, but now no longer.

Edward had suggested that politicians might be tempted to give up reality for such a game if it could be made sufficiently elaborate; politicians seldom got near any fighting anyway, so in their cabinet rooms and bunkers how would they tell the difference? Edward had explained – Of course this will not happen: but the existence of the idea might make some difference.

I had suggested introducing a random element into such a game so that players would learn that in fact they had very little power over the outcome, and so in frustration might be driven to see that either it, or they in their addiction, needed a new program. But Edward had pointed out – People don't really want control: they like to gamble. I had said – But don't they want to win? Edward had said – No, then the game's over.

One evening after I had been on one of my walks by the river – with so much going on in my head that it was as if my stitches would hardly prevent it from bursting out – I bumped into my English literature tutor, almost literally, for I had gone to his room to return some books that he had lent me. The room was dark and I could not find the light switch, and I stumbled over him where he was lying on the floor. He shouted 'Hey, that's enough!' And then when he had sat up and found a light switch and had seen my bandages – 'Good God, have they been doing it to you too?' It seemed that he was rather drunk, and had been to sleep on the floor. He asked me to stay and have a drink with him.

I had spoken to no one for two or three days, but I had all this stuff going round in my head, and it seemed that he remembered some of what we had talked about in our tutorials, because he embarked almost at once on his own monologue –

'Good God, you're the one who talks about God, of course God's a gambler, God plays dice. But he's the banker, and it's the bank that wins. All right he plays with humans, and humans usually end up bankrupt: but aren't they lucky to be in the game at all? What a story! God doubling up on his losses like a mad Mississippi riverboat player till he's got nothing left to stake except his wife and child which he does – how can anyone match that! And all because he wants a bit of risk and freedom. The Bible's like a lot of books in that it ends just where it's becoming interesting. Very wise no doubt. As Wittgenstein said – When you've learned that language makes no sense, then throw away the ladder. Belt up. Isn't that what Wittgenstein said?'

I said 'I don't know.'

'Make models. Do woodwork. Help those poor buggers in Albania.'

'What's the Bible becoming interesting about when it ends?'

'Did I say that? It tells you to throw away the ladder. Yes. Get rid of the old gods, no don't get rid of them, just belt up. If you can't stand the fire, get into the frying pan.'

'Does the Bible say that?'

'I can't remember. All that stuff about being guided by the Spirit. And the others being sent upstairs to the House of Lords. I say, that's good!'

'What about the spirit?'

'You don't know where it's come from or where it's going. It blows where it listeth. Do you know what "listeth" means? An old woman being tipped over the end of Brighton pier.'

Before this meeting with my tutor I had been thinking that I should tell him that I might not be coming back for the autumn term; but now I thought I might wait a bit longer to see what happened.

I had not been worrying about what my parents would think I was doing because they had known I was going with Edward to France and presumably they would think I was still with him. And Connie might not have got in touch with my mother about what had happened in France because – oh well, if I spent much time worrying about this

I would be doing what grown-ups liked doing, which was boring. But then a day came when my mother telephoned to the college to find out if they knew where I was, and she left a message would I please ring her. I felt I should do this, although I was reluctant to break into the conversations which I was having with myself, that I hoped in some way were like silence.

My mother said 'What on earth are you doing?'

'I've got a bit of work to finish. I hoped you might think I was still in France.'

'But you're not in France.'

'No.'

'Why didn't you let us know where you were?'

'I needed to be on my own. I thought you were saying that. It's not you, it's a psychological problem.'

'Phyllis rang to see if you were all right.'

'Yes I'm all right.'

'What was wrong with you?'

'Nothing. Things worked out all right.'

'Did you like it in France?'

'Yes and no.'

'You're being hostile.'

'I'm not, I'm keeping myself to myself.'

'Well you know what that means.'

'What.'

'Have you got that girl?'

'Which girl?'

'Never mind. Did Connie talk about me?'

'Not much. He just said he knew you.'

'So when are we going to see you.'

'I don't know. I've been thinking of going to Ireland.'

'You can't go to Ireland.'

'Why not. Have you sold the cottage?'

'No. No one will buy it.'

'It's because of those smugglers. I expect they keep their bombs there.'

'Look, what is this? What's happening?'

'Nothing's happening. Look, can I stay in the cottage? Is the key still under the stone?'

'Is it something Connie said?'

'You were going to send me that piece that you wrote, or Dad wrote, or whatever, about you and Connie.'

'Oh yes I was, wasn't I.'

'Will you send it.'

'If I can find it. I think Dad had it.'

'Is the key still under the stone?'

'How long will you be gone?'

'I don't even know if I'll go yet.'

'Why don't you just say you want to go to Ireland to see that girl. What's wrong with that?'

'Nothing.'

'Well take care of yourself, my darling, won't you.'

In the time that I had left before having my stitches out and deciding whether or not to set out for Ireland I went on searching in my head, in books, in other people's heads, to find – what – just whatever there was to be found if you looked. I picked up what I could about those Dark Age monks who had gone to Ireland: they had been fleeing from a mad world but they had hoped to get to the threshold of another world; it was this that nowadays seemed illusory. But was this all they had been doing? In my delvings in the library I came across a ninth-century monk called John Scotus Erigena who might for a time have been on one of those rocky islands off the coast of Ireland; he had also travelled and turned up at various courts in Europe or even the Middle East. He collected learning and wrote about what he had learned, but he did not just go plunging about in his head nor grope in the sky for an afterlife; he launched himself in cockleshell boats through mountainous seas; he risked himself physically in order to discover – what – about the world here and now. He said that it was in this life that one could if one chose have an experience of God; of God and humans going hand in hand, creating what happened hand in hand. In this world God was dependent on humans for what He and they did; to them He had handed over freedom: He remained that by which their freedom could operate, so of course they were dependent on Him too. But what could be learned, practised, of freedom except through exposure, risk – through trying things out by casting oneself on the waters as it were and discovering what the outcome would be after many days. But John Scotus's way of seeing things had for a thousand years been largely ignored, and freedom had been taken into custody by Church and State.

I thought – But does this stuff seem so important to me because it's already half-hidden somewhere inside me?

Then it seemed to me that, all right, I could go on forever plunging around in my head – my head with its supposedly thin skull through which I sometimes imagined messages from other worlds might come in but which recently had been almost split open as if seeds might tumble out – but sooner or later, if I was to learn any more about these seeds or bees that buzzed, I must indeed let them out and plunge after them as it were into rough seas – and did there not in fact seem to have been indicated what this implied – my just getting on a ferry-boat to Ireland?

My depression however of the beginning of the summer had returned: in particular, in the absence of Christina, I seemed once more to be massively mixed up about sex. But this was a time when the outside world seemed massively mixed up about sex: it was accepted that taboos were breaking down, but there was a puritan vindictiveness against anyone caught publicly breaking them: it was as if sexuality was reconfirming itself in its traditional colours as something savagely ambivalent – necessary for the continuation of life, yet if pursued for any other end likely to reduce humans to buffoons. But still – might there not be a virtue in humans being seen at least by themselves as buffoons? In my encounter with Christina I had not felt a buffoon. But this had occurred in such an orderly and apparently inevitable manner that it had been almost like an arranged marriage – but life-giving, rather than to do with helplessness in the face of compulsion. So what did this mean? I could not go on forever just hanging about for sex like a tick on the branch of a tree hoping to drop happily on whatever chanced to present itself beneath me.

I did have the feeling of my life now hanging on some thread – the stitches in my head not only perhaps stopping my brain spilling out, but waiting like a rope round my neck for when I dropped into the pit. And might not a jerk to immolation or oblivion be preferable to going on tumbling in free fall for ever?

I was on my way to the hospital to have my stitches out. I had removed the bandages that had been like a dirty turban round my head and I now had a large piece of plaster on the shaved side of my skull so that I appeared more like a Red Indian. During these last days the same images were recurring to me over and over again about sex and death; I was moving through a midsummer world of dust and pollen coming in on the breeze and going straight through my nose and mouth and throat down to my guts, and missing out the mind. Well how could this be stopped plaguing me except by a tourniquet round the neck? There were such stories of people hanging themselves. I approached the hospital slightly doubled up from the effect of all this; or might I be some hominid just down from the trees?

In the hospital the waiting room in the outpatients' department was as usual like a staging post for lost souls: there would be a spell in purgatory and then back to the drawing board? to the chopping board or freezer? The discomfort in my guts, groin, did now seem to have affected my mind; was there no space in a hospital for quite simple relief: there were enough beds after all. Did nursing have always to be such a cautious aid to the species?

I had had my stitches out and a new piece of plaster placed on my head and I thought I would go to get some coffee. There was a café with a coffee machine in the main hall of the building and here there was another crowd waiting but one altogether more earthy and purposive. There were families and friends of patients as if they were on some outing or picnic – and indeed hospitals now seemed to be places where families managed to gather in an increasingly dispersive world. There was a woman bending down by the coffee machine with her back to me; she was wearing a short black skirt and no stockings; the shape made by her hips was like that of the nut that is supposed to represent the shape of the female – what is the polite word for it – Hindus have some religious word, do they not? She seemed to be engaged in a more concentrated activity than just finding out how to make the machine work: it was as if while doing this she had been overtaken by some profound realisation by which she had become immobilised, until such a time as it might be able to be handled as it were like a cup of coffee. It began to dawn on me that this woman was Christina. This was so striking and yet so unlikely that my own realisation took some time to sink in. I became immobilised – out of longing perhaps that the moment should not prove to be illusory. Then Christina turned her head and was looking back at me past the line of her shoulder; but then once more remained quite still. I thought – But of course she knows me, even if this too might take some time, especially since I have half my head shaved like a Red Indian. Eventually she straightened and said 'What are you doing here?' I said 'I've come to get some stitches out of my head.' She said 'Why have you got stitches?' I said 'Something cut it open.' I thought – Perhaps the proper answer should be – So that I would come here.

She said 'It's after the end of term, I didn't think you'd be here.' I said 'No, it was just by chance that I had to stay for these stitches.' She said 'I've been away all this term.' I said 'I know, I tried to find you.'

I thought – So all this is happening like those bits of machinery that fall together in a junk yard and just happen to form a jumbo jet. She said 'This machine isn't working.' I said 'Sometimes it does if you kick it.'

She stood to one side and watched me while I pushed and pulled at the machine and got two cups of coffee. I said 'I've been coming here to have my head dressed every other day.' She said 'Well that alters the odds a bit doesn't it.' We carried our cups to a Formica-topped table and sat opposite one another. I said 'I used to have a bandage like a turban and then I hoped to look like a fakir.' She said 'You should have your whole head shaved and then you'd look like a monk.' I said 'Yes I've been thinking about that.'

She said 'So why did you try to find me?'

'I wanted to know how you were.'

'Did you want to fuck me?'

'Oh well, of course, some of the time, yes.'

'What else?'

'Of course I wanted to find you.'

I thought – We are entering that strange world of not knowing where things have come from or where they are going, but being blown along like that old lady on the end of a pier.

She said 'Have you thought about the first time we met?'

'At the women's meeting? Yes.'

'What have you thought about it.'

'What was I doing there. Why you picked me up.'

'I picked you!'

'All right, I had come there.'

'So you had picked me.'

'Of course.'

'What did you say –'

'At that meeting? About men being responsible?'

'Yes.'

'Well so they should be.'

'And women too.'

'Yes.'

She was refusing to look at me. She was gazing down at the table top. I thought – She is playing some guessing game in which it is necessary for me, for some reason, to find out the right questions; if not necessarily, yet, the right answers.

I said 'So why are you here.'

'Why do you want to know.'

'That's silly.'

'Well it's not to find out whether I've got AIDS.'

'No.' Then – 'I see.'

'Do you?'

'I might do.'

'Well I haven't got AIDS.'

It was as if I were saying to myself – Now be careful, you don't want to go over the cliff top here: or do you? Could not the old lady at the end of Brighton pier swim?

I said 'Well why are you here? And what were you thinking of doing?'

'You say "were".'

'You've already done it?'

'I might have. I had an appointment.'

'But you haven't. I mean you haven't done it.'

'The appointment's for now.' Then – 'You do know what we're talking about?'

I said 'If you want me to.'

She seemed to smile at this. Then I saw that her eyes glistened so much because they were full of tears. I put my hand across the table and held her arm.

With her head turned away from me she said 'There was a time when I thought I might want a baby. I mean before I met you. But not yet. Not then. I just wanted to know what it would be like to have what might make a baby. You say I picked you. You knew I was using you. Aren't you shocked by this?'

I said 'No.' Then – 'Why shouldn't I be honoured?'

'Oh fuck off you fool!' Tears were running down her face. But she did not try to take her arm away from my hand on the table.

After a time she went on 'When I knew I was pregnant I was furious, it was such bad luck. But then why hadn't I prevented it? You know about that? I mean the psychological thing? Part of me remembered I'd thought about becoming pregnant, so why was I furious? Was that just why? Do you understand that?'

I said 'Yes.'

'But I wasn't going to be defeated by something I hadn't planned. So didn't I have to get rid of it.'

'But you haven't.'

'Women have a right to have control, you remember?'

'Yes.'

'And then there was all the shit you said about how men should take responsibility, but how the fuck can men take responsibility, what do they think they are, and where were you God knows!'

I was thinking – I might be able to make some arrangement in Ireland.

I said 'Well I was looking for you, I told you.'

She said 'Stop it.'

'All right. But how do you think it is that I'm here?'

She was crying properly now and hitting at my arm with her free hand. I thought – It might seem that she is trying to stop me holding her arm, but she is seeing whether or not if she hurts me I will let her go: and this is how things work, isn't it – in this strange world where bits and pieces fall together as if in a junk yard to make a baby.

She said 'What can you do. What the fucking hell can you do.'

I said 'Well I can try to look after it, if you don't want to.'

She stopped hitting my arm. She said 'Are you mad?'

'I don't know.'

'That's what you said at that meeting, isn't it?'

'Yes.'

'But you don't have to have meant it.'

'How do I know what I meant? I said it.'

'What do you mean? But what do you want.'

'How do I know what I want.'

'You're mad.'

'It's happened. I said it.'

She did nothing for a time. I thought – In her heart and mind too, there are bits and pieces falling into place – clink – clunk – and causing some transformations.

Then she put her head back and let out a sort of howl.

There was a man in a white coat by the food counter who turned towards us. Christina smiled in his direction and said sweetly 'Oh yes who knows what one wants! Who cares about feelings!'

She drank her coffee. People who had been watching us turned away. After a time she said 'How can you look after it.'

'I was thinking of going to Ireland. We've got a cottage there.'

'I said how can you look after it.'

'My mother would help.'

'You're mad.'

'I might be.'

'They wouldn't let you.'

'Who?'

'Your family. The authorities.'

'Well, we'd see. I imagine it might be easier in Ireland.'

I thought suddenly – What I have had somewhere in mind all this time is that I might get that girl with fair hair to help me look after it in Ireland?

Then – Yes, but if I am mad, it is not quite my own madness.

She said 'I didn't want to ruin my life. Why should you ruin yours.'

'What's ruin.'

'All right. What about the baby.'

'What about it. It would be better dead?'

'All right. But why are you doing this? Just because you said months ago that men should take responsibility?'

'Well suppose I was right.'

'They can't.'

'They can try.'

'What do they know about babies.'

'Would you be jealous?'

'Me be jealous!'

'You'd lose some of your power to think men pathetic.'

'I don't think you're pathetic.'

'We talk about things like this, but we hardly dare try it. Of course, if they choose, men can look after babies.'

'Why should they choose.'

'They can choose to accept what happens.'

'Even if they haven't had control?'

'Who ever has control! How does anyone know what in fact will happen.'

'What about my feelings.'

'Well what about your feelings?'

'You don't think I care?'

'I don't know what you care. You haven't said, have you.'

She looked at her watch. I thought – You mean, there's still time for your appointment?

She said 'You mean, you'd let me have the baby, and then take it with you to Ireland?'

I said 'Look, I don't mind what you do, it's not up to me what you do, but I'd rather you didn't get rid of the baby, I don't know why. But I don't think I can properly say this without saying that if you don't get rid of it, and don't want it, then I'll look after it.'

'Why should you do that? Why shouldn't I get rid of it?'

'No reason.' I thought – She is on a knife edge: she doesn't know which way things will fall: she wants to stay balancing as long as she can. I said 'It's not the principle: it's something to do with what things have been leading up to.'

'What have things been leading up to?'

'This.'

She made as if to look at her watch again. She saw me noticing, and put her wrist under the table.

She said 'It's not even yet a proper baby.'

'All right it's not even to do with the baby.'

'It's my baby.'

'Yes it's your baby. But still, there are things that don't seem really to be up to us. It seems to have been like that with you and me.'

'And what if it does ruin your life. Both our lives.'

'I don't know what my life will be. I'm a fool if I think I do.'

'I know what I want my life to be.'

'Do you?'

I suddenly felt exhausted. If we were on a knife edge, it was cutting into us. I did not care what happened. I did not care what she did. It seemed that I had done what I had to do, but I had never really thought this would have any effect on the outcome.

There was an Indian family at one of the next-door tables. There were three or four children quiet, wide-eyed, attentive. I thought – All right, so we are trying to throw away our ladder.

She said 'You've got it all worked out haven't you.'

I said 'Oh for God's sake, I've got bugger all worked out.'

'Why do you think I stayed away last term?'

'Well why did you?'

'I didn't want to run into you.'

'Why not.'

'I didn't want you to give me your blather.'

Then there did seem to be some clearing as if we were looking down through clouds to the bottom of a sea far below.

She said 'Look, do you know what I was saying to myself when I was by that coffee machine? I was saying – All right, God, if that fucking creep turned up now, I'd listen to him. If he turned up with his fucking holier-than-thou shit I'd think about it, I'd be grateful, I'd see what he had to say. But of course he won't turn up now, because I'm challenging you, tempting you, God, aren't I. Oh God, you're such a creep! We all know you kick the shit out of us for doing that, don't we.'

I said 'Are you a Catholic?'

'And then I thought – But don't you get fed up, old God, with humans telling you what you can or can't do? As if you were a baby, God. Well weren't you?'

She was crying noisily now, but almost peaceably, making a sighing or sobbing noise like the wind on some strange marker at sea.

She said 'And then you did turn up.' Then quickly – 'Yes, I used to be a Catholic.'

'I wondered.'

'My mother was a Catholic. She's dead. She died on a pilgrimage to Jerusalem.'

Christina took a handkerchief from a pocket and dried her face. She blew her nose violently. Her face was strong and pretty. I thought – She would make a formidable Virgin Mary.

She said 'So you mean you might not come back to this place?'

I said 'Yes, I was thinking packing up the university, of going to Ireland anyway. This would give me some reason.'

'Why Ireland?'

'We've got this cottage there.'

'Oh yes. And Sisters of Mercy who bugger orphan children.'

'No.'

'They'd take it away from you.'

'As I said, we'll see.'

'Oh yes there's your mother.'

'And what will you be doing?'

She looked at her watch this time quite openly. But she kept her head down as if it was her face she wanted to be hiding.

She said 'I've got this job at a dig in eastern Turkey, in what was Armenia, doing fieldwork. I'd go back there, yes. I mean whether or not I'm having the baby. That would be an acceptable risk, wouldn't it?' She giggled.

I said 'Yes, that would be an acceptable risk.' Then – 'Thank you.'

'My appointment was for half an hour ago.'

'I see.'

'What do you see? I was already missing it.'

'When. Why.'

'Well what would you say – that I must have known you'd turn up?'

We were suddenly both half crying; or was it laughing; I held on to her arm across the table.

Then she said 'But this will never do. What an indulgence in feeling!' She stood up briskly and pulled her skirt down over her hips. I thought – I suppose in some quite simple way I will always adore her.

She said 'Well what would you like to do? Come back to my place? You said you were sometimes wanting to.'

'Yes I'd very much like to.'

'But I can't stand any more of the spooky stuff. Would you mind? I think we both just need a fuck.'

'Yes.'

'And nothing much more can happen this time. Would that be boring?'

'No.'

'But you know, don't you, I told you, I've got a girlfriend and I suppose I'll stick with her. She's terribly jealous of you. She says she sometimes runs into you.'

'Yes, Emily.'

'But don't get me wrong about that, either. I really do want to now.'

'Yes God knows I want to too.'

'I suppose I'll always be gay. But it's funny the other thing.'

'Yes it's funny.'

We were walking out of the hospital hand in hand. She was squeezing my hand as if she were a child. She had a grip like someone getting a hold on a javelin.

She said 'I too was getting so fed up with the university. All the intrigues, the factions. I want Emily to come with me to Turkey. There are such beautiful things there.'

'What sort of things?'

'Ruined churches. Smiling saints and animals looking down.'

'I've been finding out about old monks and hermits in Ireland.'

'There were some sort of connections.'

'What.'

'Between the people where I've been and the people who went to Ireland. You see what I mean. Spooky.'

I thought — You mean, there were those men who were blown across the sea in tiny boats?

We were towards the student hostel where we had been before. When we were in the room in which we had made love, Christina sat on the bed as if this time she was someone on the edge of a very high diving board and she said 'Look, we should try to make a bit more sense of this, shouldn't we?'

I said 'All right.'

'It wasn't that I was trying to have a baby. I wanted to see what it was like. And then you didn't take any precautions and neither did I. And I didn't try to make you. Why. What the hell.'

'Yes what the hell.'

'But then I had to promise my girlfriend that I hadn't made love to you or else she would have been so jealous. So then I couldn't then tell her I was pregnant. But if I'm going to have this baby I'll have to tell her sooner or later, don't you see, and that will have to be all right, but I don't want to have to tell her that I lied to her. So if we have a fuck now, I can tell her that it's because of this time that I'm pregnant. We'll get in a muddle about dates, but then people do, don't they?'

'Yes I believe people do.'

'But I want to be honest with you. One can't be manipulative with everyone.'

'No.'

'Do you mind if you're the person I'm honest with?'

'No.'

'As a matter of fact all this is balls. As I said, I wanted to come back here with you.'

'Well as I said, I'm honoured.'

'Oh do shut up, will you?'

'Yes.'

'But you are fond of me? You do see this is important?'

'Yes I'm very fond of you. Yes I do see that is important.'

'Well I'm fond of you too.'

'Thanks.'

'Of course we needn't make love now if you don't want to, and I could just tell Emily that I've made love to you now, but I find that it is best to keep one's manipulations down to a minimum, don't you think?'

'Yes.'

'She might have seen us come in. She might be listening. Why are you laughing?'

'Because it's funny.'

'But this time it's for real, I mean, it's for itself, for each other, no manipulation, don't you see, we know what we're doing.'

'Yes, darling Christina, yes, it's lovely, stop talking.'

So we were once more undressing – for this confirmation, commitment, highest assertion on Mount Olympus; or if one so chooses as Harlequin and Columbine in Commedia dell' Arte. But we were childlike and happy; if this wasn't love then what on earth was love; it was as if what we were doing was some promise to ourselves and the baby.

Afterwards, lying on the bed, I said 'Have you noticed how Emily looks exactly like me?'

'Of course Emily doesn't look like you!'

'She's very good looking. I thought that was why you picked me.'

'I picked you because you were the most arrogant and conceited man I could possibly imagine.'

'But you still might want me to look after the baby?'

'Of course I might want you to look after the baby!'

'Depending on what.'

'As you would say – How does one know?'

I was thinking – But it's true that it would not seem right to stay with you, live with you, marry you, darling Christina: for both of us this would not seem right. And yet I do believe that we will stay connected, yes, like those two particles who once they have made love have something the same in them even at their separate ends of the universe.

I said 'But we'll be in touch –'

'Yes we'll be in touch.'

'You'll let me know if you need me?'

'I'll let you know what happens.'

'I'll leave you my address.'

'And I'll send you a postcard of my favourite saint, Gregory the Illuminator.'

V I

Before my second encounter with Christina I had felt like
something dangling from a thread; when I set off for Ireland it
seemed that I had broken loose, taken off like a dandelion seed
and thus more like a balloonist than a monk in a cockleshell
boat; still however at the mercy of the wind and the rain, of
blasts of hot or cold air. My undertaking to look after the
baby if necessary seemed itself up in the air – in one of those
alternative worlds that would not become actual unless there
were coincidences of chances and further choices; but still the
undertaking had been given, and there were times when I
thought I had been mad. My feelings alternated in blasts of
hot and cold air.

Thus it was with the impression of both having been given
a new purpose and yet being haunted that I travelled to
Ireland: I carried a rucksack and a sleeping bag so I could feel
I was like a pilgrim with my worldly goods on my back; I had
had my hair cropped short so that I might seem unremarkable.
I travelled by bus and boat; I slept on deck, and there were the
stars which the monks had steered by: they had thought they
were travelling to the edge of the known world.

I imagined that when I got to the cottage I might find it

occupied by the people who had been using it before: would my gun still be in its hiding place in the brickwork under the sink? Did there have to be some danger for a pilgrimage to be valid?

I walked the last few miles to the cottage, coming from the other direction to that of the village with the harbour. It was becoming dusk, as it had been the previous time I had arrived here. Then I had left my father and my mother and had gone down to the sea; there I had found the boy rescuing the bird. This time I again went past the cottage and on towards the cliff. I thought I might sleep out under the stars: it was within houses that there was apt to be haunting. The wind and the cold might keep ghosts and men with guns indoors.

I found my way to the grassy knoll where I had sat a year before. Then I had tried to imagine what those hermits experienced when they felt themselves guided by God: they had chosen hardship and privation; was this simply a masochist's trick? I thought I might take my clothes off and walk up and down by the cliff edge: like this I might feel close to nature: would this be closer to God? Visions were surely engendered by a recognition of sensuality.

I took my clothes off and stood in the dark. It was in fact a warm still night, but in the air there did seem to be nudges, whispers, caresses. It was as if I were a needle in a compass being inveigled this way or that.

I walked up and down near the cliff top; I spread my arms to keep my balance, to let the air come in. One of those old monks was said to have gone over the cliff top, thinking he might fly. It was possible, yes, to feel elect, heroic: also of course absurd. I wondered – To know God, perhaps one has to feel both heroic and absurd.

And it was near here that there were those birds that might be impregnated with whatever gives rise to mutations – the cosmic radiation that is called chance, and might come from the stars. Being exposed to hardship and hunger on their rock, mutating might be open to the chances of life, while others died huddled. They spread their wings to go over the cliff top: they trusted, and flew?

I had the idea that I should make my way back to the cottage carrying my clothes and my haversack and sleeping bag; that I should confront whatever ghosts there might be in the cottage naked – even if this were quite patently histrionic and absurd. But might not just this be some protection against presumption? I was trying to understand what those monks had been up to: if it was some daft mixture of spirituality and sexuality, then was not this the stuff of life?

The darkness was now total. I had a torch in my haversack but I did not want to use it. It seemed that the whole business I was engaged in was the attempt to act out something mythological: if I had trouble in finding my way – through thorns, flints, thistles – this would be part of the journey?

– This is how a new-born baby feels; emerging into fear with closed eyes –

– You have not only to find your way, but discover what things are in the dark.

On the ground it seemed that anything was possible! Objects were not defined, they were potentialities to be felt, experienced. The softness and coldness and slight wetness of grass – the dust and these ridges where rain had moulded them – might be deserts, valleys, mountains, with myself walking above them like a giant constellation come down from the sky. In the dark you have to interpret, to build your own picture: why might you not be, as scientists suggest, on the pitted inner surface of a multi-dimensional balloon; or why might you not go tumbling over the rim of a flat earth. But you find out what is the case and what is not: you keep alert, yes, with your skin like antennae. I had to find my way to the gate of the garden; there were brambles by the gate; I could get my bearings by the thorns, the scratching. But what if there were not ghosts but in fact those men who had been waiting for my mother and me a year ago – the beams of their torches leaping out of the dark like iron bars, like baseball bats. I was anyway becoming lost; I might have to go on my hands and knees the better to feel on the ground where the path went. So it might seem that I had already been beaten up and was crawling bleeding to a ditch. And would they then leave me alone? But here were brambles, yes! I had stumbled and plunged my arms into them as if into a tub of boiling water. So get on with it: you are supposed to be learning how to survive.

I found the gate with my hands and went through into the garden. There was the short path to the door; the key to the cottage should be under a stone at the side of the porch. I found the stone but the key did not seem to be there. I had let go of my rucksack and sleeping bag and was on my hands and knees feeling the ground underneath and around the stone as if I were smoothing a small patch of earth ready to sow seeds. I felt this was funny. Perhaps I wanted to make certain I was mad; then I could be taken away and there would be no more enquiry.

I remembered that window at the side of the door had had a broken latch which we had not had mended because it had not seemed we could stop anyone who wanted to from breaking in. I found the window and pulled at it and it opened and I was grateful; I dived and slithered head-first through the opening. I was too cold and numb to feel much pain: but anyway, was not this the sort of thing I had wanted? It was as if I were a snake shedding its skin to re-enter that old and polluted garden; but hoping this time to find that other tree, what was it, the one that no one had paid much attention to because it had not been forbidden. We had left some candles and matches a year ago by the stove; but now it seemed I did not want light, I would carry on finding whatever I had to find in the dark. I was coming head-first into the front room where there was the stove at the far end; there had been a brass bedstead beneath the window through which I was tumbling; but I was landing with my hands and elbows on a table or a bench with on it what seemed at first to be the remains of a meal; there were implements that might be wooden forks and spoons and stuff that could be crumbling and hardened food; but then by the feel of this I made it out to be clay and the implements were tools – I had gone head-first into some strange workshop? I was scraping painfully down from the table or bench on to the floor; then I was crawling again, and I found what seemed to be one of the legs of the bed – thank goodness that something was what it was expected to be! And there was the mattress with something like a covering of heavy soft silk upon it; why on earth should someone have put such a covering upon it; but on the other hand why should they not? I could at least now climb on to the bed and pull the covering over me and consider my bearings.

The material was sleek and warm like a new skin. But I still had no confidence about what was around me. I thought – This is like waking up from a dream and you do not seem to be in the place which you were expecting; do you or do you not wish the lights to come on to find out the truth. It might be that those people were using the cottage again and were still here lurking in the dark. If I wanted to find what was illusion and what was not I would have to explore the room carefully, quietly; but did I want to? Would I be safer doing this than lying huddled in the dark?

I discarded my covering and set off in what I thought should be the direction of the stove; it was in front of this that there might be candles and matches: perhaps after all it would be sensible for a moment at least to have light. Almost at once I ran into something at the level of my throat; it was in the middle of the room and was hard and spiky; it was as if someone might be holding a knife against me; I put out a hand to take hold of it; I was too unnerved, almost unconscious, to dwell on being frightened; it was as if the pounding of my heart was battering fear into submission. Whatever it was that I had taken hold of was not cold like a knife: it seemed to be fluted and somewhat tattered; it was like the decaying cloth of a sleeve around bones; I might have come into a charnel house? But I felt I had to make myself explore it with my hands, or it might be I who would remain petrified for ever. It was long and sloping and slightly curved: the cloth on it might be feathers, so it was like a spread or half-folded wing. I thought – All right, not the hanged man; not a devil; you mean that bird come back – but not to haunt me: why should it haunt me? To acknowledge me: to bring some message? But where the wing joined the body there might be a head; this was what I did not want to feel. But then it was the head of a bird, yes; not a long neck; so that was according to what I remembered; almost the head of an eagle. When I came to the beak I pulled my hand away sharply; you do not want to risk more than necessary. I felt beyond the head and there was the beginning of another half-folded wing. What I had come across seemed to be the more than life-sized sculpture of a bird; I could see it in my mind; it was formed of clay and feathers and perhaps wood; it was slightly moulting; a piece had come away in my hand. It was in the middle of the living-room floor, and beneath it – but I did not want to feel much more – perhaps beneath it would be a victim with which it would feed its young; or a nest in which its young would be waiting with open mouths. I thought I should go back to the bed and lie there quietly till morning. I could pull the coverlet over my head and lie warm and curled up in my own nest. I did not even want to venture outside again to get my rucksack and sleeping bag. I wanted to be still.

There was a time in the night when I woke from sleep or perhaps I was still dreaming and I had to pee and there was a faint glow in the room as if from a break in the clouds by which some moonlight or even the beginning of dawn was getting through. I thought the best I could do was to kneel up on the bench and pee out of the window keeping my back to whatever was in the room. But I could just make out the bird, yes, and there did seem to be bits and pieces falling off it; but why shouldn't there be, why should this be unnatural? I got under the coverlet on the bed again quickly. And I must have slept again because there was light coming through the fabric of the coverlet and I was not wanting to emerge from it because I did not know what I would see clearly in the light.

When I did make the move to pull the coverlet from my head I was not after all so surprised because what I saw was what I had imagined. The living room of the cottage had been made into a workshop or studio; whoever had been using it had been working in clay and wood; there was the large figure of the bird in the centre with bits hanging from it of cloth or wire; so that it did seem, yes, that the bird might have been rising from rubbish such as one finds in the sea. But then I saw that the bits and pieces that were clinging to it and which it was either trying to lift or from which it was trying to break free, were the bodies of tiny people. The bird's feet seemed not so much to be trapped as to be trying to heave the whole rock which was its perch, its pedestal, out of the sea. And the people hanging from it might be either the food that it brought to feed its young, or perhaps they themselves were some sort of young, some dependants that had fed on it, now tumbling out of their refuge and slithering down the rock face like crabs into the sea. And then at the far side of the room, by the stove, there were two upright chairs with two almost life-size human figures seated on them; the figures were of stuffed and shaped material and seemed to be of a man and a woman; it was as if they were observing the bird and the scene; or perhaps resting from the work of having created it.

I sat on the edge of the bed. Thought – Well all right; I was wanting to be in some strange world.

Because it seemed impossible to know just what to do next, I hung my legs over the edge of the bed and swung them to and fro to pass the time. I did not feel cold although I was naked. I was aware of the extraordinary stillness of the air: it seemed it would be difficult to move from the bed without upsetting the peculiar balance of what was around me.

I noticed that the front door was open. Or had it always been open, and I had simply not noticed this when I had climbed in through the window? I thought – But if I stay still, then anyone coming in may see me as just one of the figures in this set-up.

There was someone just visible within or through the doorway; the hint of a head and shoulder; these staying still as if to give the impression of themselves being part of the created environment. But gradually more of the figure began to appear round the door – a hand, an arm, a nimbus of fair hair; the figure insinuating itself almost imperceptibly in the hope, perhaps, that it might be accepted as part of something with the stillness of a painting. I became aware – with much wonder, but is there not always wonder when one is in the presence of what one feels to be a work of art – that the figure was that of the fair-haired girl whom I had seen a year ago in the village by the harbour. When she saw me watching her she ceased to move and we each remained observing the other for a while. I thought – But then we will come alive, as things do in ballets or in fairy stories. She came on into the room moving almost briskly but still deliberately as if a false move might cause a wrong rearrangement; upset a balance or knock a chip off a piece of sculpture. She went to one of the two figures made of cloth on chairs and picked it up and sat on the chair herself and held the figure in her lap. I thought – Those figures might be representations of herself and me. She looked at me from across the room. She said 'I'll take this stuff away if you like.'

I said 'No don't take it away.'

She said 'I'm not doing this sort of thing any more.'

I said 'What sort of thing are you doing?'

It was as if we had to be rediscovering how to speak. What an extraordinary concatenation of chances had produced language!

She said 'I want to see if I can get what's required without making models.'

'You mean, make events?'

'Yes.'

'Do you think you can?'

'Well here you are.' Then – 'No I didn't say that!'

I thought – But she did say that. Then – We have to be careful that our voices don't go through this fragile fabric.

She sighed and stood up. She propped the model she had been holding on the chair. She said 'Do you mind if I take my clothes off? The tide was coming in and I had to swim some of the way.'

'No I don't mind.'

'I saw you'd taken yours off.'

She was wearing a white T-shirt and jeans. I had not noticed before that they were wet. I had not in fact noticed she was wearing clothes.

She said 'I'll light the stove.' She squatted down in front of it. She said 'You don't mind that I've been coming here?'

'No.'

'I wondered if I could look after you.' She was lighting the stove. There was a bucket with kindling wood; paper and matches. She said 'I mean, do you need someone to look after you?'

I said 'Yes I'd like someone to look after me.'

'I mean do cooking and cleaning and that sort of thing.'

'You needn't do cooking and cleaning.'

'What then.'

She was taking her clothes off. She was warm and golden as if wetness would evaporate from her.

I said 'I might need someone to help look after a baby.'

'A baby?'

'Yes. But not quite now. Some time later.'

'You've got a baby?'

'Not yet. But I think one might turn up.'

'You mean you don't want me to have a baby –'

'No. But I mean, I wouldn't mind that.'

'But that's not the point.'

'No.'

'Not at the moment.'

She had got the stove going and she was arranging her T-shirt and jeans over the back of a chair. She wore underpants. There was a kettle by the stove and she filled it from a stoup of water standing by the stove. She said 'Do you think you can make events? I mean, make art of events, rather than models?'

'I don't know. I think so.'

'Well you seemed to have done.'

'How: with the baby?'

'On that breakwater.'

'Oh I see.'

She stood with her back to me. I thought – Go on standing like that and a whole new world of events will form itself around us.

She said 'They've been trying to find out how things happen with birds. How birds find their way around. But

143

they're only interested in what they can prove, which isn't what's really interesting.'

'You know the people at the wild-life station?'

'Yes. My brother used to work for them. You know who my brother is?'

'I think so. Yes.'

'Were you frightened?'

'On the breakwater? No.'

'Why not'

'I've always thought I might die. I was pleased when I did not.'

'Oh I see. Yes.'

She went into the scullery and reappeared after a moment with a mug and a box containing tea. She said 'Anyway I wanted to thank you.'

I said 'But your brother's all right?'

'Yes he's all right. They may still be after him.'

'Who's "they"?'

'That doesn't matter.'

'And they're not after you?'

'Oh well, they might be.'

'Why –'

'They think I'm a witch.'

'With your models?'

'Oh yes, but it's quite useful for them to have me working here.' She put more kindling wood in the stove. She put the kettle on the stove and watched it. She squatted down. She said 'The mother doesn't want this baby?'

'She thinks she doesn't.'

'But she may do?'

'Yes.'

'And you thought she should have it anyway.'

'Yes.'

'And that sort of thing. And so you came here.'

'Yes.'

'I'd been wondering.'

I wondered if it might be true that if one watched a kettle it did not boil. I wanted this scene to go on for ever.

She said 'I've been coming here since the spring. I had nowhere else to work. I hoped you wouldn't mind.'

'I saw you by the harbour. Last year.'

'I know.'

'You know?'

'Yes.'

'I like your things.'

'Good.'

'I recognise the bird.'

'Oh yes you'd recognise the bird.'

'Was the other man shot?'

'Yes the other man was shot.'

'But nothing more happened?'

'They wanted someone to blame. But they couldn't, because they couldn't make out what had happened.'

'They wanted to blame your brother.'

'Yes, but it was too complex.'

She left the stove and came and stood in front of me where I was on the bed. She said 'But all this is not being a witch.'

'No.'

'I sometimes wonder if it's just how things work. I mean, it's how the brain works.'

'What —'

'Makes models.'

'And the outside world is like a brain?'

'I don't know, is it?'

'You want to see if you can make things turn out right.'

'Yes. Or make them possible.'

'Isn't that what those old monks were trying to do?'

'Oh them, yes. On their island.'

She went back to the stove and made a mug of tea. Then she came back and sat on the edge of the bed and handed me the mug. She said 'So what else did you come here for?'

'I told you.'

'You didn't know.'

'I did.'

'And you found my things here.'

'Yes.'

'I'd wondered if you'd come back, but I didn't expect you.'

'Why is making love not the point? Can you tell me?'

'Well, I suppose it takes over. You don't see things, hear things. Other things don't happen.'

'Except a baby.'

'Oh yes, but you've got your baby.'

'Would you help me look after it?'

'We'd see. It hasn't happened.'

'That could make some sort of sense of your staying here.'

'You think I could stay here?'

'Yes.'

'Or we could go to the island.'

'Could we go to the island?'

'My brother's there at the moment.'

'Is he hiding?'

'Not exactly. He's looking after it for the wild-life people.'

'That's where the birds are? Where the monks were?'

'It's difficult to get there.'

'What did the monks do?'

'Pray. Meditate.'

'Is that what you do?'

'That's not what I'd call it.'

'The birds are supposed to be changing.'

'Yes.'

She clambered up on to the foot of the bed and settled down there sitting cross-legged facing the head. I swung my legs round and up and pushed myself so that my back was against the head of the bed and I was sitting cross-legged facing her. In this position we were like those Indian or Tibetan couples I had seen pictures of who felt they had the experience of both spiritual and physical love because they were at some slight distance from each other and love did not fuse.

She said, with her eyes closed 'My brother's my twin. Our mother and father were murdered. People think we must want revenge, but I don't. People may want revenge on us because we don't want revenge. But just because things are terrible doesn't mean they matter.'

'But you're all right.'

'Yes we're all right.'

'So you have made that happen.'

'Will you come down the village this evening?'

'Yes.'

'I think it would help.'

I thought – Help what.

She now opened her eyes and looked straight at me. Her eyes were quite dry. She said 'Why have you always thought you were going to die?'

'There was something wrong with me when I was born.'

'What do you mean wrong?'

'Perhaps it wasn't so wrong.'

'People get things wrong.'

'Why will it help if I come to the village this evening?'

'They need just to see you.'

'To see what does or doesn't matter?'

'Yes.'

'And then we might go to the island?'

She opened her eyes wide. It was as if by this she might

evaporate tears. She said 'There's a wedding in the village this evening. Your father knew someone at the wildlife station, did you know?'

'I think so.'

'I don't know how much that mattered to you. But it was she who thought it might be all right if I used the cottage.'

'Yes I see.'

We sat in silence for a time. I thought – You mean, in the village we will have to go through some sort of ordeal.

In a medieval ordeal you put your hand into boiling water and then if you were telling the truth you were able to bear it, and if you were not you could not.

Or was it possible that innocence did not feel pain?

She said 'No one really wants to know what happened on the breakwater. They want to know that they needn't want to know.'

I said 'Then that's all right, is it?'

She got off the bed and went to where her clothes had been drying in front of the stove. I watched her. I thought – This is the sort of thing you think you might risk boiling water for and come out unscathed.

I said 'How will I find you in the village?'

'Come walking into town.'

'Like the lonely gunfighter.'

'Like the minstrel boy.'

I thought I might say – Did you find that gun?

I watched her dressing. I imagined her and myself living in the cottage. I had thought that looking after a baby might make this more possible for us.

After she had gone – I did not watch her beyond the door: I did not want to have an image of her beyond the door – I watched the bird like a sea eagle in the middle of the room, its feet trapped in what looked like man-made pollution but being able to lift its whole rock out of the sea; humans falling off it like ticks, like fleas; and the nest in which they had been so perilously breeding being carried off to – where – no one knew. Some humans panicked and fell, and some looked brightly out of their nest like balloonists, watching where they were being carried like seeds across rough seas.

But there was time to be filled in before evening.

I left the living room or workshop and went to the back of the cottage where I saw that there had once been a vegetable garden: there were old fruit bushes covered with brambles, and the collapsed frame of a greenhouse with bits of glass scattered like dew. There were a few rusty tools in a shed, and a heavy scythe. I could begin to clear a patch even if I never got round to planting it. What else was there to do? Imagine how by imagination one might alter the world?

If humans were no longer in the business simply of reproduction and replication (and they had not even had this in the Garden of Eden!) if they had to struggle for their living, then was this not a mercy that they were thus part of a nature red in tooth and claw: otherwise, how boring! But in this set-up what would be a state of grace? There was still a natural world to be redeemed, to be put right, was there? Humans had felt they were chosen by God for such a task (or they had chosen such a God to explain their feelings of being chosen: what was the difference!) but now this whole knot, this tie, was unravelling: so what was it to be human? If they had no task, then indeed what were humans except particular lumps of matter. What had seemed to define them had been a relationship to God – whether this had been a dream, a fabrication, something to be denied, or conceivably a reality – but what had been their experience? In so far as they felt the world was wrong, there was the implication that it might be put to rights; or at least that there might be a way of enduring it rather than not. And glimpses, experiences, of this, might be a state of grace?

Certainly things in some pattern seemed to happen to me. One still had to want to trust them.

Humans on their own seemed no longer to have instructions what to do. But if one tried things out, there were some things rather than others, as in an art work, that just seemed right?

That one could always be wrong, was a necessary condition of such responsibility or freedom.

I was having this conversation with myself in the abandoned vegetable garden at the back of the cottage. Well what if I was looking at the abandonment of not only the Garden but the myth, of all myth, then what was the message? What was it that old monk in his cockleshell boat had said – All right no myth: but some partnership with meaning that can be experienced in what happens. What was it that the girl I was in love with had said or suggested: art is that which discovers and expresses a meaning, but this meaning is there to be lived with, as well as to be formed and looked at in objects.

I was doing no gardening. I was standing in the vegetable patch like some sort of scarecrow – placed by that old gardener to tell birds to keep moving. The gardener would say to the birds – You've got enough seeds to scatter in your crop, your shit.

I had not yet looked to see if my gun was still behind the loose bricks at the back of the sink. I had not wanted to know whether I still had it; but perhaps now I should find out about it before I went to the village. Had not that old God liked to think he had a gun up his sleeve – an angel with a flaming sword, if not a flood or fire or bit of brimstone. But then, things had not gone too well for that old God: it seemed he had had to resort to other tactics.

My father had remarked when I had been with him in the beer cellar that I seemed to be quite a hero in the village. But did that mean that to others I might be a villain? Was this the danger, the ordeal, that I now had to deal with?

It might be that I should be frightened. But there had been so many events, coincidences, which had served us well so far that it was not mad to follow where they were leading?

I dozed on and off till the afternoon. I ate some bread and cheese: I drank water. I sat on the top of the cliff and looked over the sea. In the distance there were birds flying.

When it was nearly time to set off for the village I went into the scullery and knelt by the sink. Was there really a choice between entering the village as the minstrel boy or the lonely gunfighter?

I remembered how a year ago my father had put his hand into the cavity beneath the sink and had pretended that it had been seized from behind and I had thought this funny and my mother had not. I could not think now, with my hand going in, why I had thought it funny.

I could not feel my gun. I could feel what seemed to be a large envelope containing papers.

I drew this out. It was a plain brown envelope of typescript size. It had been sealed but it was easy to peel back the flap. Within it were a number of pages of typewritten script. I pulled these out and read on the first page –

I met Connie Constantine when I had my first job in a clothes shop in Knightsbridge. Connie was already an enormously rich tycoon but he was only just becoming known in gossip columns of the papers.

I thought – This is impossible. This is beyond being absurd. This is the story about herself and Connie Constantine that my mother has talked about –

–That she had said she would show to me and then had

seemed not to know where it was; that she might have handed over to my father —

Well here it is.

But how had it got here!

I had been looking for my gun.

What myth was this?

Surely too senseless to be a myth. Just something happening.

I would not have time to read whatever it was before I set off for the village. But at the moment I in no way wanted to read it.

My father had been here? He had to hide it? He had forgotten it?

I knew my father had been here. Had my mother?

My friend the fair-haired girl had come across it and had put it for safe keeping beneath the sink — after she had taken out the gun to give back to her brother?

All this was impossible to tell.

My mother was giving me some message?

I put the typescript back in its envelope and the envelope back under the sink. I replaced the bricks. I went out on to the track. I set off for the village.

The message seemed to be — Things happen; don't try to work them out; be ready for what will be happening.

The road went up and down over the hills where I had walked and bicycled with my mother a year ago. I went lumbering along like a ball on a roulette wheel; hardly like the minstrel boy or the lonely gunfighter. Sooner or later I would land up in this or that hole: and some people would be briefly pleased and others sad; but might where the ball landed really affect the fate of the world?

What was the maximum you could win on a roulette wheel?

From the direction in which I was approaching the village

I could not see the harbour; this was screened by a warehouse and barns. Then as I came round the corner by the hut from which a year ago the man in the balaclava helmet had emerged – why had I not got my gun! – as I came round the corner to where quayside was visible I could see a small crowd gathered in the roadway outside the pub: they were in smart party clothes; it was evident that they were guests at a wedding reception; there were one or two children dressed like bridesmaids, and a car hung with white ribbons. I had paused on the corner; people might not yet have seen me and I could turn back. Then I was thinking – Or this could once more be like a scene in a ballet: the first time I saw my friend she was tiptoeing like Giselle: she has ways, indeed, of fashioning shapes, occurrences, out of the air. And anyway by now one or two of the wedding party had seen me.

There was one very beautiful girl in a long flowery dress and a wide-brimmed hat on the edge of the crowd nearest to me: I wondered – She is the bride? Then she turned and waved to me and I realised that she was the girl I had been with that morning and with whom I was in love; when I had last seen her she had seemed almost naked even in her white T-shirt and jeans: I thought – She cannot be the bride! or if she is then I am in some alternative world and this is her and my wedding. She seemed delighted to see me and started running towards me: I thought – So you do trust me! this is more than playing a part. It was as if she might throw her arms around me like a garland. She stopped just short of me and she seemed suddenly shy; she said 'Oh I'm so glad you could come!' I bowed slightly formally and said 'It was good of you to ask me.' She laughed and murmured 'Yes, that's right.' I thought – This might be a shadow-play for our wedding?

She took me by the arm and led me towards the gathering. People were watching us approach; it seemed she was about to introduce me formally. People held their hands out and shook hands with me; they observed me curiously; but she did not say either my name or theirs (and I realised that I did not know her name); and once people had greeted me they moved away from me slightly as if they should not be seen talking with me for too long. She held on to my arm. She led me through the standing crowd to a table outside the pub where there was a woman in a white wedding dress sitting. My friend who was leading me said 'I know you two wanted to meet.' The woman in the wedding dress said 'We've heard so much about you.' I said 'Oh really?' The woman said 'I was a friend of your father's.' I sat down on a bench at the table and said 'Oh yes, when he was filming at the wild-life station.' I thought – But this can't be, or can it be, yes, the person called Anna he was writing to: she is the bride? My friend is a sort of maid of honour? Two or three balls seemed to be clattering round on the roulette wheel at the same time. The woman said 'I'm so glad Julie could bring you.' I thought – Julie: she is called Julie. At least now I know her name.

There was a group of men standing at the water's edge on the quayside who were dressed in dark suits and ties and who seemed to be of the party but separating themselves from it; they were watching me and the women at the table. It seemed that one of them might be the tall man who had come to the cottage a year ago when I had been with my mother; but I had no means of making sure, nor of what I was now expected to do: they might all be men who would suddenly put on balaclava helmets and come leaping along the quayside and shoot at boys lying on the rocks or indeed people outside a pub. The woman dressed as a bride was saying 'Has he done any more filming?' I said 'No, I don't think he can show what he wants.' She said 'Why not?' I said 'You can't see statistics except on a computer.' She laughed and said 'How like your father!' Then – 'He was very good to me.' I said 'Oh good, was he?'

She said 'Are you staying in the cottage?'

I said 'Yes.'

'And you're looking after Julie?'

'Yes.'

'Will you do that?'

The people in the wedding party were watching us. The group of men by the water's edge were watching us. I wanted to convey to Julie that although I had no idea what was happening, I seemed to be confident about whatever I had to do.

There was a man coming out from the pub and joining us at our table. It was the curly-haired man, I was sure, who had spoken with my mother and me outside the cottage a year ago. He was dressed in a smart suit and had a flower in his buttonhole. He put his hand on the shoulder of the woman dressed as a bride: it seemed that he might be the bridegroom: or perhaps the best man? Julie was still holding my arm. She began to say 'Do you know –' The man said quickly 'Yes.' I thought – He was the one who charmed, who was charmed by, my mother. He said 'I'm sorry you couldn't be asked properly to the wedding.' I said 'I only got here last night.' He said 'But Julie's looking after you?'

Julie said 'Yes.'

'Will you do that Julie?'

I thought – They have some feeling about what we might be to one another?

There was another group of people, both men and women, at a table outside a café further along the quayside. They too seemed to be part of the wedding party but to be keeping themselves in a separate group. I thought – Oh yes, people here are in separate factions and they have to be either balancing or killing one another. Some of the men outside the pub were getting drunk; it was now evening and they had probably been drinking all afternoon. I did not know if this would make things easier or more difficult to deal with.

Julie said 'Come along and I'll introduce you to your father's colleagues.'

The man who was dressed as a best man or bridegroom said 'Remember me to your mother.'

I said 'I will.'

Julie led me off to the café further along the quayside. When we had left the table outside the pub the tall man who had been with the group at the water's edge came over to the table where the bride and the man I had been talking to were now sitting and he leaned with his hands on the table and was talking or listening to one or the other of them. I thought – But in a ballet you can be caught up by the dancing and yet not know what is going on.

Julie was introducing me to the men and women at the table outside the café. There was a distinguished-looking grey-haired man with his back to us: Julie was saying 'This is Mr Kevin O'Reilly, the director of the wildlife station.'

Mr O'Reilly said without looking for long at either myself or Julie – 'Are you part of Julie's experiment?'

I said 'Yes I think so.'

He said 'Ah you don't know!'

Julie said 'And these are the rest of my friends who can exactly predict just what they know can be exactly predicted.'

A woman said 'You're a silly girl Julie.'

Another woman said 'Did you predict him?' She indicated me.

A man said 'If you had done, would we have been here?'

The bride and bridegroom were climbing into the white-ribboned car behind us. The bridegroom paused to look along the quayside towards Julie and me. I realised he was a different curly-haired man from the one I had been talking to earlier. I had no idea why I thought this important. Julie was looking up at the sky. I thought – She is expecting something to happen?

One of the women said to me 'Your father really wanted to make a film about human beings.'

I said 'Yes I know.'

'But genetic differences are tiny. You only notice when things go wrong.'

The other woman said 'Things aren't identifiable when they go right.'

Julie said 'I won't be a minute.' The bride and bridegroom were driving away. People were running after the car throwing flowers and confetti. The car was coming in our direction. As it was passing us it stopped, and the bridegroom leaned out of the window and gestured as if he wished to say something to Julie. Julie went over to him. She listened to him through the window of the car. The rest of us watched them.

The man called O'Reilly said 'The things we will do for the beautiful Julie!'

One of the women said 'I don't do it for Julie, I do it because I've got nothing else to do.'

Julie was coming back to the table. She said 'Now I want you all to sit and not to look up.'

O'Reilly said to Julie 'Was that all right?' Julie nodded. Then O'Reilly turned to me and said 'You know Julie's test about how things might go right if one doesn't try to identify them.'

I said 'No.'

One of the men who had not spoken before said 'And what do you think you'll prove from this, Julie?'

Julie said 'I won't prove anything.'

I thought – Have you been trying to arrange for us to go to the island?

O'Reilly said to me 'Your father was trying to film the birds.'

I said 'He didn't find the birds he wanted to film?'

Julie said 'As soon as the sun goes down I want you not to look up.'

A woman said 'And they'll come if we're not looking for them?'

A man said 'Pigs will fly.'

Julie and I were standing. The others were seated round the table.

A woman said 'You can't intentionally be unaware of something.'

One of the men said 'You can be aware of being unaware of something.'

The man called O'Reilly said 'And that's the trick?'

One of the men in dark suits who had been watching but not waving as the car with the bride and bridegroom drove away came over to our table and faced me and said to Julie 'Well aren't you going to introduce me?' I thought he might be the short man who had spoken to my mother and me a year ago. He appeared drunk.

Julie said 'Oh piss off Matthew.'

He half sang 'Wedding bells, wedding bells, weddings all the way.'

The tall man who had been in the group by the water's edge came and took the drunk man by the arm and said 'Stop that now.' He tried to pull him away. The drunk man resisted.

Julie said quietly and quickly to me 'It's all right if you go back to the cottage tonight, I fixed that.'

I said 'Right.'

'But come down to the village again tomorrow night.' She seemed to be saying this for the benefit of the short and the tall man.

I thought – Yes, I need to get back to the cottage to read that story of my mother's.

The people round the table were looking down at their cups and glasses as if they were embarrassed. I thought – But they are looking down because they are alarmed by the drunk man, who is belligerent, not because they have been told to by Julie. Nearly all the wedding party had left the roadway and gone into the pub: the men in dark suits on the quayside seemed to be waiting for their two companions by our table to rejoin them. The sun had sunk low behind clouds which made the sky blood-red and orange above the horizon. The man called O'Reilly said 'Julie, as scientists, we hear the sound of laughter.' I was looking out over the sea and somewhere above the strips of colour there were birds circling; I thought – Julie has not told me that I should not look up. There was a small formation of birds coming in from the sea lower and faster like bombers; approaching from the direction of the sun so that it was difficult for them to be seen; as if avoiding being picked up by radar technology. Then they were overhead and past, and gone – with a faint whirring noise like a tearing of fragile cloth. And it did seem that perhaps no one might have seen them except myself; and indeed, they were hardly worth seeing. Julie had not bothered to look up. Then the drunk man was laughing and he let the tall man lead him off to rejoin his fellows. And O'Reilly kept his head down and laughed and said 'Julie, is your miracle occurring?' Julie said 'Oh yes.' One of the women said 'It's a miracle that I've been sitting here for you young lady.' Julie held my hand briefly and said 'Thank you.' I thought – Those birds have come from the island? They are going no one knows where? They are mythical birds that are supposed to stay up in the air for ever?

VII

One reason I had wanted to get back to the cottage was so that I could take out and read my mother's story, which I had left in its hiding place under the sink. There seemed no use in my speculating further about how it had got there: my father had had it with him when he had visited the cottage from the wildlife station? He had had to hide it and then had forgotten it? Could my mother have been here without my knowing it? None of this made much sense. Why should it make sense: why should I think I might know things?

I had bought some supplies in the village and I lay on the bed in my sleeping bag with two candles propped up precariously on a chair, and gusts of wind came through cracks in the frame of a window and blew the flames towards the pages that I was holding. Ghosts seemed to dance on the walls of the shadow-filled room; it was as if they might be anxious about my reading the story. I wanted to tell them – But that's all right; ghosts, presumably, want to give information.

On the envelope there was written in capital letters – MEMOIRS OF AN ADULT CHILDHOOD. This seemed to be in my father's writing. The typescript had occasional corrections that might be in either my mother's or my father's writing. I read –

I met Connie Constantine when I had my first job in a clothes shop in Knightsbridge. Connie was already an enormously rich tycoon, but was only just becoming known in the gossip columns of the papers.

I had started work as soon as I left school. My parents were conventional people with an eye on the social ladder. They had sent me to boarding school from which I had run away; they had sent me back; children are supposed not to rock the social ladder. I wanted to go into the world of fashion because this was something that my parents had nothing to do with and even disapproved of, but which they held in some awe. I thought I might get a few rungs above them on the social ladder.

I got the job in the dress shop because I had an affair with the husband of one of the rich young women who had put money into the shop; he had picked me up at some party. His wife had recommended me to the manageress of the shop because she wished to know where her husband would be in the afternoons. He used to take me out to lunch after which we would go to some hotel while his wife presumably was with her own lover. My parents were impressed that I was being taken up by such a friendly couple.

The fashionable world is different from the conventional world in that it makes no bones about society being a jungle. Humans are predators: why should not instincts be pursued without shame? Predators however require exotic shapes and colours to protect themselves and to attract victims. Conventional people admire them from a distance through magazines.

Connie Constantine came into the shop one afternoon with someone who I think was the daughter of an earl:

this was a time when daughters of earls might still just be thought fashionable. Connie was in his fifties: he was thin and rather lizard-like but attractive. I did not know much about him, but I sensed that he might be a hunter in the jungle who wanted more than trophies to hang on his wall. With the earl's daughter he looked bored; like a leopard that has eaten and is resting on the branch of a tree.

When he and his companion came into the shop the manageress was out for lunch (this was her day to be with her lover in the afternoon?) and I was in charge of the shop. Connie and the earl's daughter had come in from lunch; they were themselves presumably on their way to wherever they would seal their own bargain. He was telling her that she could choose any dress she liked. So she had the choice (this was my view of things) between selecting either a dress that she actually liked, or one of the most expensive in the shop which she could sell later for cash. She pranced around not making up her mind while Connie sat on one of our high-backed chairs with his hands on the top of a silver-headed walking stick. He had a high sloping forehead and somewhat thick lips; there was something mournful about him as well as formidable that made him attractive. He was like an impresario remaining impassive while his protégée chattered and performed. I thought I might say to her – But you are doing this all wrong: you should be aloof and enigmatic; then he would be impressed.

When the girl went into the changing room to try on a dress Connie asked me how much it cost. When I told him he said 'Do you think it's worth that?' I said 'It depends what you want it for.' He did not smile, but he looked at me as if I might have made him happy. He said 'I don't think I want it for anything.' I said 'Then it might still be worth it.'

At this time I had learned my own lures and wiles for the purpose of attracting or protecting myself from predators in the jungle. I wore a mini-skirt and had bare legs; I cultivated an air of waifishness and yet disdain. I hoped to give the impression of being both vulnerable and in control.

When the earl's daughter emerged wearing a very expensive dress she preened and pirouetted and Connie scarcely watched her. I leaned against a pillar with my hands behind my back: thus I might be Andromeda chained to her rock, Saint Whoever-it-was shot through with arrows. Connie said to me 'What do you think?' I said 'I've told you.' Connie said 'All right I'll have it.'

I wondered – Now how clever is he?

When his protégée was back in the changing room Connie stood up and without quite looking at me said 'Fortunately I have to go now. Here is my card. Will you let my companion take the dress, and will you kindly bring the account round to this address this evening, when I will give you a cheque.' I said 'All right.' I thought – He did say 'fortunately'? When his friend came out of the changing room she said 'Where is he?' I said 'Unfortunately he had to go, but he says you can take the dress.' She said 'What a duck!'

When the manageress returned she said 'You let her take the dress? He hasn't paid yet? Are you mad?' Then she looked at Connie's card and said 'Or bloody hell darling, are you clever!'

When I went that evening to the address that Connie had given me it was an apartment on the top floor of a building overlooking Hyde Park. He let me in himself. He had made out two cheques – one payable to the shop, and another one with the line for the payee left blank. He said 'I don't know your name.' I said 'Thanks.' He said 'Aren't you going to ask – What do I do for it?' I said 'No.' He said 'Why not?' I said 'Because we don't know what I'll do for it.'

After a time he said 'I see.' He walked up and down. He

took deep breaths. These seemed to be a sort of exercise. I thought – But he doesn't look like someone who will hurt you.

He said 'Have you got a boyfriend?'

I said 'No, but I've been going out with the husband of one of the women who own the shop.'

'Yes I'd heard that.'

I thought – Oh had you.

He said 'I could buy the shop.'

'I don't think that would be necessary.'

'I wouldn't want you to lose your job.'

'I don't think I would.'

'You mean he might be impressed?' He smiled.

I was thinking – So he is clever, yes.

He said 'Where do you live?'

'With my parents.'

'Would they mind if you moved out?'

'I don't know.'

'I'd like to get you somewhere to live where I could see you in the evenings. I don't like having to go out.'

'I see.'

'I'd prefer it if you didn't see other people there.'

I said nothing.

'I'd have no other conditions.'

'Conditions?'

'I apologise. Expectations.'

'Why not?'

'I'm a gambler. I like seeing what turns up.'

He stopped walking up and down and came and stood in front of me. I thought – All right he's a gambler. He thinks he knows the odds.

He said 'When I saw you in the shop I felt I had to know you. Do you understand that.'

'Perhaps.'

'I like to be able to be with a person who means something in my life.'

'Well I do want to get out of my parents' house, yes.'

'Then you must do that. What will you tell them?'

'That I'm earning a lot on commissions and I think it's time that I moved out.'

'That seems proper.'

'My parents are impressed by money.'

'And you're not impressed by your parents?'

'No.'

When Connie smiled he became like one of those clock-work toys that make a whirring noise before they snap at you.

That evening he took me out to dinner. I had wondered whether I should suggest that I go home and change, but I thought it better if I did not. He took me to a smart and expensive restaurant and I was in my working clothes of black mini-skirt and white blouse and I was young enough to be his daughter, but this was the sort of place where people might think I really was his daughter, or would not be much interested in whether I was or not.

During dinner he talked about his business which was with computers. Computers were still somewhat primitive at this time, used mainly by government departments and universities and big businesses. Connie had inherited a newspaper and a publishing business from his father but he had started his own company with the aim of simplifying the technology and software of computers so that they might be used without too much difficulty by individuals. Connie was one of the first people who had the dream that everyone who wished might own a computer and thus be components in a vast network that would bypass the methods of information and control that were at present wielded by people in authority. Connie's view of Western society was that although shackles of poverty and class prejudice had been largely shaken off, power was still held and guarded by an established elite, and individuals found themselves alienated and ineffectual. Connie's vision was a Messianic or an idealistic Marxist one of a world in which ordinary people, linked up in what would come to be known as the Net or Web, would participate actively in not only the recreational but the political exercise of liberty, equality and fraternity.

I said 'But in front of their computers, won't people be just the same as they are now?'

'They'll feel they have power.'

'But power to do what?'

'Whatever they like.'

'They'll like the same rubbish.'

'That doesn't matter.'

'Why not?'

'They'll learn.'

'Learn what.'

'Whatever matters. You can't learn what matters unless you've got the means to know the truth.'

He seemed to be meaning what he said. I wondered whether or not people who did this were slightly mad.

I said 'But they won't really have power. It'll keep them quiet. It'll be a bluff.'

'Ah!' When Connie said Ah! it was as if a number that he had backed had come up at roulette.

He said 'But what isn't a bluff? All power is a sort of bluff. But we're not talking about what things really are, we're talking about what will give humans a feel of satisfaction and empowerment.'

'Then you don't mean what you say.'

'Everything starts as a bluff. Then you find out what is and what's not.'

'And that's what you're doing?'

'Right.' He did his crocodile smile. I thought – So do I want to be gobbled up?

I said 'And I mean that's what you're doing with me?'

'I hope so. To be sure. Why not.'

It was then that I began to be a bit in awe of Connie. But in the jungle, did I not want to show that I was a bit of a gambler too?

I had thought that when we left the restaurant we would be going back to his apartment and there, in spite of what he had said about no conditions, we would go through the usual routines. I was prepared for this; and did not quite know what I would do about it. In the jungle you become used to bluffs, and only ask that people should play the game with enough style. It was only in my parents' jealous world that bluffs were called lies.

But then outside the restaurant Connie opened the door of his huge black Mercedes while his chauffeur stood waiting, and he watched me climb in. He said 'Lennie will drive you home.'

I said 'Thanks. And thanks for the dinner.'

'You'll think about what I said?'

'Yes.'

'You know that my leaving you now does not mean that I'm disappointed in you.'

'Yes I think I know that.'

'Good.'

I thought – I am in some fairy-tale world where options are put to the test.

– One does not even know the nature of the test?

The next day when I gave the cheque for the dress to the manageress, Mrs Lupescu, she held it gingerly between finger and thumb and looked at the figures; then said 'What did his ladyfriend have to do for this!'

I said 'I don't think his ladyfriend did anything. It was a pay-off.'

'Then what did you have to do you dreadful creature!'

'Nothing. He took me out to dinner.'

'Darling, where did you learn such tricks?'

I thought I might say – I took fairy stories seriously when I was a child.

I told my parents that I was thinking of getting a flat. They were torn between being suspicious and relieved that I was getting on in the world.

My parents' morals were like those of characters in a Jane Austen novel – respectability was judged mainly in terms of money. I wondered how many billions Connie would have to be known to have before he became eligible for the role he had chosen to play with me.

Connie took me out every other night for a week. Lennie the chauffeur would wait to pick me up in a side street near the shop and would drive me home after dinner. Lennie was a handsome dark-skinned man who wore a black uniform so that he was like a shadow. I wondered – What do Connie and his shadow do on the nights they are not with me?

Or indeed – What does Connie get up to after I have been driven home?

I learned from Mrs Lupescu that Connie was married. Little was known about his wife except that she spent most of the time in New York where Connie had an apartment.

At the start of the second week Connie came himself with Lennie to pick me up at the shop. He waited on the pavement while Mrs Lupescu watched through the window. He said to me 'Have you cashed that cheque I gave you?'

I said 'No.'

'Why not?'

'I wanted to see what would happen.'

'Well what has happened.'

'I'll cash it one day.'

'It takes some time to find a flat.'

'I see.'

I thought – But you were waiting to see what would happen.

He said 'Have you told your parents yet?'

'Have I told them what?'

'That you're moving out.'

'Yes.'

'Well come and see.'

As I climbed into the car I thought – But of course I know I am entering a dark cave that leads down into the underworld –

– And Connie has stage-managed this scene so that Mrs Lupescu would be watching, and thus it will become public property and I will not be able to get back.

The flat that Connie had chosen for me was in a modern block with a porter and a restaurant downstairs and facilities for having food sent up. It was luxurious, with good modern furniture. I wondered – If I was a tart, would it be mock antique?

I said 'This is very nice.'

He said 'Perhaps I'd better explain.'

'You don't have to.'

He sat in a deep armchair as if deliberately to be on a lower level than myself who stood in front of him. He said 'I'm very fond of you and I want to know that I can see you, as I said, when I want to. But I don't want at the moment to make love to you.'

'Why not.'

'I think that fucking is the ruination of love. I think that's what's wrong with the world. I believe what it says in the Bible is right about that.'

'I see.'

169

'Fucking's a battle. Fucking's power. And of course when you want that, you get it. But not making love is calling the bluff.'

I wondered – He's impotent?

He said 'It's caring that matters. Giving to people what they need.' Then – 'You must tell me if you think I'm using you.'

'I don't mind your using me. I suppose I'm using you.'

'Would you mind if I held you?'

'No.'

He leaned forwards and put his arms around me so that his head was against my groin. He there remained quite still, as if he were getting some sustenance from me. I thought – If he is impotent, he may be wanting not to be? After a time I put a hand to the back of his head. I thought – Poor old snake, always crawling on its stomach.

After a time he let go of me and said 'Thank you.'

'That's all right.'

'Now shall we have dinner, or would you like to look round your flat?'

'Let's have dinner.'

'Here are the keys, anyway.'

The next morning when I arrived at the shop Mrs Lupescu was excited and was pretending to be angry or upset. She said 'Can you tell me what you're up to you horrible thing!'

'I've got a new flat.'

'I know you've got a new flat. I've been on the sprinkler for half an hour with your parents.'

'Oh God, what were they on about?'

'What do you think they were on about?'

'Did you tell them they could go fuck themselves?'

'They don't have the same opportunities darling.'

'I just told them I was getting a flat.'

'Well I didn't tell them anything I hadn't seen.'

'As a matter of fact he doesn't want to fuck. He says he wants to look after me.'

'Oh my God it's like that is it?'

'Like what?'

'Never trust a man who doesn't want to fuck.'

'He says he thinks that that's what's wrong with the world – that no one wants to do anything but fuck.'

'Well he's right there. And that's what he puts into his disgusting paper.'

'What does he put?'

'The sanctity of family life, darling, and the wickedness of anyone who goes against it.'

It turned out that what Connie liked to do when he came to visit me in my new flat in the evenings – it is difficult for me to describe this even to myself: we are programmed not to see how we behave – what Connie liked to do when he came to visit me in the evenings was to treat me I suppose like some long-lost ideal daughter. I gathered that he had no children. And perhaps because my own experience of being a daughter had been so bleak I found myself curiously enchanted by Connie's attentions in this make-believe world; I suppose something was being exorcised in me of my eleven-year-old self who had been sent away so furious to school, whose father had wanted but had been too nervous to take me on his lap, and whose mother had taken out on both of us her scorn for his reluctance as well as his desire. But now Connie and I might be able to indulge in such needs and fantasies as had got stranded like fish when the tide has gone out – because he was in fact not my father and I was not his daughter. And so the conflicts between affection and propriety, impulse and restraint, that seemed to bedevil families in the real world, for us provided a sort of glamour in the games we felt we were permitted.

Connie would come home from work and I would perhaps

sit on his knee and he would hug and caress me; soon he began kissing me and this did, yes, seem to be encroaching on a taboo; but were not both the taboo and the encroachment what we wanted? I might half-heartedly demur; but this was part of the game, and at some stage Connie would shy away as if he knew he was on forbidden ground; but this was part of the game too – a situation in which he could enjoy what he felt guilty about without the danger of losing it. It was loss I think that Connie above all wished to avoid: the sense of something having been consummated and thus being over. I felt I understood this – that if you want to possess something and keep it alive then you dangle it, you don't devour it; you play with it like a cat with a mouse.

So when it came to my bedtime (I mean the bedtime of me as an eleven-year old girl: after Connie had gone I would get up and revert to my nineteen-year-old self and have a drink and watch television – though would this not be the dream of an eleven-year-old girl!) – when it came to my so-called bedtime Connie would watch me as I got ready for my bath and then come and sit by me and would sometimes help to wash me and dry me; would show concern about me; would pretend to be solicitous about any real or pretended bruise or blemish. I had gathered from friends that their fathers sometimes behaved like this; and my friends had not minded; why should they? it was only later that it had been borne in on them that they were expected to have felt affronted and their fathers ashamed. And so a taboo on tenderness had been added to other taboos. I sometimes wondered about this – about what were necessary taboos and what were not. So many restraints seemed the equivalent of wounds.

Then Connie would tuck me up in bed and sit on the edge and we would talk of inconsequential things, of the trials and personalities of his business, of what had been going on at my shop. His hand would sometimes stray under the bedclothes as if we were both hardly aware of what was happening; as if this had remained in the unconscious; and he would stroke me, and I would both not respond or perhaps respond as if to something not to do with him. And then Connie would give me a sudden lurching and indeed not very fatherly goodnight kiss and would rush away in flight from shame or in accordance with his game – as if he had caught himself over the edge of forbidden territory and had brought himself to his senses just in time. And thus were we acting out repressions and fantasies in a form in which they might be harmless – or might they not? But was there anything in this area that humans were supposed better to do?

And then, yes, after Connie had gone I could get up and have a drink and watch all the ghastly repressed and deprived people on television complaining and yelling and bashing one another about. And I wondered if they might be more free of their violence and frustration if they indulged in a few games like Connie's and mine; or was whining and bitching in fact just the game they liked?

Becoming rather drunk, I tried to work out –

With his network of computers Connie wanted to turn the world into a game – one in which virtual worlds would be available and by which frustrations and disappointments would be trivialised and gutted. The real world would be an unknown space to which actors need never go because they were always on stage. So how might reality be known to exist? Perhaps only when rain and wind and cold came in so that pipes froze and electricity failed and walls and roofs were carried away in a flood. But then, was it an unacknowledged fear of this that turned more and more people to trivial performances on stage; or to try to exorcise fear by enjoying and practising displays of disgust and violence.

But if sexuality became a game in a make-believe world without fucking, then what would happen to life?

I should have liked to talk with Mrs Lupescu about this; but I think she was upset and jealous.

Then one day Connie himself seemed to step outside the role that he had given himself, and tried to talk about it objectively. I welcomed this as some sort of coming down to earth: but then might it not be just a move in a more complex game?

We had gone back to the restaurant to which Connie had taken me the first evening when he had talked of his vision for sorting out the world. He now said –

'But what may be impossible for humans is that there's something built in that stops them getting what they want. It's not just that when they get it they no longer want it. It's because we've evolved a mind that hopes for sophistication and control which is still tied to a Stone Age nervous system designed for the perpetuation of the species. People are ashamed of their desires and they can't accept their shame. So they can get everything but satisfaction.'

I said 'But you say they can play games.'

'So they do.'

'Then what's wrong.'

'In reality they feel they need to be punished.'

I was not sure if this made sense. Was he talking of other people or of himself? He was looking down at his plate. I thought – Yes how does one distinguish between reality and games.

He said 'That's the theology.'

'What is?'

'Humans are out of sync. They have a need to be punished.'

'In a game –'

'No not in a game –'

'Well in reality people are punished all the time.'

'But for satisfaction you need a game that isn't a game.'

I thought – You mean, you don't want it to be too real. But it can't be just like a game or else it wouldn't seem like being punished.

– But in reality, should one not change?

I had heard of course of the men who got satisfaction, pleasure, from in one way or another being punished. In newsagents' windows in London there were innumerable advertisements offering forms of abasement, to such an extent that it seemed that this might indeed be at the heart of what men desired – and so might provide an explanation for much of human history. I had explored these advertisements with a friend during my last year at school: we had giggled – What an easy way of making money! I wanted now to ask Mrs Lupescu – Is it powerful men especially who want to play this sort of game – to compensate for the shame of being powerful?

– But wouldn't this just incur shame on another level?

– Or if it was simply funny, would it change?

When Connie and I got back from this evening at the restaurant he sat in the low armchair that he usually sat in and I did not sit on his lap because he was watching me like the effigy of a stern god fallen on its back in the sand; and I wondered if he might want to punish me rather than I punish him, for something he desired but did not know the trick to make it feasible. And for the first time I felt sorry, not only for him but for all screwed-up humans; it seemed that if I were a god I might put out a hand to help him. I was standing in front of him as I had done the first evening we had been at the flat, and I said 'Well what else do you want me to do?'

After a time he said 'Fortunately, something that seems impossible.'

I thought – He uses 'fortunately' in such clever ways.

I said 'What –'

'I've only just realised this.'

175

'What –'

'If you want a game that isn't a game –'

'Yes?'

'That isn't possible.'

'Why not.'

'I'm very fond of you.'

'Well I'm fond of you.'

'So there it is.'

'What.'

'Our reality.'

He laughed. He bounced up out of his chair, not with his crocodile smile but with the energy of a predator scattering lesser scavengers. He said 'Our deal is that I look after you, not you look after me.'

I said 'But you need looking after?'

'Oh yes, yes.' He went on laughing. It was as if there were rival predators all around him. He said 'We're all like children sometimes.'

I said 'I wouldn't mind growing up.'

He began to move towards the door, but not in his usual dash as if to get away, rather as if he were trying to keep one foot in what might be reality. He paused and said 'You're not getting fed up with me?'

'No.'

'But you're not getting any fucking.'

'I don't mind.'

'I'm sorry.'

I thought – But it's you who are getting fed up with me, surely, if you want, and can't get, reality.

– But as you say, it's not behaving like babies that's reality.

Mrs Lupescu was due to go away for her summer holiday, and she was anxious to know more of what was going on before deciding whether to leave me in charge of the shop.

She said 'He wants you to go on working? He still doesn't fuck you?'

'He sees me as the little seamstress round the corner.'

'You sew him up, darling, before he gets restless.'

'What do people like that want?'

'I don't know, darling. Some people say he gets his bodyguards to do it for him.'

'He hasn't got bodyguards.'

'He's got that chauffeur.'

I thought – Dear God, yes: Lennie?

Lennie was the only person I saw of those who were presumably in Connie's entourage. I had begun by seeing Lennie as a shadow.

Then Connie telephoned to say that he would be away for a few days, and Lennie would keep an eye on me, and take me to do any shopping.

And thus I did have a feeling of my own shadow coming to get me; like something bursting through the walls in a film about demonic possession.

When Connie was away I had nothing to do in the evenings. I had lost touch with my friends, because I had not wanted to explain to them about Connie; and most of them were away now anyway in the summer. My old boyfriend had stopped trying to see me; and my parents were leaving me alone; either out of shame, or ignorance, or because they were awestruck by Connie's billions.

Then Mrs Lupescu decided to close up the shop for her two weeks holiday; she must have suspected that things might go wrong. And I had nothing to do during the day.

Lennie would come round in the afternoons and take me to wherever I wanted to go. He would follow me at some distance when I went for walks in the park. I had not tried to become friends with Lennie because I had thought Connie would not like this. Now I wondered if Connie had been trying to fix it so that I would be friends with Lennie.

I had got into the way of spending most of the mornings in bed. I thought – Perhaps I am going back towards being a baby.

One day when Lennie arrived at lunchtime to see what he could do for me I left the door of the flat open and wandered through into the kitchen. I said 'Lennie –'

'Yes?'

'How long have you been working for Mr Constantine?'

'Many years Miss.'

'Has he had relationships with other people like he has with me?'

'I don't know what sort of relationship he has with you Miss.'

'Oh come on, Lennie, you know what I mean. And you needn't call me Miss.'

Lennie was a tall loose-limbed black man with rather prominent hooded eyes. He followed me into the living room. I suppose I felt resentful towards Connie because he had abandoned me and had seemed to fix me up with this new game.

'I don't know what Mr Constantine has told you Miss.'

'What he's told me about what.'

'I think he'd like us to be better acquainted.'

'Oh do sit down, Lennie. Why do you think that?'

He was looking up towards the corners of the ceiling. It suddenly struck me that the room might be bugged.

He said 'I think you shouldn't be here so much on your own.'

I said 'I could ask people round here. But I don't think he'd like that.'

'I could get you some dope.'

'Dope!'

'Don't you smoke?'

'Do you get dope for Mr Constantine?'

'Would you like to?'

Lennie had sat down. He was in the chair that Connie usually sat in. He was lying back with his legs stretched out in front of him. He was acting as if he were at home. His legs were like the roots of a tree that you trip over.

I said 'Why do you think Mr Constantine would like us to be better acquainted?'

'You should ask him Miss.'

'He's in America.'

'What should I call you if I don't call you Miss?'

'Call me Melissa.'

'Hey, Melissa! I thought you were going to make us some coffee!'

Lennie jumped up and went into the kitchen where I had left the coffee pot to boil. I thought – He knows how to do this: he is in charge in a way that Connie never wanted to be in charge. And this is what Connie wants? This is what I may have wanted?

– And Connie really might have cameras in the corners of the ceiling?

When Lennie came back he stood in the doorway of the kitchen and was rolling what seemed to be a joint. I said 'That was quick.'

He said 'Mister Magic Man.'

'Lennie –'

'Yes?'

'What does Mr Constantine do on the evenings when he's not with me?'

'Hey, do you want this?'

'Is it good dope?'

'Is it good dope! It's ice! It's rivers of fire!'

'I'll try it.'

'Don't be frightened now.'

'Lennie —'

'Yes?'

'What does Mr Constantine do on the evenings when he's not with me?'

I had not smoked much dope since I had left school. I liked to think this was because I had been ambitious rather than unadventurous.

I thought — But indeed this is just one more game: that business in the pantomime where King Rat comes up through a trap door and there is green and red smoke and all the children begin screaming —

— God knows this is not reality.

Lennie said 'You don't want to worry your head about that. You've got your problems.'

'What are my problems.'

'You don't know your problems?'

'No what are they.'

'Mr Constantine didn't tell you your problems?'

'No.'

'Mr Constantine has his problems. You lie back. Relax.'

The smoke was making me feel rather sick. I thought — The point of this sort of talk is that it eases one down through the cave into the underworld but not too fast, so that things become blurry but one does not quite get the bends as one goes towards the bottom of the ocean.

I said 'Lennie —'

'Yes.'

'What are Mr Constantine's problems?'

'Mr Constantine didn't tell you his problems?'

'No.'

'I wonder why he didn't do that.'

'Lennie —'

'Yes.'

'What does he do that he doesn't do with me?'

Lennie and I were like sharks circling in a goldfish bowl. I had the impression, yes, that Connie might be watching us through a two-way mirror. This would make sense of why he had told Lennie to keep an eye on me.

Lennie said 'Mr Constantine likes to solves his problems.'

'What does he do.'

'He gets his recompense.'

'What's his recompense.'

'You don't know?'

'No.'

'Then, Miss, I'm not going to tell you.'

I began to see Lennie as the head eunuch in an Arabian Nights harem: then it turns out that he isn't a eunuch at all, but someone smuggled in to keep the women happy while the Caliph is away. This may have been arranged by the Caliph himself; the Caliph may be a eunuch. These images float round like droppings in a goldfish bowl.

Lennie said 'You want to know about Mr Constantine saying he'd like us to get better acquainted?'

'Yes.'

'It would give him pleasure.'

'What would?'

'You think about it.'

'I am.'

'He wouldn't like it if he thought I was talking to you in this way.'

'I thought you said he would.'

'I said it would give him pleasure.'

'I see.'

I felt as if I were in a bathyscaphe getting close to the bottom of the ocean and looking through a small round window at the strangely shaped fishes. The fishes were like

the organs of a body removed and preserved in surgical spirit.
I said 'Would he be watching?'

'Would he be watching!'

'Yes.'

Lennie laughed. 'Oh he'd be watching! He'd see everything!'

I laughed. I said 'Does he want you to make love with me?'

'I never said that.'

'No.'

'He doesn't treat you right Miss Melissa.'

'He told you to look after me?'

'Yes he said that.'

'He said what.'

'You should be a queen! Nothing should be too good for you. That's what I say, Miss Melissa!'

I had begun to feel lost very quickly. I could hear myself saying 'Lennie, what is this stuff?' He was coming over to the sofa where I was lying – where one part of my mind was watching the other through its own two-way mirror. Lennie was leaning over me and cooing and touching me as if I were a baby. I thought – I am at a much earlier and more helpless age than I was with Connie. What was it that people said – was it true? – that much of the sexual abuse of babies is done by mothers. So what did mothers think they were doing: looking after them? Lucky children! Lennie was saying – Come along then, my beauty, my sweet baby girl then, who's a pretty lady, your mummy could eat you. And so does one not want to be pushed and pulled around; gobbled up again. This seemed to be Lennie's and my game – Ah what an unloving daddy! baby girl deserves better.

And I could tell myself – This is part of what I signed on for; in the jungle.

By the time Connie returned I had been smoking quite a

lot of dope both with Lennie and on my own. And still none of this was like proper fucking: for the most part imagination got us where we wanted; and it did sometimes seem that Connie might be watching. We would lie on the warm bright surrounds of dope, as if it were a swimming pool.

When Connie reappeared he looked glowing, confident. He said 'Well, did old Lennie look after you?'

I said 'Yes thanks, Lennie looked after me.'

'I thought we were being a bit hard on him.'

'Hard on him?'

'He wasn't getting much fun.'

'That's it?'

'That's what? Is anything wrong.'

'Nothing's wrong.'

'Has Lennie been misbehaving?'

I realised that after all I had no idea what had been happening. Had Connie really wanted Lennie to have been misbehaving? He wanted to be duped about Lennie's mis-behaviour? I told myself – But this fog, this dope – this is reality?

Connie took me out to Sunday lunch in a restaurant in the country and Lennie was in the front seat driving us and Connie carried on as if there was nothing particular happening. Or was this a sort of gangster-film game in which the big man is being friendly to the lesser man he is going to kill, putting his arms round him and patting him on the cheek. But then who was Connie going to kill? We were going into some snuff movie?

I said 'How did the Hollywood deal go?'

Connie said 'They'll play but they're not playing yet.'

'Is that difficult for you?'

'Difficult? Oh, it's fun.'

Connie was now making excuses not to stay with me in the evenings. And I only saw Lennie when he was in the front seat of the car or waiting beside it on a pavement. I thought – Connie thinks he is tormenting us? Connie might like us to be tormenting him?

I began to miss seeing Lennie on my own in the evenings. I did not know if this was a need for pleasure, or for the pulling of the roof down over my head. I thought – That would be reality?

One evening Lennie came to the door of the flat and when I stood back for him to come in he stayed where he was on the landing. He frowned and put a finger to his lips. He came in slowly and looked up at a corner of the ceiling. I thought – But he's done that before. Then he said 'What have you told him.'

I said 'I've told him nothing.'

'Then what's he doing.'

'I don't know.' I was raising my eyebrows and shrugging and making a gesture towards the corner of the ceiling as if letting him know I knew we might be bugged.

Lennie said 'I know where he goes in the evenings.'

I said 'Oh do you?'

'To a place in Bayswater.'

'In Bayswater.'

'Yes.'

'And what does he do there.'

'But you know.'

'Do I?'

'Yes. And he wouldn't like it if you knew.'

'No.'

'I could hurt you.'

I thought – I've always wondered if Connie gets himself beaten up. But then what's the reaction, the recompense, for this – You turn on people –

– And Lennie wants Connie to hear this?

Lennie said 'He's being blackmailed.'

'How?'

'They've got a tape of him.'

'And you're telling him?'

'Yes, that's it. I'm telling him. You want to be in on this?'

'On what. On what they do to him? On telling him?'

'That's what I'm saying.'

'What –'

'He might be in danger. He might be dangerous.'

'You're blackmailing him?'

'No, it's these people. I'm trying to help him.'

I suddenly felt enormously tired. The game did not seem to be working. I wanted either to smoke, to make it amusing, or to switch it off.

I said 'Does he know about this?' I thought – This is too boring to be one of Connie's tricks.

Lennie said 'Yes he knows. Will you be in on this? Will you tell him?'

'Lennie, I'm tired. I've got to get out of this.'

'Where do you think you can go.'

'Anywhere.'

'You're not going anywhere. Look, I've got things lined up.'

'What.'

'You said you liked people watching.'

'Did I?'

'Yes.'

'I don't remember.'

I had to think of a way of getting rid of Lennie. Perhaps Connie could get him dumped in the river with his feet encased in concrete. Perhaps the people in Bayswater could get them both crushed in the big black car.

Lennie said 'He'll let you stay here. You get him to let you stay here.'

'Yes I'll do that.'

'Then I'll come here. We'll see.'

'Lennie, what are you talking about?'

'I'm talking about money.'

'You are in with these people!'

'You'll like it. You like it here.'

'You want to film me? Pimp me?'

'I haven't said that.'

'You say you've got a tape of him? He likes being beaten up?'

'Yes he likes that. He wants this. I'm talking about you.'

'He wants you to do things to me?'

'We've done that.'

'He wants people to come here?'

Lennie watched me. I thought – This is a nothingness. Evil is a nothingness.

I said 'Lennie you must go now. I don't like it.'

'You don't like these games?'

'No.' I waited. I thought – I must just be still.

After a time Lennie left. I suppose he knew that Connie was coming round that evening. He might have told Connie anything, or nothing. It seemed that it was me that Lennie was blackmailing.

It was as if there were a lot of old film clips going through my head – the sort of trailers with quick flashes that are fashionable now but were not so much then – rainy streets, screeching cars, men running up stairways, a woman in a dressing gown in an upstairs room with acid being thrown in her face. Then the arm over the side of the bed, the empty bottles of alcohol and pills, then a flood of flame enveloping everything, coming from anywhere – a truck, a ship, a plane; the storage tanks of an oil refinery. I thought – These images are lodged in our heads, they are what life has to adapt itself to.

When Connie came that evening he was as he had been all week – bright, confident, almost shining; as if he had been through a reprocessing plant to reconcile what people were with what they might be. He said 'Has Lennie been here?'

I said 'I thought you wanted him to.'

'Did I? He's blackmailing me.'

'What about –'

'He says he's got a film.'

'Of what.'

'Not of you?'

'Of me!'

'Or of me. I don't know.'

'He said he took a film of me?'

'Well I wouldn't mind having a look at that!' He laughed.

He prowled up and down. I thought – He's not acting. He's like some shark that has smelled blood.

He said 'I may have to abandon you for a while. Will you mind that?'

'I'd be sorry.'

'Have you got anyone else?'

'No.'

'You say Lennie didn't get up to no good with you?'

'But I did think you might have wanted him to.'

Connie laughed. He said 'But he shouldn't be blackmailing me!'

I thought – But of course you can switch off these games. You can simply pull the plug out –

– Or download, if you like, on too much whisky and pills.

I said 'I thought it was other people who were blackmailing you.'

'What other people?' Then – 'Lennie's been talking?'

'No.'

'Ah those people, yes. They sometimes get films for me.'

'Lennie does?'

'Does Lennie do what? Why do you go on about Lennie?'

'Get films. Fix things for you.'

'Did he fix things for you?'

'No.'

'You can stay here if you like. I said I'd give you the flat.'

'I don't want the flat.'

'Then you can sell it.' Then – 'You needn't worry about Lennie.'

'Why needn't I?'

'Poor old Lennie. He got a bit out of his depth.'

'Haven't we all.'

'No no no, you were fine. I adored you. You were never out of your depth.'

I thought – Connie, why weren't you laughing and full of energy like this when I first met you? Then we might have had some reality.

When Connie had gone I walked round the flat as if I were waiting for someone to burst in through the door because that's what happens in horror films. I thought – It's easier to die with some outside help.

I took to going for long walks in the park. I tried to look at the flowers, at the birds on the lake. I thought I would like to be getting to a place where there was no language. One afternoon there was a band in a bandstand playing.

Mrs Lupescu came back from her holiday. She reopened the shop. She said 'You've survived have you? I didn't think you would.' Then – 'Have you thought of getting some help, darling?'

After a time it seemed that I was not going to hear from Connie again. I learned that the flat had been put into my name: I finally cashed the cheque that he had given me at the beginning. I imagined that Connie might be in New York or Paris or Hollywood. I wondered if he had taken Lennie with him: or would he have got tired of his shadow.

I sometimes worried that Lennie would try to see me again. But Connie had told me that I need not worry about Lennie.

Then one day the bell rang and I opened the door and there was a man whose face seemed familiar. I thought – But he might be bringing a message to say that someone's dead.

He said 'I've come from Mr Constantine's office. He wants me to take some pictures of you.'

I said 'Mr Constantine wants you to take some pictures of me?'

'Yes.' Then – 'I've seen you.'

'Yes.'

'You were in the park.'

'Yes.'

'You were being followed by a man like a shadow.'

'He's gone.'

'Yes so I see.'

'What were you doing in the park?'

'I was making a film.'

'What of.'

'Well you, amongst other things.'

He had followed me into the living room. I was not walking very steadily: I had either drunk or smoked too much. This did not seem to matter. I thought I remembered this man from the park. He had been by a bandstand. There had been a band playing.

I said 'Why does Mr Constantine want you to take photographs of me?'

'Well I suppose he would, wouldn't he.'

'But I mean, why you.'

'Oh well, I was rung up by his secretary.'

'Do you know his secretary?'

'She's the mother of an old girlfriend of mine.'

'Have you got a girlfriend?'

'No.'

'Is that what you do?'

'What?'

'Take photographs.'

'I make films. I want to make films. I take photographs for the money.'

'What else were you filming in the park?'

'There was a band playing. There was this man following you. There were one or two other things happening. I want to know if by paying attention you can make a story.'

'He was supposed to be keeping an eye on me.'

'I supposed so, yes.'

'But how did you know where I was.'

'Mr Constantine's secretary gave me your address.'

'I see.'

'I mean I don't know Mr Constantine. I haven't met him.'

I sat down. I thought – This is ridiculous.

Then – But it's not a game.

He said 'Anyway now he's dead.'

I said 'Who's dead?'

'Your shadow. Not Mr Constantine. The man who was following you.'

This person who said he had come to take photographs of me had sat down opposite me; he had avoided as if by instinct the chair that Connie used to sit in. He carried none of a photographer's usual paraphernalia; he held just one small camera. He said 'At least I suppose it was him. It was in the papers.'

'What was in the papers?'

'Mr Constantine's chauffeur found dead in mysterious circumstances. Mr Constantine in New York. That sort of thing.'

'You're making this up.'

'No. Though I suppose I might be.'

'How did you know he was Mr Constantine's chauffeur?'

'It said so in the papers.'

'But I mean the man who was following me.'

'Oh well, there was a photograph of him. But I didn't really recognise it. Then Mr Constantine's secretary rang me up. And then there you were when you opened the door.'

'And you didn't know I was the person in the park.'

'Of course I knew you were the person in the park!'

'I mean before I opened the door.'

'No.'

'And then you recognised me.'

'Yes.'

'And that's your story?'

'Yes.'

'So it's all by chance.'

'Yes.'

'That's what's good about it.'

'Yes.'

'It's not manipulated.'

'No.'

We sat in silence for a time. He was frowning, then smiling, as if there was some sort of music playing in his head. Then he said 'Well something had to get me here.'

'You didn't follow me from the park?'

'No.'

'Why not?'

'Oh well, I did in a way.'

'What way?'

'I recognised the building.'

He made a face as if in response to an emotional piece of music.

I said 'Then why didn't you come round earlier?'

'Would it have been any good earlier?'

'No I don't suppose it would.'

'I was keeping where you lived up my sleeve.'

'So you knew this might happen.'

'Of course I didn't know this might happen!'

'Why not?'

'Oh well perhaps I did in a way.'

'So you didn't seem surprised when I opened the door.'

'Well you didn't seem surprised when you opened the door.'

'Look, I've got to get out of this.'

'Out of what?'

'Everything.'

'All right.'

'It doesn't all have to be by chance.'

'No indeed it shouldn't all be by chance.'

'So can you manage it? I can.'

VIII

At some stage while reading this story by and of my mother (and my father? I assumed that the man who came in at the end like an annunciating angel was my father) I had fallen asleep, not indeed with boredom though probably with an overdose of intimations coming down like volcanic ash around my head (my mother might even have wondered if the man called Lennie could be my father? but this seemed unlikely) – some time in the night I had fallen asleep and was woken by a page of the typescript I was holding in fact having been set on fire by one of the candles in the light of which I had been reading. I thrashed about putting out the fire and bits of burnt paper flew around like moths. A few words at the end of a blackened line or two I had to reconstruct, but this was not difficult: and the story was of people, my mother at least, being nudged along as if by flames. It seemed to be not so much a confession, a cry, as a story of how there might be a way of dealing with flames; the flames being part of human nature, but another part being that which could see it was tied to a stake, and that if one trusted the ability to see this there might nevertheless be a way of surviving. I thought – Oh really? I felt that the story might have been written by my parents for me: containing the sort of information about attitude, risk, wariness, that, in addition to genes, parents might want to pass on to children. I thought – All right, I will be learning; and I may be able to pass on something more.

I went out into the morning sun and sat by the edge of the cliff and looked out over the sea. The sky, the sea, were extraordinarily still. It was as if light had been caught between the two and had become motionless.

I tried to remember about the birds on their island that had been dying from pollution: what chance was there of a strain emerging that would be immune (had my mother's story been in a sense about this?). Not immune in the sense of being able to prevent pollution (for how could this be up to the birds?) but by learning to recognise pollution and to feed off it even (there were microbes, insects, that did just this) manage to survive, this having come about through a readiness, yes, to adapt to what occurred. And what about those monks, hermits, who had turned their backs on worldly pollution and had hoped not to prevent it nor even to transfigure it but rather to gaze out from their rock towards another world that would be free from it, that would be pure and holy. But then it had been this hope that had seemed to fail; because pollution, even for hermits, was in the mind that they carried with them; and anyway had they not been told before they gazed out to sea that whatever there might be of another world, their entry into it would be through this one.

I saw Julie scrambling over the rocks by the landing stage; I realised I had been expecting her, although she had not said last night that she would be coming up in the morning. I did not go to meet her; it was as if we were each on our own finely balanced trajectory. She arrived at the top of the cliff and sat down beside me. We looked out to sea. After a time she said 'What exactly is it that's happening about your baby?'

'I said I'd see to it if its mother didn't want to – that is, if she'd decided to have it.'

'And you think she has decided?'

'I'm not sure. She may change.'

'Change whether to have it or whether or not to look after it?'

'Either.'

'But you think what you said might affect this.'

'Oh I don't know!'

'Of course it did!'

'I don't know what I believe. It might make things possible.'

'Anyway that's what I believe.'

We looked out to where the ocean went up to the rim of the world. People once thought they might go over. Then it had been worked out that if one travelled far enough one arrived at the back of one's own head.

I said 'I've been trying to see what those old monks felt – if you prayed, you thought God might nudge things one way or another.'

She said 'God was their word for being able to think that if you believed then what happened was for the best.'

'And then it was.'

'Perhaps.'

'But one thing or another happens anyway.'

'Yes.'

'You needn't call it God.'

'You needn't call it anything.'

There were some gulls wheeling and floating at a level with the top of the cliff. They seemed to be watching us without quite acknowledging our presence.

I said 'Can we go to the island?'

She said 'There's a shelter built for the people who were collecting stuff about the birds. It's made from the old hermits' meeting place. My brother went there when he was getting over his wound. The wildlife people like to have him there. They'd given up on what they could find out about the birds.'

'And what about the others.'

'The people who shot him?'

'Yes.'

'They don't know what they want.'

'That's supposed to be peace?'

'That's still words.'

'It can go one way or the other?'

'But depending on what.'

'On what nudges things?'

We sat side by side like statues placed on a hill. Perhaps some markers to give information to travellers.

I said 'Isn't the island supposed to be holy?'

'You think that affects things?'

'It protects your brother?'

'It might do.'

'They wouldn't know what affects them.'

'I sometimes think something quite simple, like a grain of sand, might start an avalanche.'

I put my arm round Julie and pulled her towards me. I thought – We are like the clapper and the dome of a bell, reverberations from which go off to assist sailors.

I said 'And we can stay on the island?'

'It's difficult to land there.'

'The sea looks calm.'

'One can't keep a boat there. When one person lands, another has to take the boat away.'

'Your brother's there now?'

'Yes.'

'Does he want to stay?'

'I was going to take stuff out to him anyway. He may want to get away.'

'Have you stayed there?'

'I've stayed there with him. On one's own it's quite frightening.'

'Why do I want to go there.'

'I suppose you want to produce an avalanche. Some sort of baby.'

I put my head down against her shoulder. I thought – We are like the two poles of a magnet, joined together in the middle.

After a time we got up and went towards the cottage. When I was side by side with Julie it was as if there was, yes, a force that both impelled us apart and held us together, like those particles at opposite ends of the universe.

She said 'People from the village used the cottage when they were running guns. But you know that, don't you.'

'Yes.'

'And now it's drugs.'

'Is that better?'

'I suppose so. Do you think what those holy men were doing on the island was a drug?'

'It wasn't what they were looking for.'

'No.'

'Some sort of peace.'

'But that should be possible.'

'Why did the people from the village let you use the cottage?'

'I was useful to them. Camouflage.'

'Did you find that gun?'

'What gun? Oh that gun, yes.'

'Did my father stay at the cottage when he came to the wildlife station?'

'I don't know. Did he?'

'I was just wondering.'

When we were in the cottage Julie looked at the model she had made of the bird with the humans crawling and tumbling out of its nest. She said 'You will come to the village this evening?'

I said 'They want to see more of me?'

'There's another party. A celebration.'

'What for.'

'For what might be called peace. For the re-ordering of war.'

'And what do they want from me?'

'I think they want an excuse.'

'An excuse for what?'

'You needn't say anything.'

'An excuse to do nothing?'

She was touching her sculpture. She seemed to be seeing if bits would fall off it.

She said 'We need to be set free.'

'From what.'

'From revenge.'

'Who, your brother?'

'Him, me, you. All of us.'

'And then we can go to the island?'

'We'll go to the island anyway. What will happen then.'

I thought – But could there be an avalanche?

She took her hand away from her bird. She said 'Maybe I'll just leave it here.'

'Yes leave it here.'

'I must go and get things ready.'

'I'll come down in the evening.'

'Yes, and we'll see.'

When Julie had gone I had another day of nothing to do. I thought – The island is the place where one learns about staying alive: how does one get to the island; what does one find when one gets off it.

I tried to work out what I should do if confronted by the people in the village. Yesterday at the wedding we had all been on our best behaviour; they knew something of my part in the shootings a year ago – but what? It might not be in their interests to make too much of it now, if they wanted to get on with their new businesses. But I might still be able to damage them?

This was like a game that my father used to talk about – the Prisoner's Dilemma. Two rebel colleagues are captured and are being interrogated separately in order to extort information from each and check it against the other. If one stays silent then the other might gain immunity by betraying him; if both talk then there is no chance of immunity; if they neither of them talk they will both be tortured but in the end may be set free. So – what are the advantages of loyalty? But how did this apply to the villagers and myself? We were enemies to whose advantage – to the advantage of everyone – it might be to become colleagues. In real life strategies for such games could not be accurately assessed because of the complexity.

Then there was the other story of the acolyte who was being tested by the Zen master: The master says – If you say I am holding this stick I will hit you with it and if you do not say I am holding this stick I will hit you with it – and the lesson to be learnt is for the acolyte to leap up and snatch the stick from the master and even to whack him or to threaten to whack him with it – and then the master bows, and gives the acolyte his blessing. But in reality, this would just mean becoming interested in something quite different?

In the medieval trial by ordeal you plunged your arm into boiling water. Well I had plunged my arm into that hole under the sink; I had read my mother's story; and I had not felt pain.

I put my things into my rucksack and tidied the cottage. There was a chance I might never come back. I would leave it, yes, to the beautiful and hungry bird that was trying to rescue humanity from pollution, but humanity was dragging it back, and humans were tumbling off it like lice, like fleas; like junkies.

In the afternoon the heat and the stillness became so intense that it seemed a thunderstorm was brewing. I lay on the bed and imagined myself walking along the beach at low tide to the village; I would sit on the rocks of the breakwater and wait for Julie; she would appear in a cockleshell boat like a Venus coming in out of the sea. I fell asleep and dreamed and I tried to remember my dream: I had been to the village and there had been people running as if from an avalanche. Julie and I had talked of an avalanche. I remembered the physics Professor my father had interviewed saying – The future can be affected by what might happen, or what might have happened, as well as from what happens: from events that are almost imperceptible there can occur an avalanche.

I seemed to be both anxious to get down to the village and to put it off. Timing is important for the occurrence of coincidences.

When I did get to the village – having walked along the misty moonlit road as if puffs of cloud had come to the ground to give the occasion an air of theatricality – lights had come on, and at the far end of the quayside there was a building like a large boathouse or warehouse which was hung with coloured bulbs. When I had sat on the breakwater a year ago I had imagined the façade of houses as the backdrop to a stage set: now more than ever the lights were making it like a virtual reality game in which one was invited to participate; somewhere within reach there should be knobs and levers, but how did one find them, and was it this that would be like plunging one's arms into the fire of an ordeal? Or did one rather have to trust the way things fell out?

From the lighted building there emerged the booming and groaning of a band warming up: amplified noises from a torture chamber: roll up, roll up, to the dungeon of delights! People were gathering outside the door and an altercation was taking place: how terrible to be so close to hell and not yet to be allowed to enter! Then when the band began to play it was a heavy metal band and the noise seemed to hurtle about inside the building like glass and china breaking, pots and pans being flung about, a massive domestic catastrophe – how exciting! One might become deaf, go blind, become catatonic: a consumer opportunity surely not to be missed.

I sat on the breakwater and behind me the sea seemed unnaturally calm. There was a path made by the moon like a pattern cut by a diamond. At the building the light was being shattered into coloured bits and pieces but beneath the moon there did not seem to be light: there was just the pathway cut on the water. To one side of this there was a boat approaching keeping to the darkness: it had no lights, it was like a shadow cast upon shadows. It appeared to be travelling quite quickly but was making no sound: if it had an engine this was drowned by the noise from the village. The boat might be one that crept up stealthily to ferry souls away from hell; it was the boat, I was sure, in which I had first seen Julie's brother. Julie was in it now; of this I was sure too, though I could not quite distinguish her; but what else should be happening? The boat was approaching the breakwater from the ocean side which it could do without danger because the sea was so calm. I climbed down on the rocks to catch the boat as it came in; Julie seemed to have expected me, for she kept her back to me and was paying out a rope attached to an anchor over the stern. Then she came to the front and threw me a rope so that I could pull the boat in; she manipulated the rope from the stern so that the boat would be held just off the rocks. Then she pointed to where there were some black plastic bags just above the waterline which I had thought must be flotsam; it appeared that they contained provisions that Julie had collected earlier and placed on the rocks. I handed them to her and she loaded them on to the boat and I gave her my rucksack. Then she climbed out adjusting the ropes to maintain the boat just off the rocks; then she stood looking along the pathway made by the moon and put her head against my shoulder. I thought – We will always be trusting about doing things without quite knowing why we are doing them.

Well why does one go into the world of rave up, beat up, carve up; the enjoyment of bombardment, the celebration of war; it is by chipping away at stone, at rock, that one gets clearance for life, for the avalanche? We climbed over the rocks of the breakwater, Julie and I; we walked along the quayside hand in hand. I thought – But if we are on our way to a party, can I not put my arm round Julie and kiss her? We will have to get used, sooner or later, to normality. So you plunge your mouth, your soul, into the fiery furnace, and angels are there for you. Julie responded. And then with her cheek close to my ear she said 'I'll be ready.' I said 'All right.'

There were, and had been for some time, cars arriving on the quayside and disgorging people who converged on the building hung with flashing lights. They had the purposive but slightly dysfunctional movements of drunks or computer-animated figures; so surely one should be able to outwit people whose communication systems were limited to the speed of light. At the door of the lit-up building there were gate-keepers, security men, taking tickets, taking money, even briefly feeling under raised arms and down trouser legs, for a grope. Julie was holding me by the hand

and was speaking to one of the bouncers; I was leaning away as if trying not to overhear what they said, like someone in a high wind on a pier. The men at the entrance made a way for us to go through.

Inside it was, yes, as if there were bits of white-hot chain being hammered out on an anvil, so that if you picked one up your skin might glow. Or if you were guilty you would scream, but who would hear you? For everyone was screaming, and being poured into a mould. There were laser beams and smoke and mirrored globes and arms rising up like maggots out of a tin can: or, if you could thus imagine them, like strands of DNA. The music was hitting at the walls and the walls were punching back; perhaps with enough violence you do not feel pain. But the mind was besieged and would soon be having to capitulate to battering rams and boiling oil, to be put to rapine and the sword; how uncompromising; what fun! Then trophies and relics could be gathered and hung on the walls of galleries and cathedrals. Julie squeezed my hand and then left me. I was ready for this. There are myths about this: survivors have to make their own ways through the burning city to the boats drawn up on the shore.

I got my back against a wall and was moving along it with my hands behind me. This was the start of the journey to – where – beyond the abode of the dead: to the cave, the worm-hole, that went underneath the sea? But how soon did one lose consciousness if one was being burned at the stake? To be sure, it might seem like eternity. I was making my way along the wall; it seemed that if I could get to the end of the room I might find a niche where I might prop myself like a martyr or crusader, and people might find me if they wanted to speak to me. I caught a glimpse of Julie who was in the crowd in front of a man with a beard who appeared to be talking to her although it did not seem possible that in the noise she could hear. Julie had her hands by her sides and one foot in front of the other and she was looking up at the man with her head thrown back and her eyes half closed; she was like a drawing of a dancer. Then she did begin to dance: not jerking with her arms up as other dancers were doing; but slowly, sinuously, like a snake in front of a snake-charmer; but it was Julie who was the charmer and the man was the snake. She still kept her arms by her sides; she gave little flourishes with her feet like kicking up dust; the man began to respond to her. Communication seemed to be being conveyed through the stillness, the uprightness, the antennae, of the upper halves of their bodies. I thought – So things may be all right.

I had come to the end of the building where there was what seemed to be a low stage. It might be that the structure was not a boathouse or a warehouse but a village hall where people put on performances and plays. I climbed up on to this and there were one or two props and bits of painted scenery; a door here, a window there; they might have something like a stool to which one might be tied and hurled into a river. In front of a back wall there was a cloth hung like a curtain; it broke into waves when I touched it, like that special effect in science-fiction films where there is vertical water. Then someone took hold of my arm from the back. But it was as if I had been expecting this.

The man who had taken me by the arm was the bearded man who had been dancing with Julie. He led me to the end of the wall in front of which there was the curtain and he pulled the cloth back and there was a door which he opened and beyond it there was an annexe to the building which might be used as an actors' dressing room. There were four men seated round a table: they were like poker players. I thought – They have been seeing too many films. They looked up when we came in; they seemed to have been counting not cards but money; all except one put their hands under the table. The bearded man had closed the door behind us but the noise of the music was still very loud. The man gestured to me to sit in a chair that was facing the table; but I acted as if I had not heard him and remained standing. The man frowned and made a face of irritation; not at me, but at the music. The men round the table were shuffling their money again and putting it into a tin box on the table.

I had been imagining that the point of my being here was that I was going to be questioned about what had happened on the breakwater a year ago; about my being a witness to who had or who had not shot whom. Julie had said that I need not tell them anything and this had seemed to me to make sense; were there not many things everyone would rather not know than know, and why should these make sense? But then would not these people have to go through the motion of wanting to know, because this was how they had been programmed. Though in fact the music was so loud that it might be quite easy for those who thought they should know but did not want to know, to frown, make out they were getting somewhere, but hear nothing.

I sat down and frowned and cupped a hand behind my ear. I thought it would be helpful if I could be seen to be talking so long as they did not hear what I said, so I said 'It's useful, isn't it that there's this terrible music playing, so we needn't hear a word of what we're saying.' The man I was facing at the table frowned and shook his head; he gestured towards the bearded man who went out of the door and past the curtain that was like water and into the big room: I supposed he was going to tell someone to stop the music. I smiled and said 'With any luck there'll be a riot!' The man I was facing moved his mouth so that he seemed to be saying – What? Or perhaps – Wait! Or perhaps – To Whit to Woo? I had no idea what I should be saying if there was no music.

And indeed how could I remember just what had happened on the breakwater? It seemed such an unlikely story. Would it not be truthful just to say I had no idea?

The music suddenly stopped: the bearded man must have pulled out a plug. So now one was in free fall. I said 'There'll be a riot.' The man I was facing said again 'What?' I said 'Without the music.' The man said 'Why have you come back?' I said 'You mean why have I come to the party?' The man said 'Why have you come to the cottage.' There were roars and moans and jeers coming from the room: I imagined the man with the beard and the disco people struggling with the plug; a mythical wrestling match between snakes and men in balaclava helmets. I said 'Oh why have I come to the cottage —' but the music had begun again, and I did not think that anything I had said would be heard. The man with a beard had reappeared through the door from the hall, but then when the music began again he turned and shot back through it as if he were one of those men who hold guns in front of themselves as if they have been taken short and have to be hanging on to themselves. I said 'All this makes a good cover.' The man I was facing cupped his hand behind his ear. I said 'What?' The music stopped again. He said 'You're in the cottage?' I said 'What?' Then — 'I mean yes.' The man said 'You're selling it?' I said 'I don't know.' There was a burst of music like machine-gun fire: then it stopped, started, stopped again. I had a vision of the people round the disco equipment ducking and raising their heads and ducking again and the man with the beard spraying them with machine-gun fire. Three of the men at the table got up and ran to the door. Noises from the big room made it seem that fighting must in fact be going on there. Then there was a shot. And then everything was silent.

The man I was facing across the table seemed unperturbed. He said 'As I was saying, are you selling the cottage?'

I said 'I don't know.'

'How much do you want for it.'

'How much are you offering?'

'We don't want it.'

'I see.'

'We can stop other people getting it.'

'Yes.'

'Why don't you keep it?'

'Well I'd quite like to.'

'Julie's got her things there.'

'Yes.'

'That suits you?'

'Oh well —'

'Is that agreed then?'

'What.'

'You'll tell your mother?'

'Yes I see.'

'She's a charming lady.'

'Isn't she.'

'Does she want rent for it?'

'I suppose it would help.'

'It can't be official.'

'No.'

'I don't suppose your father will be coming back here.'

'No.'

'It's obvious why we don't want to buy it.'

The music began again. I thought — Oh well, now, that's perfect timing.

— Words need not work out too badly, need they —

— If there's hardly any time for them.

When the music had begun again the man I had been talking with got up from the table and made a movement with his hands over his head as if the roof might fall down; then he went to the door. I thought that after a moment I would follow him, and could now rejoin Julie. So who would she be dancing with. Might someone in fact have been shot? Would anyone notice?

The party in the big room was hotting up again. The dancers seemed to have taken the chance of the breaks in the music to top up with dope; shadowy figures were round the walls as if in a classical frieze of obeisance to dark gods; bowing, scraping; then returning to the floor in a *danse macabre* of twitching skeletons, bodies hung from ropes; teeth, tongues and fingernails wrenched and flying from racks. The smell of dope was in the air; chemical weapons were being tested; and were doing nicely, thank you.

I was making my way along the back wall opposite the entrance door past the loudspeakers of the disco. I was hoping to get a glimpse of Julie. But it seemed that if one stayed beneath the bombardment too long one would become like that frog in a saucepan of water which is being heated; the frog has no instinct about the exact moment at which to jump, and so it doesn't jump, and it gets boiled. I thought – And so the human race, yes, is becoming boiled.

I caught sight of Julie across the room; she was dancing with a different man, but still keeping her arms by her sides, flicking her feet as if this was a way of keeping the floor cool beneath them. She did not seem to have been looking for me. I thought – But we have an instinct.

Julie turned from the man she was dancing with and went to the door which led into the night air. She still had not looked at me. I thought – But that is right because she will be thought to be abandoning me. I pushed my way through the crowd. At the door the bouncers were watching where Julie had gone; they watched me as if I might follow her. I stopped and gazed after her. Julie was walking back the way we had come along the quayside: it seemed likely that she would go to the beginning of the breakwater and then, if no one was watching too closely, go along it to where the boat was tied. I began to walk away in the opposite direction with just that air, I hoped, of dejection and liberation; would an audience go home happy if Julie and I never saw each other again? I imagined that when Julie had got the boat she would row along on the ocean side of the breakwater; but then, where the pier ended, she would have to move across the open mouth of the harbour before she could get out of sight again behind the rocky promontory beyond the dance hall, in the direction of the island. Though with luck by then no one would be watching. And I would have wandered lonely to the end of the promontory – to throw myself over? It might even have been that Julie had said something about meeting at the end of the promontory when, before entering the dance hall, she had put her cheek against my ear. But I knew that the island was somewhere beyond the promontory, and we were on our lines of trajectory.

I was on a path that went off from the end of the quayside beyond the boathouse; I left it where it curved to the top of the promontory and I went some way down on the rocks towards the sea. I sat on a rock just above the water line and looked to where I could see the end of the breakwater. It was possible that Julie might wait for me where the boat had been tied; but I did not think so. Would she not have looked back to see that I was following? Though it seemed to be a point between us that we should not look back.

There was the shadow moving again at the end of the breakwater; it was coming to the place where it would have to cross the moonlit path at the end of the harbour, where it would become quite clearly a target. So there was the boat quite visible, yes, with Julie rowing steadily across the gap between the end of the breakwater and the rocks where I was sitting; she had not started the engine; perhaps without the engine the scene might be taken to be mythical. I went down to the water's edge; it did not matter now if we were seen; we would get away quickly. Julie was bringing the boat in; we could do this expertly; we had had our rehearsal. I held the boat off and jumped in. The boat bobbed up and down appreciatively.

Julie left the seat in the middle and went to the back; she was leaving the oars to me. They were heavy like the trunks of small trees; there were pegs with ropes for rowlocks. I manoeuvred the boat round and rowed towards the end of the promontory. Julie was lowering the outboard motor so that its propeller was in the sea. I thought – I suppose those old monks knew what they were doing.

Julie sat facing me on the seat at the back. As I stretched forward to row I was almost, but not quite, touching her: I thought – This is like the mechanism of that huge pendulum by which one can tell that the earth is turning. And once Julie had started the engine I could go to the front and see where we were going.

The sea was still almost unnaturally calm: and was it phosphorus, or were there stars reflected in the water? Julie was looking down, and steering by the stars? Her own image would be a constellation?

Julie gave two pulls on the cord of the engine and it started. I went to the front of the boat to balance it. We were that chariot with horses plunging through the sky.

The monks who had made this journey had been escaping from burning cities and bodies writhing on stakes. They had hoped to find a place where horror did not matter. Now there was reproduction horror: it was more fun to reproduce horror than to go on journeys like seeds or would-be-fertilised eggs.

The flashing lights of the boathouse were growing distant behind us. Somewhere beyond the battlefield there would be provision to make love?

Looking down into the water it was as if I could feel the gigantic effort of the sea to keep us afloat: why did we not sink down to those cold depths of unknown shapes and compressed creatures. There was such buoyancy on the surface: this was what had given an image of heaven?

I became aware that the nature of the light, the darkness, was changing: there was mist rising up from the sea, drifting in front of the moon whose path was no longer cut as if by a diamond on glass. And then there was the shape of the island looming up like a giant whale: it was extraordinary how I had not before had a sight of the island; it had been hidden by the two headlands that were between it and the cottage. It was in the shape of a story-book illustration of a whale – with high black sides and a dip towards the tail where there might be, on a calm night, a chance of landing. And if it was difficult to land, then that was just why the monks had come here. Birds could land; and it might be isolated enough for them to mutate, but not for the people watching them to prove this. Had the monks mutated? They would have had their own strange means of recording this.

As we came closer to the island the mist cleared and a cold breeze began to blow; there was a place against the rocks where the sea, rising and falling, seemed to breathe; as if it were keeping the island alive like a life-support machine. Julie was lowering the speed of the engine; the boat was coming in to the dip by the island's tail; perhaps there should be a primitive landing step like the one below the cottage. The boat would have to be held off again, we would jump and scramble, but was this the point, that we should become expert at this? But how would the boat be made safe; how would we ever get off the island again.

There was a pale shape moving down the side of the island which might be that of a bird; well birds do come floating down the face of a cliff, don't they? It ensconced itself just above what did seem to be a landing step; then it became apparent the figure was human; it squatted with its hands round its knees, or was it some resident deity come to greet us? Then it became distinguished as, of course, the fair-haired boy who was Julie's twin brother; I had forgotten for a moment that he would be on the island; I had been so much imagining myself alone with Julie. But it would be he who would take the boat away again, and leave me alone with Julie.

Julie switched off the engine and brought the boat in. I was leaning over the front again to hold it clear: this was now not so easy because the water was rising and falling. Julie's brother had come down on to the landing stage to where the back of the boat was swinging round; Julie was handing up the bags and my rucksack to him; he was handing down to her a bag which he had on the landing stage; I was becoming stretched, elongated, between my feet in the boat and my hands on the rocks with the sea gasping and groaning beneath me; but it was I who seemed to be having my insides pulled out, being drawn and quartered; or was I rather like one of those representations of the sky as an arched human with the earth sheltered beneath it. Julie was climbing out of the boat and her brother came and reached over me as if to take on the holding of the boat off from the rocks; but I was so extended that it was difficult for me to let go without collapsing and being crushed; or could I be used as a bridge? When there was a particularly big heave of the sea I kicked with my legs and I seemed to be doing a hand-spring on to the landing step; at the same time Julie's brother was doing what seemed to be a rather neat somersault over me into the boat and Julie was catching me before I could fall back; so that it was as if we were a group of tumblers, and I had ended up with my head between Julie's legs. Julie called out 'When are you coming back?' Her brother said 'When do you want me?' Julie said to me 'When do we want him?' I said 'I don't know.' Julie called out 'We don't know.' I had crawled through and round Julie's legs so that I was facing her brother. He said 'Hullo.' I said 'Hullo.' We began laughing. He had got an oar and was paddling with it as if the boat were a gondola. The boat was wriggling this way and that as if it were being tickled, laughing.

Julie and I picked up our bags. The path that went up from the landing step to the top of the island was not much more than a series of ledges connected by where there happened to be footholds between each. This side of the island had been in deep shadow from the moon which had made it seem smooth like the flank of a whale; but to hands and feet it was encrusted and precipitous and craggy. Julie led the way from ledge to ledge; I handed the bags up and followed her. The moon was behind the hump of the island but there was now behind us in the east a faintly glowing light. As I climbed using my hands I became aware of rustlings, murmurings, on either side; at first it seemed that the land as well as the sea was coming alive; then as our eyes and minds became accustomed there emerged among the black rocks the shapes of birds; they were not on the so-called path itself but on the ledges on either side; they were almost motionless, mostly in ones and twos, but in places packed tight like objects being found room for on a shelf. For a moment it seemed they might be models, dummies set up by Julie or her brother in the style of the figures she had made in the cottage. Then there was the occasional hiss, the movement of a head, the strange gape of a beak that was indeed like rocks breathing. The birds seemed neither particularly hostile nor friendly; it was as if they were aware that they were there for their purposes and expected us to take care to keep to ours. As we approached the top of the island the path became easier and the birds became fewer: they knew that for safety their niches, their nests, should be on precipices and crags. And the monks? I remembered that they had built a chapel, a meeting place, on the gentle slopes on top of the island: and there they had been safe from most predators, but perhaps not always from those in the mind.

At the very top of the island there was a concavity like a crater that might have been gouged out by nature or by hand. There were the fragments of stone buildings round the edges of this depression; then a slope and steps leading down to a doorway that might be the entrance to a cave or a crypt. The light from the eastern sky was now making the outlines of things more clear; above and beyond the doorway was a mound like a beehive-shaped dome. I followed Julie down the steps carrying my haversack and some bags; she pushed on the door and went in. There was a hurricane lamp alight on a table. The interior was like a cave in that the roof glistened with what seemed to be crystalline stone; it was like a crypt in that there was a central pillar to the arched roof that seemed man-made although it was gnarled like the trunk of a tree. The space of the shelter was circular and not large – about five paces in diameter. It was possible that the central pillar might be a stalactite that after millennia had become at one with its stalagmite rising from the floor; but then there were other indications that the whole structure had been fashioned.

As my eyes became accustomed to the gentle light there came into view round the walls shelves close-packed with provisions – tins and packets of food, jars and bottles and cans: also books and papers and implements of various kinds. Also interspersed with these were bits of stone and coloured glass so that it was like a small and well-stocked village shop that sold not only provisions but curios and antiques and precious stones. All this was lit by the flame of the hurricane lamp by the central pillar. The scene was precise and glittering, but also malleable like wax.

Then it became apparent that the vault of the ceiling

glittered because the whole of it had been inlaid like a mosaic with coloured stone and glass; the effect thus presented was that of the leaves and branches of a tree. The trunk was the central pillar that had been made to seem as if it might have grown from earth; the branches were the dark spaces between the leaves and flowers that spread in shining profusion across the ceiling and then hung down to where their fruits interspersed with the fruits of everyday life on the shelves. There were bottles of wine like the strange nests of birds that hang from trees; packages like the elaborate homes of insects. I thought – This is the Tree of Life! Of course it is underground! It was never forbidden; only hidden and difficult to find.

Julie had put down the bags she had been carrying and was sitting on one of two chairs that faced each other across the small central table. She put her arms on the table and her head on her arms and she seemed to go to sleep. I thought – So we are tired, yes; we should let this place take us over for a time.

I put down my bags. I wondered where beneath or within the shelter of this tree there might be a niche where it would be customary to sleep; where one would not fall out of the branches. I went round the table and the trunk of the tree and beyond it there was a gap between the shelves which was the opening to a tunnel. I went along this with my head slightly bowed; at the end was a faint light from a window. This would be looking out over the far side of the island – to the west, away from where the sun was now rising – so that it would be when the sun was setting that the light would stream in like a sword. Just short of the window the tunnel opened into alcoves on either side within which were ledges like bunks on a boat: I wondered – This arrangement was made not for the monks, but for Julie and her brother. One of the beds had blankets laid out on it; on the other there was a rolled-up sleeping bag. I thought I should unroll the sleeping bag and lie down: it was as if I were already half-sleeping. Julie might come and join me on the bed or she might lie across the passageway with the sheathed sword between us. This was a place that would have its own way of ordering things; of timing.

IX

The island that for six hundred years had been a refuge for hermits and monks had been abandoned in the fourteenth century and most of the outlying cells in time became indistinguishable from natural outcrops of rock. But the beehive-shaped dome in the hollow at the top of the island remained, and became of interest to archaeologists when in the nineteenth century they began to come to the island in pursuit of an understanding of history rather than of God.

It was thought at first that the dome might be the covering of a tomb; then excavations unearthed the underlying chamber which seemed to have been an oratory or chapter house where monks had gathered. The unusual central pillar was thought to be a megalith of an earlier date, brought in for the construction and support of the roof. There were faint carvings on it of foliage or snakes.

It had been noted by researchers that there were similar beehive-domed constructions in early Christian settlements in the Middle East – notably in eastern Turkey, in what had been Armenia, which had been the first nation officially to embrace Christianity, and from which an early and cheerful form of Christianity had spread. This was manifested not so much by decrees and dogma as in subtle representations of the wonder of God's creation – carvings and illustrations of birds and animals, and whimsically smiling saints who seemed to be amused at their predicament in being a self-conscious part of creation.

It was when Christianity had become the established religion of the Roman Empire that violent antagonisms within the Church took over from persecution from outside: dispute and the pursuit of dissenters became the business of prelates as well as of politicians. Devout monks and would-be hermits retired to deserts and mountains; some peregrinated (this was their word) in their cockleshell boats to wherever the wind would take them – to some edge of the known world where they might either live in peaceful communion with God or topple over as it were into His presence. They carried with them their illustrations and representations of God's wondrous works: some reached the cliff faces of islands off the west coast of Ireland, and halted there.

Then when after several centuries it had seemed that living in expectation of the end of the world was not the point, that there was work to be done with civilisation, cells and hermitages had been abandoned, to the future delight of archaeologists.

When later still it began to seem that neither religion nor history were a sufficient means of understanding creation, then ecologists and biologists had come to the island bringing their measuring and recording instruments to study the anatomy and habits of birds. They had got permission to use the underground chamber as a storeroom; few antiquarians came to the island any more, since there was not enough of interest there to make worthwhile the risks of the hazardous journey. But as a diversion from the repetitive business of collecting and tabulating scientific data one or two of the wildlife people – notably Julie's brother, who by now I had discovered was called Peter – had carried out further excavations and had opened up the tunnel that had been cut from the chamber to the cliff face, probably by pirates in the sixteenth century to serve as a lookout post. And then when the study of birds was coming to an end through lack of suitable evidence, Peter had been encouraged to stay to look after the site; and he had come across in a hitherto unearthed alcove a chest containing bits of mosaic and lustrously coloured glass. He had not told anyone of this; but during his time of seclusion on the island had set about constructing his own version of what he imagined monks might once have planned in the way of decorating their place of worship – a representation, as Peter saw it, of the Tree of Life – that according to the myth had been in the Garden of Eden but which had remained unnoticed. It was Peter's idea that the Tree should be underground, like roots, so that each person had to search for it for themselves.

I learned most of this later, but I had come across some of the relevant history and indeed theology when I had been doing my reading before I came to the island. What struck me now were the extraordinary resonances that there seemed to be on and around the island – not only concerning its own past but between this and my own present circumstances. I realised that the place to which Christina had said she was going to rejoin her archaeological dig was what had once been Armenia, from which it was thought that some of the monks who landed on this island might originally have come. Christina had told me she would send me a postcard of St Gregory the Illuminator, who I learned was the patron saint of Armenians and of their particularly benign form of Christianity. I imagined those amused, smiling saints looking down through the foliage of trees on Christina and our baby.

The usual inhabitants of the island however are birds,

though when Julie and I had landed just before the sun came up we were aware of them only in that they were by the side of the path up the rock face like sentinels, like markers to keep us out of a minefield. Then before I had gone to sleep in the alcove at the end of the tunnel I had become aware of a vague screaming which I had taken to be the pleasure of birds as they greeted the sun; this had become mingled with a dream or fantasy I sometimes had of crowds fleeing from a burning town towards a river. When I woke there was light coming in through the window at the end of the tunnel and I saw that Julie had come and lain in the alcove across the passageway from me; she was sleeping. I felt such happiness in her presence that I hardly knew how to handle it; it did not seem that time could stand still for so long. I thought I should get up and go along the passage and find a drink of water. When I came into the dome-shaped room there was only a dim light from the passage but the foliage and flowers of the tree still glittered as if light from the glass and stone shone from within them.

When I went on into daylight there was a scene overhead that was as if leaves were becoming detached from the tree and were blowing in a gale: these were birds that were gliding and swooping and soaring overhead as if to demonstrate the skill needed to be alive; the exuberance of having achieved this. The hollow in the ground on to which the beehive-domed chamber opened was like a defence work against all this energy; it might be safer to keep one's head down below the level of the moss-covered parapet. Had those old monks ever mentioned the birds? Had they seen them as the demons that had plagued St Anthony?

When I did go over the top (had those men in the First World War felt themselves getting close to God?) there was a beautiful no-man's-land of green and mossy grass with just the aerial dogfight going on overhead. There were no birds on the ground here; presumably they were all in the air or protected by the ramparts of cliffs. As I walked the ground fell away towards a cliff. Then birds came into view as they squatted on or around their nests on narrow ledges.

I knew almost nothing about birds. I had wondered a year ago if the bird that I had helped to rescue with Peter might be an albatross; I had learned it was probably a gannet. Many of the birds that nested here seemed likely to be gannets: they had sturdy white bodies with black wing-tips and short curved necks: I could not be sure that they were the same as my bird for my bird had been covered with oil and bedraggled; but then I had imagined that my bird might be a mutation – one that might not on its own be able to deal with pollution, but might be ready to be helped with it. It was from the birds on their ledges that now in the daylight there was coming the most clamour: the birds in the air were uttering cries but these were intermittent like the huzzas or warnings of spirits that have been freed. The uproar on the ledges seemed to be due to the determination of adult birds to possess and protect their nest or narrow patch of ledge and to nag at their young: they stretched their necks and waggled their heads and made gasping or gagging noises like disturbed and angry parents. Their young were grey and rather dumpy-looking birds who seemed to be trying to stay aloof from the antics of their parents; they sometimes flapped their wings, but seemed still trapped in dependence. I thought I would find a place where I could sit and watch the birds without their noticing me; this should be possible because they seemed so intent on their business of possession and aggression. It occurred to me that if I were a God looking down on earth then this is how I would see humans. But then birds are not naturally fitted for much more than survival and procreation.

There was one young bird at the back of a ledge of rock which seemed to be eyeing wistfully the edge beyond which was a precipitous drop and then the sea. The bird seemed to be trying to make up its mind to fly from the frightful racket of adult life; but between it and the edge from which it might jump were its parents and those with whom they seemed to be in an almost constant rage – so how in fact does an adolescent get away? Do some not leave too early before they can fly? But there seemed to be some understanding between the adult birds and this particular progeny: perhaps they longed to be rid of it: anyway the time for an attempt at flight seemed to have come. The dumpy bird waddled its way towards the rim of its ledge as if through a gauntlet of mocking but nevertheless goading relatives: it was like a child being warned and yet not prevented from jumping into the deep end of a pool. It paused on the edge and tried out its wings rather mournfully as if waving goodbye; then it flopped over towards the sea some hundred feet below. It did not seem even to be trying to learn how to fly; it landed on the water with a splash; there it bobbed up and down top-heavily. There were other young birds on the ledges stretching and flapping their wings as if in applause or envy; then after a time they seemed to get bored and turned away. Then there was a quick flurry on the water and the bird I had been watching disappeared. I had not seen exactly what had happened; there was just a swirl; perhaps it had been taken from underneath by a fish. Do fish eat birds? I did not know. I remembered the monk who had thought he might fly and had jumped from a cliff; had he been eaten by a whale? I felt upset. What had happened to Jonah? Had after a time the whale simply been sick?

I saw Julie crawling or clambering from one ledge to another along the cliff face below me; she was moving amongst the birds carefully as if trying not to disturb them or to be apologetic to them if she did. She moved starting and stopping, as in the children's game in which the person you wish to get close to must not see you moving. There was a ledge not of gannets but of some smaller gull-like birds that were still nesting; when Julie was near to them she put out a hand tentatively as if she were asking permission to touch them in a way they might not like; the birds seemed to grumble but not altogether to discourage her. She got a hand underneath one of the birds that in fact raised itself slightly from its nest; she was taking one of its eggs. The bird made a formal pecking movement at her hand, and she put the back of the hand to her mouth and looked at the bird reproachfully; this hand held the egg so that she seemed to be showing the egg to the bird and to be waiting to see if the bird would make any further objection. The bird settled back on its nest. Julie moved a step or two along the narrow ledge towards another nest. I wanted to say – Julie, Julie, you need not do this! You are on a cliff face with an egg in one hand and if you get an egg in the other you will not be able to hold on; it will be a miracle if you do not fall! I do not need an egg for breakfast, people who come to this island do not expect an egg for breakfast! Or are you saying – why should they not?

Julie and I were reclining in the grassy hollow in front of the beehive-shaped construction and we were eating boiled eggs and biscuits as in a *fête champêtre*. I said 'Do the birds spend the winter here or do they migrate?'

Julie said 'The gannets go somewhere in the south, or young ones do. The older ones sometimes seem to hang around.'

'And they come back to the same place?'

'So people say.'

'And how do they find their way.'

When Julie and I talked we did not confront one another: it was as if this might be unnerving. We faced slightly away from each other, as if our voices, to be acceptable, had to travel through some circuit, some mediation, like that by which whispers travel round the walls of certain caverns or cathedrals.

Julie said 'By the sun, by the moon, by the stars. By some response to a magnetic field. They don't know.'

'They've done experiments?'

'The wildlife people took a bird – I don't think it was a gannet, perhaps a shearwater – and they carried it in a closed box to America. There they let it go, and it found its way back in a fortnight.'

'And they admit they don't know how?'

'Peter came across this bird – he says it was the one, it had been marked with a ring – and he tried to communicate with it as it was coming out of its burrow.'

'What did he say?'

'There's not all that much genetic difference between humans and birds, so it shouldn't be totally impossible to have some to and fro. But humans have language, and birds know how to find their way. Humans don't; and language doesn't seem to help them. I think Peter thought he might pick up something from this bird.'

'And did he?'

'Well, I suppose he was feeling he had to get back to the mainland anyway.'

'What will he do there now?'

'I don't know. I suppose it's by what turns up that one finds one's way.'

Our words seemed to hover in the air like fragile observation planes. I thought – If they become too presumptuous, will they be shot down?

Julie said 'Did the people you talked to say they wanted to go on using the cottage?'

'Yes.'

'Will that be all right?'

'I suppose so.'

'They were threatening to burn it down.'

'Who were?'

'Does it matter?'

'No.'

I was wanting to make love to Julie, but it was as if we were making love all the time, and what form this took depended on the sun, the stars, on some magnetic field.

I said 'Perhaps we should give up language.'

'Us?'

'Everyone.'

'We shouldn't give things up. We should make them sing.'

'That's what everyone tries to do.'

'Did you? With those people?'

'No. I said very little.'

'The music helped?'

'Yes. It drowned them. Perhaps that's what music should do.'

It was such a bright summer day. The dip in the ground where we lay was like a saucer, or dish, by means of which we might pick up messages from the sun or moon or stars.

Julie said 'When we were young Peter and I used to do experiments. No not experiments, because if we thought of them like that then nothing happened. You could only see them as experiments when you looked back.'

'You tried to communicate?'

'Yes.'

'You didn't talk?'

'No.'

'You didn't know whether or not you'd communicated?'

'No.'

'But this or that happened.'

'Yes.'

Julie was lying on her side with a hip and shoulder jutting up and a dip as if down to a landing stage at her waist so that she was like an embodiment of the island on which we lay.

I said 'There was some language before the Tower of Babel. Perhaps it was silence. People thought that by this they were getting up to heaven.'

'Perhaps it was an instinct, as with the birds.'

'God knocked it down.'

'Why.'

'Perhaps because people had things to do on earth.'

'It's when things are too good they get knocked down.'

'Only if you try to build them into a tower.'

'What were those monks doing when they prayed, do you know?'

My wanting to make love to Julie, and yet it being as if we were making love, was like a membrane stretched so tight that vibrations might be received and sent out that would otherwise be beyond the range of humans.

I said 'I suppose they were imagining they might start an avalanche.'

'To clear away – what –'

'What was wrong on earth?'

'But now. Here. What are the things to be done on earth.'

'On the mainland?'

'Yes.'

Julie sat up. She raised her knees and put her forehead down against them, so that she was in the position of someone who has been pulled up from dreaming.

I said 'Birds that don't adapt die.'

'People, God knows, on the mainland die.'

'You want to stop them?'

'Don't you?'

'I don't know. Why shouldn't they.'

'People should be different from birds.'

'Yes.'

'They might stop.'

'How?'

'Those birds that flew in from the sea the other evening –'

'Yes?'

'They usually come at that time of the evening.'

'Things should just happen?'

'You can imagine. Can't you? Try.'

Four people on the mainland are approaching the wide steps that lead up to the portico of a monumental building. They are walking in twos, coming from opposite directions; their trajectories are such that they will not meet.

The eyes of cameras are upon them. The light that travels from them to the cameras turns them into a negative which will be turned into noughts and ones which will be transmitted round the world and turned into print. This will become lodged in minds and will have no chance of change until it and what contains it crumble to dust.

The four people begin to climb the steps to where there is an array of microphones. When they see each other, two by two, they stop: they do not want to meet. But each pair wishes to get to the microphones first. The sky is becoming dark as if for a thunderstorm.

One of the men from one of the pairs risks a move and reaches the top of the steps and takes hold of a microphone. He turns to face the photographers at the bottom of the steps. As he does this a large dollop of birdshit lands on his head. He looks up. Another dollop lands on his face.

No one can see the birds under the portico. It was thought they had been cleared out by poisonous gas and explosives.

The reporters at the bottom of the steps begin to laugh. The photographers jostle and work their cameras. The man at the top of the steps has nothing to do but laugh. He feels in the top pocket of his jacket as if for a handkerchief; when he cannot find one he makes a face like a clown. The reporters and photographers give him a cheer.

One of the other pair of men who have stopped on the steps sees the man splashed with birdshit getting an ovation from the crowd. Because he cannot bear this, he hurries up the steps holding out a handkerchief to the man at the top. This man, with the eyes of cameras upon him, has to take it. He dabs at his forehead with it and smears the birdshit; then he examines the handkerchief. The owner of the handkerchief has turned and is acknowledging the cheers of the crowd. Just then there is a flash of lightning and people half duck; they have become accustomed to explosions. Then the thunder comes, and with it rain like bullets. The two men at the top of the steps have remained upright; the one holding the handkerchief hands it back to the one who had handed it to him, and this one absentmindedly wipes his face with it and finds his face covered in birdshit. Suddenly the crowd is not laughing; it is as if the rain on people's faces were tears. The rain on the faces of two at the top of the steps is melting and spreading the birdshit so that it is like the stuff of their eyes as well as tears.

I was sitting on the grass with my back against a rock not trying to collect my thoughts but to let them fly. I had been watching the birds overhead. A bird had been the symbol of the Holy Spirit; and in so far as those monks had seemed to pay little attention to the birds, what attention had they paid to the Holy Spirit? They must have felt it was what had brought them here, and sustained them gaunt and transfixed staring out to sea. It was just that one cannot talk about this much? One can let imagination fly? Send birds winging to the mainland where they can find their way?

Julie had been sitting with her head against her knees in the position of a child pretending not to be watching.

The rocks on the island were covered with birdshit. Somewhere there were islands from which birdshit was carried to a mainland and used to fertilise the fields. Had the monks had no use for birdshit? There was not enough soil on their lonely rock?

The baptism of the Holy Spirit might be like a dollop of birdshit on one's forehead?

There were moments when being with Julie was like being in contact with some magnetic field; but how could humans become at ease with the impression that they might be able to find their way? Of course they would have to work for it; to come across it by tilling the soil; by procreation and nurture. Though then there would be presences like dandelion seeds taking off and floating in the wind. But to what new lands would they go?

I thought – Come on birds, shower us with your blessings.

Julie had turned her head so that with one eye she seemed to be laughing.

She said 'Can you fish?'

I said 'I suppose I can fish.'

'Do you know how to dig vegetables and carry water up a slope?'

'Yes.'

'Peter must somewhere have made a vegetable patch.'

'Then it will be facing south to catch the sun, and high up to be out of the reach of spray.'

'The things you know!'

'Yes.'

'I think we need fish before vegetables.'

'All right.'

'Look what's happened to you!'

She came crawling over to me and dabbed with her finger at my forehead. She said 'Did you know it was there?' I said 'I wasn't sure.' She said 'It was black and white and now it's grey.' I said 'Make it into the shape of this island.'

The wandering monk called John Scotas Erigena who might have come to the island centuries ago and whose story I had come across just before I set out for Ireland had had the idea that although humans were part of animal creation they were obviously different from it in that they had intellect with which they could consider it and try to understand it and even order it, and thus might be partaking of an activity that might be called God's. It might be that they needed no further justification for the use of this word; but still, how was their potential power to be understood? They had the curious experience of both having freedom and yet not having it; of being able to control things and yet being helpless. So what were they to do?

I tried to imagine John Scotus as he went about his business on the island: how did he experience his partnership with God? Was it equivalent to Julie's idea of being able to make life, living, a form of art – trying out this, trying out that, and then when you get it knowing what is right; but even from the beginning perhaps having an instinct for what to try. And this sort of thing with regard not only to oneself, one's own life, but to the events and experiences of those with whom one is in contact; even (and perhaps as importantly) to people one is in no discernible contact with at all. Of course there was a tie-up here with the old monkish idea of prayer and meditation: you attend to what seems to you to be at stake; you watch and listen; and then perhaps through your attentiveness there may occur what it is beyond your competence to occasion or even imagine. This sort of possibility had been talked about by the science master at school; it had been called action-at-a-distance: you can know that almost ubiquitous connections exist, but you cannot send messages through them; you have to accept (and what better is there to do?) that such things work on their own.

I imagined myself bumping into John Scotus on this island: I would know what to do? We would meet on a narrow rocky ledge, and in order to get past each other we would have to hold on – not on to the rocks, but on to each other, face to face; with our backs to the precipice and rocks. And thus we would be together for a moment; between the ends of time and the universe. He would have a rough face like something on the tongue. We would not talk; because what is faster than light is silence. After we had moved on, somewhere, there might be an avalanche.

Even when the sea was calm it was unnerving to go fishing. Peter had set up a system whereby a net was draped across an inlet on the south side of the island with the lower edge weighted and the top end threaded with floats so that in theory when one drew the net in it would be bulging with fish. But to do this one had to be perched perilously on a rock or even straddling two rocky projections, thus risking the chance of a wave or a swell of the tide pulling one into the sea and even entangling one in the net so that one would become a catch oneself for crabs and fishes. Peter seemed to have managed the net on his own, fastening one end to a rock and then scrambling to the other side of the inlet to pull the net in; but it was easiest to imagine him flitting from rock to rock somewhat magically, pulling on the two ends of the rope at the same time and steadying himself with as many hands as might be required. I would have liked to have tried to manage the net myself, but felt I had to recognise (which for once I did not want to do) that I was too clumsy; that if

I had fallen my head was likely to have cracked open like an egg. But Julie seemed to have recognised this too and took charge, wedging me in a gap in the rocks with one end of the rope while she clambered round the inlet with the other. And watching her as she moved with her hands and feet clinging to the narrow ledges like notations on a stave of music I thought – This is what is at the back of music; this is what people wish to express with music: Julie spreadeagled on the black rocks like a butterfly and still moving; the sea below her in a ground bass breathing, and unseen fish like bits of light fallen from the sky. And it seemed that I was lucky to have a sickness so that I could be a witness to such things; and if one day it all became too much for me then of course I could die, and life would have had some ecstasy.

Julie and I sat in the sun by the vegetable patch that Peter had planted in a small but comparatively protected piece of earth which was showing faint signs of life in shapes like dragon's teeth that emerged from the thin soil and seemed to make the point that nothing was easy, nothing was to be taken for granted; what you sowed grew curled over on itself like a question mark. Julie and I had made a fire of a few pieces of driftwood and were eating the fish that we had caught. There was nothing edible on Peter's vegetable patch, so with the fish we had opened a tin of fruit that Julie had brought from the mainland. I said 'When Adam and Eve were turned out of the Garden of Eden they were told to till the soil but God didn't much like it when they did; I mean he didn't like Cain, who was a tiller, he liked Abel, who was a hunter. So Cain killed Abel out of jealousy.'

Julie said 'God makes cock-ups. I used to think Peter wanted to kill the people who'd killed our parents. But you think God wants us to put things right?'

'Where do you think Peter is now?'

I still had not made love to Julie. We used to lie holding on to one another at night. This was becoming increasingly hazardous; but if we made love, might we not lose paradise?

She said 'I think Peter wanted to find out about other Trees of Life – about places where people had made images of those birds and animals that seem to be trying to tell one to find the way; of those figures amused at God's deliberate cock-ups.'

'Christina's gone digging, or recording, or restoring, in a place like that. I mean where there are those images; our beehive constructions.'

'Do you think of Christina?'

'Sometimes.'

'There are these connections?'

'Yes.'

It was evident that one day Julie and I would have to leave this island. We would wait for Peter to fetch us? There seemed to be no way of letting him know.

She said 'Those people were wiped out, weren't they?'

'Who, the Armenians? Very nearly.'

'By people who were envious?'

'I suppose so.'

'One has to be cunning.'

'Yes.'

It seemed to be a matter of timing. And what was time (as my science master used to say) except that which prevents everything happening all at once. Except that in a way everything was happening all at once.

I said 'Do you think about Peter?'

'Yes.'

'What might he be doing.'

'I don't know.'

'I used to be told I was lucky to be going on living.'

'Peter thinks he's lucky to go on living.'

233

'That can be a way of finding out what to do?'

'I sometimes feel like that, yes.'

Then one night there was a storm. Julie and I had left the net down on the rocks and the sea would be coming in high and violent and we would lose the net, it would be torn, it would be carried away. The night was dark, one could not see the shape of the moon, but it seemed to make slightly luminous the lashes and sheets of rain. Julie and I had been lying holding on to one another as we usually did in our alcove at the end of the tunnel; we got up to see if we could rescue the net. Julie said 'No you stay here.' I said 'Why?' She said 'Because I don't want you to die.' I had been trying to work out as I so often did why Julie and I had not made love and the words had gone round and round – We have come to this island to put something to the test; things have to happen in due order; once we have made love we may have to go; did not those old monks know this? They were renouncing possession but that was because they wanted to possess – what? – certainty? unchangingness? what they thought might be life beyond the grave? But when they stretched their arms out they had held the air. So what had God thought of this: was there something that they had had to learn: what is procreation? If you want to practise non-possession do you not have to be in possession of what you choose not to possess? Or what is freedom: and what is the due order for things to happen in.

On the night of the storm Julie went ahead of me to the top of the cliff above the inlet. I followed her. I was wearing nothing but shoes; so was Julie. There seemed to be just enough light by which to see; perhaps even the sun was rising. I thought – If we get through this, all right, we will make love. I said to Julie 'No you stay here.' She said 'Why?' I said 'Because I don't want you to die.' She said 'All right we can both die at the same time.'

I felt my way down the rocks. The sea was coming up in spray that seemed quite solid, like the tentacles of whatever the giant squid is that lives at the bottom of the ocean. On the island we always seemed to know what we were doing: of course we had to rescue the net! Julie was coming down the rocks behind me. When the waves hit me I wanted to say to them – All right, do your worst, I have to be risking this. The force of the water made it difficult to breathe. I got handholds on the rocks but then it was as if my hands would be torn off; my feet slid away from me and it was as if my body would be flayed. I reached down to where the net had been and a fling of the sea cast up and caught me; I thought – Bloody hell, now you've done it! While I was under water I managed to get hold of the net and then it seemed – Well all right, this is funny. I was climbing up on the net not as if I were rescuing it but as if it was rescuing me. Julie was leaning down and holding out a hand. I was thinking – Well, I am like that bird; and now we can make love. A wave lifted both me and the net who were in each other's arms and landed us violently at Julie's feet. I was cut by the rocks but had been saved by the net and Julie's legs. Julie wrapped the net around us both like a towel. It was as if we were fishes having caught the net and landed it. We draped it over our shoulders and set off to the top of the cliff. I thought – We'll find a hollow and spread the net out and lie on it; and there will be waves crashing and rain lashing and the thunder and lightning that people talk about in story-books, but here it will be true. And there will be the taste of blood and tremendousness, and a body forming perhaps between God's legs.

When I had left Christina at her lodgings after our meeting a week or so after the end of term I had had no sure idea of what she would do. She had talked of joining her archaeological field group who had been working in what had once been

Armenia – I had hardly known where Armenia was – she had wanted to learn more about what she had found in her first visit to eastern Turkey: something about those androgynous, whimsical figures that had seemed to recognise and convey the farce of being human; the enmity between men and women that had come about as a result of sexuality (it had been surmised); but this need not be the point; had not those smiling saints and knowledgeable animals known this: it was not necessary to be a predator to make love.

In Armenia according to legend there had been not only the Garden of Eden and the place where Noah's Ark had come down but also the building and the collapse of the Tower of Babel – but was this the story of a curse or a liberation? What had people been doing thinking they could build a ladder to heaven? The people who had lived in that place later and built their churches with their rueful, comic figures did not seem to have felt themselves under a curse; or if they did, it was just telling them bluntly to be in harmony with nature. But then like other such cheerful people before or after them – the Etruscans for instance – it had seemed they were destined to be wiped out by the envy and resentment of neighbours who indeed might seem to be perpetrators of a curse, but would not see it like this, would just be bitter and triumphant against people who were happy. Over centuries Armenia as a nation was obliterated; its churches laid waste – their images indeed being given something to be ironic and rueful about, looking down on waste and rubble. And it was to this countryside and this history that Christina had gone or was going; to record or preserve or learn what she could – of the outside world, of herself, of what might be her attitude towards her baby.

And Julie and I had come to our island – to a place to which some seeds had blown from the place to which Christina had gone. So I mean, God doesn't exactly tell you what to do, does he? You just notice, or you do not, things that happen apparently naturally.

And Peter had come here and had built his own all-enfolding image from bits and pieces left behind by the monks. Then Peter had gone – perhaps to try to learn, like Julie, what, after one had done one's images, they were images of: what was the knowledge being attended to by such wide-eyed saints and caring animals.

So that when we lay together at night, Julie and I, on our sarcophagus-like bunk in the alcove at the end of the tunnel that was like a root going off from Peter's tree (we had in fact come back here the night of the storm to make love; we had not needed the thunder and the rain) we did not need to cling to each other so tightly now, our birds had flown, our seeds were away wherever they would go in the wind; forces beyond us were waiting to see what we would do. We lay side by side with an arm lightly around each other – like those Etruscans indeed on their tombs that did not seem to be tombs but rather a platform from which celebrants could make their declarations about eternity and life. Now when I held Julie I could let my thoughts once more fly – they need no longer go round and round – they could fly to where Christina might be with the baby that she carried in her womb or what still might be a tomb; to Peter who might have reclaimed the gun I had hidden and might even now be prowling on the mainland like a hungry lion; even to my friend Edward whom I had not thought about for some time but who had played such an odd part in these events – taking me to see Connie and somehow getting me hit on the head so that when I went to the hospital I bumped into Christina. All this by chance of course; to mention which was not forbidden. And then had not Edward's friend Stanislaus, the pilot who had flown us to France, come from this part of the world; I mean the part to which Christina had gone and from which seeds had flown; and had he not been like some ruefully apologetic leopard in a tree; probably not a saint. And had not he and Edward been planning some journey, some escape, some sortie, back to where he had come from? So what was chance; and what were God's patterns, or cock-ups; and how ironic for God to be blamed. But what in fact was happening there now: was there not some sort of civil war in what had been Armenia? Edward and Stanislaus would be flying to it in their small plane?

Lying at nights now with Julie after we had made love I would imagine Christina on her archaeological dig standing by a ruined tower by a lake in a settlement which has been bombed; she was holding our baby perhaps and was looking ruefully up at the sky; was not this the sort of picture that would be carried all over the world; but was she ready to cry or laugh. And I saw myself and Julie perhaps in the air with Edward and Stanislaus and we would swoop down like a bird – the sort of bird that Julie had fashioned and Peter and I had rescued – and we would rescue Christina and her baby just in time, pick them up in our talons. For men on the plains with guns and deformed faces would be running to capture us if we landed or let her go. And Julie and I were lying side by side with our arms lightly over each other in our alcove. And I wondered what Julie would be dreaming. I wondered if I could be part of what Julie would be dreaming. The light was beginning to come in through the window at the end of the passage. The leaves and fruit on Peter's tree would be shining. There would be a new figure coming to life in its branches.

One of the tasks that Julie and I had set ourselves while we were on the island was to repair and make smooth the roof above the beehive dome so that it would appear from the outside to be no more than a mound; then what was

underneath might be more protected and hidden. It seemed
that Peter had begun to do this but had run out of time, and
it was not in fact clear what form the roof should take. There
might once have been a cairn above the half-underground
dome – there were enough stones for this lying around –
and a cairn might have been in a traditional style of both
guarding a mystery and marking it with a finger pointing to
heaven. Julie said 'But do we want people to come here?'

I said 'What did Peter want?'

'I think he would have wanted people to find their
own way.'

'Do you think you should be finding out about Peter?'

'Do you think you should be finding out about Christina?'

The stones that were lying around fitted quite well into
repairing and strengthening the dome. I handed up the
heaviest stones to Julie and she manoeuvred them into place
and then I climbed up and we both filled in the cracks with
earth. We found enough turf to cover the surface so that the
whole thing looked smooth and unremarkable. I thought –
So how are people going to come and rescue us?

There was a morning when we had set our last piece of
turf into place and we were standing back and admiring our
handiwork and Julie said 'Peter and I sometimes wondered
if he and I might have a baby. But it seemed right that that
wasn't right.'

I said 'If we had a baby then it could one day have a baby
with Christina's baby.'

She said 'Yes I'd thought of that. But they'd have to find
their own way, wouldn't they.'

A cold wind had begun to blow. It was as if we had done
what we wanted and autumn was coming on. We sat in our
shelter. The tree seemed to be shedding its leaves by crying.
Julie said 'I'm so sad.'

I said 'Don't be.'

At the back of our time on the island there had been the thought of when Peter would be coming for us. I had both dreaded this and yet accepted it: there was a sense of fatality imparted by the island. I said 'Perhaps Peter won't come.' I thought – Do I mean, he may be dead? I felt the cold wind entering my heart. I thought – I suppose the wind will blow us to find out.

We were beneath or within the branches of our beautiful tree and there it was, all around, with its leaves and flowers and fruits and animals and birds. But we humans had to go – this was our liberation or curse – we had to go over deserts and plains, in cockleshell boats over rough seas; we had to set things to rights; we had to die in order that things could come alive. And I felt I might be becoming ill with the illness that came on me every now and then; that one day indeed should kill me. And I thought – But this is autumn and it is just that seeds fall in autumn; and some do come alive again.

Julie had gone to the end of the tunnel and was tidying the bedding in the alcove; we had already, as part of our task of completing the roof, tidied the equipment and the shelves beneath the tree. When Julie came back to me she seemed to have grown older than me. She said 'You're not well.'

I laughed and said 'It doesn't matter now.'

She said 'Of course it does. We have to have something to teach it.'

She laid a hand on my forehead. Then she took my hand and laid it on her stomach. She said 'It's reality that changes, not you nor I.'

Then still holding me by the hand she led me out into the sun. Some clouds had appeared in the sky and were casting shadows that moved on the sea. The sea was glassy as it had been the night we had come here; it was as if one might walk on it or skim like a stone to the mainland. There was a column of smoke rising in the distance; I wondered if it might be the cottage burning. There was a small flotilla of boats on the sea.

I said 'I'm not ill.'

She said 'This may be all part of it.'

The boats were heading towards the island. There were in fact only two, but the patches of dark and light as they moved with the wind on the sea made it seem as if they were a flotilla. Someone stood in the prow of the leading boat: it was not Peter: I had not expected it to be Peter. I thought – And it may or may not be marauders coming to ravage the island. Julie said 'If they're coming to the island, which they seem to be, I think we should get off now, and not wait for Peter.' I said 'All right.' We got our bag and rucksack from the shelter and it was as if leaves and blossoms were no longer weeping; they were, as they usually were, regarding us gravely. And we were not saying goodbye to them.

When we got down to the landing step the boats were coming in and there were people in them holding poles and tripods like Odysseus's men; or a film or photographic unit. I thought for a moment – Oh God, not my father! But then – Why should it not be my father? Julie was saying to the woman in the front of the leading boat 'While you're here, do you think one of your boats could possibly take us to the mainland, and then it could come back for you?' The woman was saying 'Who are you? What have you been doing here?' Julie said 'We've been doing some work on the island.' The woman said 'You've not been shooting, have you?' Julie said 'No.' I was handing my rucksack and Julie's bag to the man in charge of the second boat: I wondered if I might recognise him from the village by the harbour, but he did not seem to recognise me. Julie said to him 'Would you mind doing that?' He said 'No problem.' Julie said to the woman 'I'd love to see some

241

of your pictures when you've got them.' She said 'Yes I think I'll know where to find you.' I thought — It's not even reality that changes; it's just the tree shaking its branches.

X

When I got back to London I had some idea of what I was doing but if I tried to put this into words it drifted away as if insisting on a life of its own. I had felt I should try to find out what was happening to Christina; but I did not think it would be right, after our last meeting which had seemed to happen and unfold so miraculously, for me to be checking up on her. So I thought I would try to get hold of Edward, imagining that he might have some news; but this made little sense; why should Edward know anything about Christina? Perhaps this was a way of acknowledging that I felt I should find out what had happened to Edward.

Julie had gone in search of Peter. It had seemed right at the time that we should travel separately; but it was this that it was becoming difficult to make sense of.

The boat that had picked us up on the island had taken us to a town further down the coast. From here I could catch a bus to Dublin and Julie could go to the village by the harbour to make her enquiries. When I had left Julie at the bus stop: she had said 'I'll join you in London.' I had said 'When?' She had said 'As soon as it's possible.' I had thought – She is thinking that Peter may still be involved in some vendetta. I gave her the address and telephone number of my parents' house, and the place where Edward stayed with his computer-freak friends when he was in London.

In Dublin I bought a newspaper and it did not seem that anything had changed about the situation in Ireland: people were saying – This is the last chance for peace; there is nothing more to be said; take it or leave it. But people did not want to choose between peace or war, they wanted to go on talking, beneath porticoes, in front of microphones, with the eyes of cameras upon them. About persecutions and war in the Balkans and the Middle East there did not seem to be any news at all.

I arrived in London off the early morning train and was handed a pamphlet outside the station saying that there was going to be a big demonstration that day as a protest against the iniquities and self-destructiveness of life under capitalism. This was advertised as a 'Carnival', though at the same time there was going to be a 'two-pronged attack' on the Houses of Parliament and the financial district of the City.

I rang up the house in London where Edward stayed and there was no answer. I rang Connie Constantine's house in Chelsea and asked the man who answered the telephone if he knew where Edward was. The man said 'Just a moment.' After a time a woman came to the phone and said 'I think Edward's gone to some demonstration or other.' I thought – But that's not the voice of the woman called Phyllis: it sounds like my mother. I put the receiver down. I had not wanted yet to get in touch with my father or mother. I thought – My mother has moved in with Connie?

I set off to walk from the station down to the Embankment where the demonstrators were assembling. During the spring Edward had been working on his idea for a computer game in which there would be simulations of diplomacy and warfare in the Balkans and the Middle East: atrocities would be committed, and there would be reports of the manufacture of chemical and biological weapons; UN observers would be sent in; there would be demands for the end of persecutions and the dismantling of sites; and then when nothing happened bombers would be sent in. After a time of death and destruction the participants would get bored and the situation would revert to much the same as it had been before. Edward had taken the plan for this game to a director of one of Connie's companies who had said – But where's the entertainment? Who wins and who loses? Edward had said – But no one wins or loses, that's the point; the game can go on for ever; the entertainment is in seeing how long it takes before it gets boring.

I had said to Edward – But you don't really see things like that. You're like my father; you think there should be, will be, some catastrophe, virus, that will bring the whole thing crashing down.

Edward had said – But it's individuals who can change.

The crowds were thick in the streets before I reached the Embankment; they were like a routed army rejoicing in the lack of leaders under whom they might regroup. They stood beneath banners which drooped so that the crowds were like people with hair over their eyes. When I had left the island I had imagined that Julie and I might be like secret agents parachuted on to the mainland; but it still would not be clear just what we were agents for. Thus we would be unable to give secrets away if we were captured?

On the Embankment there was indeed the impression of a carnival more than a protest. There were the usual groups with their banners – the feminists, the gays, the Eastern mystical people in orange or white smocks and with shaved heads or long hair. There was a jazz band and an eighteenth-century dance group with tambourines; there was a troupe dressed as fairies or angels. There were conventional-looking couples with children in pushchairs who did not form a group but rather seemed to be visitors or observers from an alternative world.

I sat on the grass in the public gardens just across the road from the river. In the papers that morning there had been a report of how both the Israelis and Arabs were claiming success in their attempts to produce a biological weapon which would spread a lethal virus that would kill only people of a certain genetic type and not others – it having been discovered how to pick out relevant genetic differences for such a purpose. Thus the restraining fear of biological weapons killing one's own people as well as one's enemies in theory was removed; but how without testing in practice could it be proved there would not be general annihilation?

There was one group in the gardens which appeared to consist of transvestites in drag or perhaps a collection of middle-aged actresses. I had been wondering whether in theory there might be any group that it would be beneficial to humanity to eliminate; and I had thought – No of course not, anything that has survived so far has its ecological use. One of the men in drag or actresses reminded me of Edward; or perhaps of the huge bird that Julie had fashioned in the cottage, but that had reminded me of Edward. And Edward had reminded me of Mephistopheles, whose trickery and disguises could yet be a force for good. I had realised before this that I had been missing Edward. After a time it began to dawn on me that the person in drag probably really was Edward – and why not? It had always seemed likely that Edward might have a secret life in London.

I thought I would move up the gardens casually as if I were setting off on another stage of pilgrimage – I was carrying my rucksack and had picked up somewhere en route a stout stick – and I would approach the group who were like exotic birds on their ecological ledge and I would get a close-up of the person who might be Edward without appearing to be intrusive – I had become practised at this with birds on the island – I did not want the person, whoever it was, to think I was trying to pick him or her up. Or might I not even be able to recognise Edward? The person was wearing make-up and a wig and a large picture hat. I went past trying not to gaze too intently. Then Edward said 'Hullo dearie.' I thought – It must be Edward, because surely no one else would actually say 'Hullo dearie.' I said 'I was wondering whether or not to try to pick you up.' He said 'About time too.' He detached himself from his group and put his arm through mine: he waved goodbye to his friends as if he had made a successful pick-up. But what if after all this was not Edward? He said 'And what are you doing dressed up like a fucking scoutmaster!' I said 'I've been in Ireland.' He said 'The things you do!' Then – 'Yes, a most unexpected but welcome bird told me.'

We walked down the garden with people taking a moment or two off from absorption in their groups to watch us. We found a space and sat on the grass. I thought – By 'most unexpected but welcome', he means my mother? He said 'They've been looking for you. Did they tell you?'

'Who's been looking for me?'

'Your father and my father. They've got some big cheese from Hollywood interested in their film.'

'Is this true?'

'Haven't you spoken to them?'

'No. I mean I spoke to someone at your father's house.'

'And what did they say?'

'I asked where I might find you.'

Edward was taking off his high-heeled shoes. He was making a face such as women do when they're thinking that their feet are killing them.

I said 'And did you get whatever you were looking for in your father's house in France?'

'Does one ever get what one is looking for?' Then – 'Oh that, yes. You mean the secret of my father's power, like Samson's hair. No I don't think that matters any more. My father's changed. He doesn't think people should be given what they want. He sees they may want to destroy themselves.'

'So you won't be trying to stop him.'

'Won't I? No. I don't know. Perhaps if my father's changed, I'll have to change too.'

There was a television crew filming the people in the gardens, probably for a news or current affairs programme. A man with a camera had squatted down in front of Edward; another man hovered with a pole with a fluffy microphone on the end. Edward had taken his hat and wig off. We had sat down next to a banner saying 'Carnival Armageddon'.

I said 'But they're going ahead with the film? The film about Jerusalem?'

'I don't know. My father says what's the point if it's all just happening anyway.'

'But they can film that?'

'That's what your father thinks.'

'What.'

'Except that your father thinks there's nothing going to happen. It's Sitcom Armageddon.'

The woman who seemed to be in charge of the film crew had squatted down by the cameraman and was gazing at Edward intently. The cameraman seemed to be trying to film up Edward's shirt. The woman said 'You think there may be Armageddon?'

Edward said to me 'Have you got a change of clothes in that rucksack?'

I said 'I've got a vest and underpants.'

'That'll do.'

Edward began to peel off his elaborate dress; he was like

248

a snake shedding its skin. It appeared that he was wearing nothing underneath. He held my spare pair of underpants in front of him like a figleaf and said into the camera 'My friend and I have been ruthlessly evicted from our garden, and we are demanding compensation.'

The woman said 'You're anxious about what may be happening in Jerusalem?'

Edward said 'Artichokes.'

The woman said 'Artichokes?'

Edward said 'Causing the release of a biological agent into the atmosphere.' Then to me – 'I've been trying for days to get that line in somewhere.'

Edward had stood up and was pulling on my underpants. I handed a T-shirt to him: I was putting his dress in my rucksack. The cameraman had lowered his camera. A man came hurrying up to the woman and said 'There's a bomb scare at Victoria Station.' The woman turned away. The camera man exclaimed 'Jerusalem artichokes!'

Edward was now dressed in what looked like running gear. He jogged up and down. He said 'But what I say is, in the end, all we can do is go out and do our best.'

The camera team were moving away. Edward called after them 'Would you like my hat?' He spun it like a frisbee, and it came back on the air and I caught it. I said 'I'm afraid I haven't got a pair of shoes.'

We moved out of the gardens on to the road by the Embankment. Edward said 'What were you doing then? Were you walking over hot coals in Ireland?'

'In a way.'

'But it was good?'

'Yes.'

'How was your head.'

'Oh that worked out all right.'

'You look better with your hair off.'

'Thanks.'

He seemed to know where we were going. He had turned right on the road towards the Houses of Parliament.

I said 'And what did you do? What were you up to with Stanislaus.'

'His family are under sentence of death in Turkey.'

'Oh yes, I see.'

'There might be something I could do.'

'Your father might help?'

'Not really.'

It was difficult to make one's way through the crowd that had been herded on to the pavement: the police were trying to keep the road clear for traffic.

I said 'Why have your father and my father been looking for me?'

'Have they? Oh yes, I said so. About the film. I think it was something you said when we were in France.'

'What.'

'I don't know. Do you? Something about survivors.'

'Oh yes. Make a film about survivors.'

'Survivors are very unfashionable. I don't think my father cares much about survivors except himself.'

Edward and I had been halted by the congestion on the pavements. There were television vans in the road with cameras perched on top of them. Edward was dressed in my pants and vest, so that it was as if he were at the start of a race.

He said 'Perhaps I can say I'm carrying an urgent message for the Prime Minister.'

'You might be on your way to pick up the Olympic Torch.'

'You can be my back-up man. With brandy.'

'I should know where we're going in case you run too fast for me.'

'We're going to my father's house. As a matter of fact you don't look very fit.'

'I may be dying.'

'You don't happen to have any brandy?'

'I've got some biscuits.'

'I don't think that would do the trick.'

Edward pushed his way through the crowd on the pavement on to the road and began running. A television crew on top of a van turned their camera on him. The police made as if to stop him, but the television van was following him and the police had begun to clear the road. We became a small escorted cortège, with Edward rolling slightly and wagging his head like someone approaching the end of the Marathon. I was thinking – But how on earth does a back-up man behave carrying a picture hat and a rucksack?

At the turning into Parliament Square the police made another lunge to stop Edward but our cortège had got up too much momentum, and people are wary about interfering with a television crew when filming. Somewhere by the House of Lords the van was finally stopped but Edward got through and disappeared into the crowd in the gardens beyond the Houses of Parliament. I pushed my way on to the pavement and made out that I was a spectator. If we were on our way to Connie's house, then this was about a mile away at the end of Chelsea Embankment.

I thought – It is Edward who has taught me about making use of virtual reality.

I caught up with Edward somewhere short of the Tate Gallery. He had stopped at a van selling hot dogs and coffee. I said 'Perhaps you'd be less distinctive if you put on your dress again.'

He said 'I think at the finishing post they'd prefer me to be athletic.'

We walked on. Edward was more than ever like a bird –
a gaunt seabird that had lost its feathers in some ecological
disaster and has new skin growing like a human's vest and
underpants.

I said 'Is my father really at Connie's house?'

'And your mother.'

'I thought it was my mother when I rang.'

'You don't mind?'

'No.'

'Why not.'

'I'm not sure.'

'Neither am I. They're having this meeting.'

We had come to a crossroads and had to wait for the
traffic. I said 'I think the thing I said about survivors was, that
life-giving things have to go on secretly.' Edward wrapped
his arms around himself as if he were cold. He said 'And all
that boloney.'

I said 'My mother wrote a piece about her and Connie
when they first knew each other. I read it when I was in
Ireland.'

'And you didn't mind that?'

'No.'

'I think there was in fact some tape of them.'

'Yes possibly.'

'And why on earth should she mind. No.'

'Are you going to Turkey with Stanislaus?'

'I hope so.'

'You're packing up here?'

'Yes.'

'Good luck then.'

'Thank you.'

He began running again. I tagged along behind. I thought
– Everyone's going to Turkey: that's where the Ark took off
from, as well as came down.

While he was running Edward said 'It wasn't your mother I was jealous about, it was you.'

'And you're not any more?'

'No.'

We were going under a railway bridge. There was a train stuck on the bridge. I thought – Perhaps the train is having to wait because of the bomb at Victoria Station.

I said 'So what do they want to make a film about.'

Edward said 'How can you make a film about what goes on secretly?'

'Well, you just film it.'

'And would anyone see it?'

'If they wanted to.'

Connie's London house was one of a row of grand houses set back from the road behind its own front garden. There was a huge American car with darkened windows parked outside; a policeman was chatting with the driver. Edward turned in through the garden gate and the policeman moved to go after him. When Edward reached the front door he continued jogging on the spot; the policeman caught up with me on the path and Edward said 'It's all right we live here.' The policeman said 'Can I see in that rucksack please?' Edward said 'He's bringing some clothes for his mother.' The door was opened by a Chinese-looking man. Edward said to him 'Thank you Gung Ho. Can you please take my friend straight through to where he can plant his bomb under the table.' I was leaning with my hands on my knees trying to get my breath with my rucksack still on my back; the policeman was opening the rucksack and was pulling out Edward's dress and holding it up. Edward had gone past the Chinese man and had disappeared into the house. My mother had come to the front door and when she saw me she said 'Oh I thought it was you.' I said 'Yes I thought it was you.' My mother said 'We didn't know where you were.' I said 'I've been in Ireland.'

She said 'Oh I know that.' I thought – Oh you do, do you. The Chinese man said 'I must close the door.' My mother said 'Are you coming in?' I said 'Yes.' I got Edward's dress back from the policeman and went past my mother into the house. She said 'Your father's here.' I thought I might say – Oh I know that. I said 'I read the piece you wrote about you and Connie.' She said 'Oh did you? I thought I'd lost it.' 'It was in the cottage.' 'Did you bring it?' I thought – I suppose this could be said to be making sense. My mother was going up the stairs ahead of me. She led the way into a long drawing room on the first floor at the back which had french windows looking on to balconies and a large garden. There was a large sofa facing away from where we had come in, at one end of which was my father who had his back to us, and at the other a dark-haired woman with a suntanned face and bright blue eyes to whom he was talking intently. I thought – It's now her he's carrying on with? The woman did not seem to be listening to him, but was rather watching where we were coming in. My father was saying 'But the Russians may still be getting fed up at being left out.'

The dark-haired woman said 'But that's not going to start a third world war.'

'Why not.'

'I thought we were talking about Jerusalem.'

My mother and I had come in quietly and we sat on two upright chairs near the door. I was trying to get my rucksack down off my back without making a noise. I thought – We are like children who are embarrassed and embarrassing in this grown-up world.

My father was saying 'All right there are still thousands of people coming into Jerusalem for what they think will be the Second Coming. They're getting ringside seats on the Mount of Olives. What more do you want? An epidemic?'

The woman 'I thought there was going to be one.'

'Well there may be. And an attempt to blow up the mosque.'

'You mean all this will still be happening?'

The dark-haired woman was very good looking. She wore a black trouser-suit, and was in her mid- or late-thirties. I thought – But if nothing that my father does like this is secret, does it mean it's not important?

My father was saying 'And they'll let us film. We needn't script it.'

My mother said 'I thought you said nothing was going to happen.'

My father said 'Oh well, then we'll film that.'

The dark-haired woman said 'You mean make a documentary?'

'No there'll be a story.'

'What –'

'Of us filming. Does that make any difference? That's always a good story.'

'Well does it?'

'We'll see.'

'You mean we don't do anything to stop it?'

I had not at first noticed that Connie Constantine was in the room. He was at the far end, half-hidden in an armchair, and was watching a large-screen television. I had the impression that it was we, the people in the room, who were performing for his benefit, but he was not watching us.

The woman said 'But if nothing does happen –'

'We've been through all this.'

'Oh yes. People have to make out something to be happening –'

'So what is it really.'

The charade that my father and the dark-haired woman were engaged in was being watched by my mother. Connie was watching, I could just see, a news item of the demonstration or carnival a section of which had been assembling on the Embankment. On the screen there were scenes of people running and throwing stones, of police coming after them with shields and truncheons. I thought – But we have become so used to scenes like this that they still seem like a carnival.

The dark-haired woman was saying 'But who would see what's really happening? Who would the audiences identify with?'

My father said 'They wouldn't. That's it. They'd have to think.'

A man holding a mobile phone had come in through a door at the far end of the room and he stood by Connie and held the phone out to him. Connie went on watching the television. The man bent down and whispered into Connie's ear. The dark-haired woman had turned to Connie and was saying 'Connie, can you help us with this please?'

I was thinking – And what is my mother seeing? Those times when Connie sat her on his knee and played with her as if she were his daughter?

My mother said 'Connie, are the streets blocked?'

I said 'There's supposed to be a bomb at Victoria Station.'

My father turned to where my mother and I were sitting. He did not seem to have noticed me before. He said 'Hullo.' I said 'Hullo.' He said 'Are you all right?' I said 'Yes.' He said 'We were worried.' My mother said 'You weren't.'

My father said 'Did you go to the wedding?'

I said 'Yes.'

'Did all go well?

'I think so.'

'Everything was all right.'

'Yes it seemed to be.'

I thought – My father is really saying that reality should not be so secret?

Connie had taken the mobile telephone from the man standing by him and was saying into it 'Yes? Yes?'

My mother said to my father 'So are you going to Jerusalem?'

My father said 'I've told you.'

My mother said 'No you haven't.'

The dark-haired woman was saying to Connie 'Is that Jerusalem?'

Edward was coming in at the door beside which my mother and I were sitting. He was wearing his white trousers and a striped blazer as if he were on his way to play cricket. He said 'Oh I'm so sorry, I thought you'd finished.'

The dark-haired woman was saying 'Connie, is it the Prime Minister?'

Connie said to the man who was standing by him 'I thought you said they'd got him.' Then he put his hand over the mouthpiece of the telephone and said in the direction of my mother and myself 'Well what do you think we can make out is happening?'

The man who was standing by Connie said 'They said they'd got him.'

Edward said to me 'He's talking to you.'

I said 'Oh is he?'

Connie took his hand away from the mouthpiece and turned back to the telephone. He said 'Ernst? Ernst?' Then to Edward 'You've been on television.'

Edward said to me '– So what do you think we can make out is happening –'

I said 'I think Jerusalem's like Sodom and Gomorrah.'

Connie said into the telephone 'Ernst, I've got a young friend here who thinks Jerusalem's like Sodom and Gomorrah.'

I said 'But I don't think it matters.'

The dark-haired woman said to me 'Then what do you think matters?'

Connie looked up from the telephone and said 'They seem to have had some sort of warning.'

I thought of saying – Edward, can I tell them your joke about Jerusalem artichokes?

The man standing by Connie said 'There seems to be some breakdown in satellite communications.'

I said to the woman 'I suppose one finds out.'

Connie handed the telephone back to the man and said as if to the room in general 'Who lives and who dies. Who's damned and who's saved. That's what matters.'

Edward said 'The end of the technological revolution as we know it.'

The dark-haired woman stood up. She said 'I've got to go.' She turned to my father – 'Are you coming?'

My father said 'No.' He was watching my mother.

I wondered – How long has my mother been staying here with Connie?

I noticed for the first time that there had been another person in the room – a young woman holding a tape recorder. She was now putting this away in her bag.

Connie said 'Can you stay for a moment please?'

The dark-haired woman had been on her way to the door. She stopped. She was standing by my mother. My mother was staring at my father who was watching the dark-haired woman who had her back to him and she was looking at the ground.

Connie stood with difficulty. He spoke as if he were rehearsing a speech. He said 'The gods have decreed that the human race should be wiped out. This is a commonplace story. On what grounds might they decide that it should not be? Traditionally, the gods look round to see if there are any people it might be proper to save. Or for the sake of whom it might be proper for the rest of humanity to be saved. Who are these people? The theme is still relevant even if there are no gods.'

I thought – Connie is ill. He is dying.

Edward said 'Traditionally everyone thinks it is himself.'

My father said 'Traditionally you get people in a cinema, lock the doors, turn on the taps, and call it entertainment.'

The dark-haired woman said to me 'Can I give you a lift anywhere?'

I said 'Me?'

She went out of the room heading towards the stairs. I followed. My father got up from the sofa and made as if to follow but then stopped at the door by my mother. My mother paid no attention to him; she was staring across the room towards Connie.

Edward came to the top of the stairs and said 'Where are you going?' I said 'I don't know.' I was thinking – Might I be about to be offered an enormous Hollywood contract?

Outside the huge American car was waiting. The chauffeur opened the door and the woman was climbing in. I was following her. My father had begun to come running down the stairs but then had gone back and had caught hold of Edward, and seemed to be giving him some instruction. I was thinking – Well I suppose a lot of this sort of thing is usually filtered out. The woman was saying 'Are you coming?' I said 'Yes.' I climbed into the back of the car which was like the cabin of a small boat. The young woman with the tape recorder was settling in at the front with the chauffeur. I sat on one of the small seats facing the dark-haired woman who was sitting on the large seat at the back. She said 'I'm not going to bite you.' I said 'Aren't you?' She said 'Or do you want me to.' There were curtains that one could pull across the windows on the inside of the car: I thought – Do film people usually make love in this sort of car? The woman said 'Oh for God's sake, I just don't want you looking at me.'

I went and sat on the back seat beside her. I thought – If you don't filter things, do you see what's happening? I said 'So are you going to make this film?'

She said 'There isn't going to be a film. He's mad. They're going to get rid of him.'

'Who, my father?'

'No not your father. Connie. Though your father's mad too. What was it you said about finding out what matters?'

'Well, I suppose, I thought one could make a film about no one knowing what's happening, and then, if one recognised this, things sorting themselves out.'

'And do you think things do?'

'I don't know.'

'But that's what all films are about.'

'But nothing really gets sorted out. It's all convention.'

The car was moving along the Embankment back in the direction of Parliament Square. The woman was extraordinarily good-looking; rather like an older Christina.

She said 'Jesus, is this going to work itself out?' Then – 'How much do you know about me and your father?'

'Not much.'

'Why do you think I asked you to come in the car?'

'I suppose to annoy my father.'

'God, you are a genius!'

'You're angry with him because he stayed with my mother.'

'He didn't stay with your mother.'

'Oh.'

'Who the fuck does he think he is.'

The car was becoming held up in the traffic. I thought – There may be demonstrations further on and then I can get out and walk.

She said 'I'm sorry, I shouldn't have said that. He knows very well who he is. I don't know who he is. Who is he?'

'I don't know.'

'Will you stop saying you don't know.'

'Right.'

'You think you can make things different just by assuming they'll come out all right?'

'Well, I suppose you might notice things more and take advantage of them. And then they might come out different.'

'When you were in Ireland, did you meet anyone your father knew there?'

'Well there were people he'd been filming with.' I registered – Everyone seems to know I've been in Ireland.

'He said something about a wedding.'

'Oh yes there was a wedding.'

'Whose?'

'I don't know. There's a girl I'm in love with in Ireland.'

'It wasn't her who was being married?'

'No.'

'Oh yes, there was a message for you.'

'A message?'

'Yes. Didn't your father tell you? I suppose he didn't have time.'

The car had been moving more and more slowly. Now it stopped altogether, with traffic piled in front of it. I thought – But now I can't get out.

I said 'What message?'

'I'm afraid I wasn't listening.'

'Was it from a girl?'

'I don't think so.'

'She's got a twin brother.'

'Oh has she?'

'It might be him. They're much the same. They used to

try to communicate with one another. No I don't mean communicate.'

'Really. Was he the one with whom you took on the terrorists single-handed?'

'Me? No. That's what my father told you? How did he know!'

'That's what I'd like to know.'

'Yes I see.'

'More than I do.'

The car had stopped short of the railway bridge that went over the road and the river. There were people on the road trying to peer in through our windows. One or two tapped on the glass as if we were fish in an aquarium.

The woman slid open a panel of the window that separated us from the seats in front and said 'Charlie, what the fuck's going on.'

The chauffeur said 'They're not letting anyone through Miss Eva.'

'Betty, can you find someone to ask what's going on?'

I said 'Perhaps it's the bomb at Victoria Station.'

The woman called Eva said 'It's probably been planted by your Irish girl.'

I had been thinking – A message? What message? Then – The bomb might be something to do with Peter?

I said 'My Irish girl's not a terrorist.'

'Isn't she? I thought she was.'

The woman called Betty had got out of the car. The people who had gathered round backed away, with the ones behind pushing forward to see who might be in the huge car.

I said 'She sometimes seems to use it. Take advantage of it.'

Eva said 'Take advantage of what: of being a terrorist?'

'Of what turns up.'

There was a train still stuck on the railway bridge – probably the one that had been there an hour ago when I had been running with Edward.

Eva said 'Your father thinks that nothing gets better until there's a disaster that makes things worse.'

'I think things do get better if you see them as they are but you may not at once notice this.'

'How smug can you get.'

'I suppose it's easier not to be.'

'And that's what you'd like to make a film about?'

'Yes.'

'And you think that's what's happening with you and your girl and all the shenanigans in Ireland?'

'I don't know.'

'But it might be.'

'You can't say.'

Betty came back into the car and knelt on the front seat facing backwards and said 'They're stopping the traffic. There's a bomb at the station.'

Eva said to me 'For fuck's sake how did you know? How do you use this?'

She opened the door on her side of the car and got out on to the road. People crowded around her. Betty was saying 'Can you give us a bit of room please.' I was thinking that Eva did look like a film star. Perhaps I might have made love to her in the back of the car. She made her way across the road towards the river. I got out and followed her.

Eva and I stood side by side on the pavement just short of the railway bridge. There were people leaning out of the windows of the stationary train like the inmates on the top floor of a prison.

Eva said 'What about feelings.'

I said 'Oh yes, there are feelings.'

'So they do they come in.'

'I suppose so.'

'And motives.'

'Oh motives, I don't know!'

There were police cars with flashing lights under the bridge. The police were trying to get the cars nearest the bridge to turn back but this was not possible because of the cars piled up behind them. Beyond the bridge there were more police and then another jam of cars. We were a long way from Parliament Square.

Eva said 'Why isn't it easy to see things as they are.'

I said 'I suppose everyone's programmed to see things according to their own feelings.'

'And that's no good?'

'I suppose things don't have a chance to sort themselves out.'

People leaning out of the windows of the train stuck on the bridge were waving and calling out. I thought – They're wanting to escape.

Eva said 'For you to sort things out.'

'No. Things just happen.'

'How?'

'I don't know.'

'I don't know, I don't know. For someone who thinks he knows everything why in God's name do you say you don't know?'

I thought of saying – Just because of that, I suppose.

There was a patch of grass guarded by railings between the road and the river; I thought I would go through and stand by the river. People on the train were waving at the people on the road.

Eva followed me through a gap in the railings. The river was running sluggishly inland with a high tide. The patch of grass was not far below the people on the train. Eva said 'There's someone who seems to know you.' I said 'Where.' She said 'On the train.'

I thought I should wave back at whoever was waving at

me as one does with children at the side of a road in a foreign country. I said 'Oh that's Emily!'

Eva said 'Who's Emily?'

'The friend of a friend.'

'Of your Irish girl?'

'No not my Irish girl.'

'She seems very keen on you.'

'Perhaps she's got a message for me.' I waved and shouted 'Emily!'

Emily shouted 'We've got to talk to you!'

Emily seemed to be being pulled back by someone inside the train. She disappeared, and Christina appeared at the window. I thought – They are like clowns, or like those comic saints on buildings in Armenia: but why isn't Christina in Armenia? She shouted 'We didn't know where to find you!' Eva said 'Who's that?' I said 'That's the other one's girlfriend.' Eva said 'You mean they're on the train and they wanted to talk to you?'

Christina seemed to be trying to climb out of the window. I was shaking my head and frowning and making pushing movements with my hands. Eva said 'She's crazy.' I said 'She's pregnant.' Eva said 'How do you know she's pregnant?' I said 'Because it's my baby.' Christina shouted 'If we get out on to the bridge, can you help us get down?' I shouted 'I expect so.' Eva said 'For fuck's sake, she's not your Irish girl, she's got a girlfriend, and she's having your baby?'

The end of the bridge this side of the river went over the road and was supported by a massive concrete arch curving down on to the bank. This was guarded by iron spikes to prevent people climbing. The structure containing the railway track projected beyond the concrete arch. I shouted 'It will be difficult.' Christina shouted 'Perhaps we can jump.'

Eva said 'Does she want to get rid of the baby?'

I said 'I don't think so.'

Emily and Christina seemed to be struggling for who should be climbing or stopping the other one climbing out of the train window. Emily emerged head-first and got a hand on to the parapet of the structure at the edge of the track. She pulled and shoved herself clear of the window with her feet and nearly went over head-first into the river. Then she moved along the space between the train and the parapet until she was almost above where Eva and I were on the bank on the patch of grass. She said 'We want to keep the baby.'

I said 'Oh good. Well that's all right.'

'I mean we want to look after it.'

'Good.'

'You don't mind?'

'No.'

Christina had begun to squeeze out of the train window. Emily saw her and shouted 'Oi!' and then turned and ran back towards her. I shouted 'Be careful!' Christina had got herself half out of the window and Emily was trying to push her back. Christina shouted 'I just wanted to tell you how grateful I am to you!' I shouted 'Oh that's all right!' She shouted 'I do hope you'll always want to see it!' I shouted 'I'm sure I will!' I suddenly found that I wanted to cry. There were people peering out of windows along the train to see what was happening. Two officials in yellow jackets were running along the track from the direction of the station; two policemen who had been dealing with the traffic had come into the bit of grass where Eva and I stood and were looking up at Emily and Christina. Emily's arms that were supporting Christina suddenly gave way and Christina collapsed out of the window on top of her. They picked themselves up. They saw the men in yellow jackets coming along the gap between the train and the edge of the track towards them. Christina clambered on to the parapet and teetered there. One of the policemen by Eva and me on the patch of grass called out to the men in yellow jackets 'Grab her!' Eva said 'She'll kill herself.' But the water of the river with the high tide was not in fact so very far below. Christina held her nose and jumped over the parapet into the river. She made a small splash, but hardly seemed to go under. I thought – Dear God, now swim quickly or you will be like that young bird that was eaten by a fish. I had become frightened and I ran along the river bank to where there was a wooden construction that might serve as a landing stage: I shouted 'Here! Land here!' One of the policemen had come with me and seemed to be waiting for Christina; Eva had come with him and was saying 'It's all right, we're filming.' He said 'You're filming?' Eva said 'Miramar Films, Hollywood.' Then to Charlie and Betty who had followed us on to the grass – 'Get the camera.' Emily had climbed on to the parapet of the bridge and stood poised with her arms above her head; then did a perfect straight-bodied dive into the river. Christina had reached the landing stage and she put an arm up to me and I held it and pulled and she came up out of the water like something extraordinarily buoyant. I said 'Oh God I'm so glad!' She said 'It's all right about the baby?' I said 'I'm glad about you.' She said 'But you will love it won't you.' I said 'Yes.' She said 'And it will love you.' I had begun to cry, and Christina put up a hand and touched my cheek. She said 'Everything's all right!' I said 'I know, that's what's so difficult.' Betty had reappeared on the patch of grass and was holding a hand-held camera. Emily had reached the landing stage and Charlie was putting down a hand to help her. The policeman was saying to Eva 'Is this how you do it now?' Eva was saying 'Yes it's the new way of seeing things.' The policeman was saying 'You don't want too many rehearsals for a scene like that!' Eva was saying 'No we want to keep it as close to real life as possible.'

X I

The script for a film that my father had originally written about Jerusalem told the story of a plot by Jewish religious extremists to blow up the Islamic Dome of the Rock, which for centuries had stood on the site where there once been King Solomon's and King Herod's temples. This building was felt by the extremists to be an abomination in their holy place; it had to be destroyed, even if there was a danger of Arabs in neighbouring countries retaliating against Israel with chemical and biological weapons. It was also possible that a gang of Arab secular extremists were themselves plotting to do some damage to the Dome, so that this would inevitably be taken to have been done by Jewish extremists and thus might instigate and even seem to justify an attack that would annihilate Israel.

In my father's story there had been an Arab boy and an Israeli girl whom chance (or whatever) had put in the way of possibly undermining the plots of the extremists. I sometimes imagined myself and Julie in these roles: but how might such things happen in real life? Were there any possible connections between the threat of mass destruction and what people could do about it who had no apparent power – the one or two people like those in the myth mentioned by Connie for the sake of whom the gods might consider saving the world.

Or if anyone imagined this, they were crazy?

The scene by the railway bridge in which Christina and Emily had jumped and dived into the river had continued, with Eva organising the occasion as if it were taking place on a film set; her conversation with the policeman occupying his attention without it seeming to make much sense. Charlie the chauffeur had been handed the camera; Betty the secretary fetched a rug from the car and with it helped Christina and Emily to dry; these two seemed to have accepted the idea that it would get them out of trouble if they played the parts of actresses or stunt-girls. We moved towards the road as if it were being assumed that we all, including Christina and Emily, would pile into the car: it was not so much that our acting was at odds with reality as that it seemed to be taking reality over. I had begun to feel ill: the sickness that had been hovering since the day before when I had been in Ireland seemed to be taking its chance to play its own role; as if as a result of the bizarre meeting with Christina and Emily my defences against it had come down, and indeed what need was there now for me to have defences? With the baby preserved and the question of who would look after it settled, what more, biologically, might I have to do? Should I not reasonably, like some male spider having done its stuff, find some corner in which to die?

It was true that I was expecting to be rejoined by Julie, but there were times when a renewal of the miracle of my time with Julie seemed almost too much to hope for. One should not expect to repeat or cling to miracles; when one has known a miracle, might one not die?

Then when we were by the car at the far side of the road by the river Edward appeared on a bicycle manoeuvring in and out of the jammed traffic; he was in his cricketing clothes and was wobbling like a clown on one wheel. He propped himself against the roof of our car and said 'There's been an earthquake in Turkey.' I said 'Oh has there?' Charlie the chauffeur seemed to be undecided about whether or not he should be filming Edward: the policemen said 'How does this fit in?' Betty said 'I'll have to look at the script.' I said to Christina 'You never got to Turkey then.' She said 'No, we had to go and talk to Emily's father.' I said 'Did that go all right?' She said 'Yes.' Edward said 'Hullo Emily.' Emily said 'Hullo.' I said to Edward 'Has there been a message for me?' He said 'Yes, your father asked me to tell you.' I said 'What?' He said 'Come to my place.' I said 'But what was the message?' He said 'That was the message.' Betty said 'We're all going to catch our deaths standing here.' Eva said 'Why don't you all come back to my place.'

My illness was taking the form of too much coming in, filters were breaking down; there was no means of understanding by moulding things into patterns. Intimations were invading and churning within my brain: my blood and guts did not seem to be able to handle this; they were in revolt, threatening their own pre-emptive strike. I thought – But for there to be miracles there have to be almost too many coincidences; that's what miracles are; understanding goes into abeyance. The policeman was clearing a space in the traffic for the car to turn round. Edward said 'You know where it is?' I said 'What.' Edward said 'My place.' I put my head in my hands. I thought – But I am at least now sufficiently ill for it to make sense if I stagger away to be on my own: I will be seen to be overwhelmed, overwrought by Christina's news. Then I can find some corner in which to lie down and at least seem ready to die. The message to me might conceivably have come from Julie; but where would she have sent it; how could she have had time to send it? It struck me that I might be feeling ill just because events were moving out of the form in which one usually notices them. But why should one worry about this.

Edward pushed himself off from the car and balanced himself upright for a moment and then crouched over his handlebars and pedalled away fiercely in the direction of the bridge. Betty said 'I thought there was a bomb under that bridge.' The policeman said 'No, it's at Victoria Station.' I said to Eva 'Will you really do that?' She said 'What.' I said 'See that Christina and Emily are all right.' The policeman was holding open the car door for us. He said 'But only the detonator went off, and blew off the man's thumb.' I said to Christina 'I must go now, I'm so happy, dear Christina and Emily.' I began to move away. I thought – Now this is a proper end to this scene: cut! don't let it go on.

I thought there might be somewhere under the bridge where I could lie down, but there were too many cars and people. The railway line continued on a viaduct across waste ground after it had left the road; here there were arches beneath which I might hide like an animal in its lair. With everything happening all at once in my fuddled brain details began to be unclear – how long ago had I left Julie? Might it even be Peter who had something to do with the bomb, with disarming the bomb, at the station? I had had no sleep the night before on the boat from Ireland; perhaps it was because of this I was feeling compelled to find somewhere to curl up and wait for the pain and sickness in my head and guts to go. But I had had these onsets of illness, fever, before; when it seemed that my system of immunities, my thin skull, were too fragile to keep things out.

No one was following me. Would Christina be explaining to Eva – Leave him alone, he is all right; he has to let things work themselves out.

The waste ground across which the railway line continued

was like a disused parking lot or junkyard; a branch of the river must once have come in here where barges tied up. The waste ground was protected by a wire fence which I clambered over with difficulty. I flopped down on the other side and looked around to see where I might be; was this not indeed a graveyard? I had been warned of the speed and determination with which my illness might strike. And was it not I myself, by having presumed to build a ladder up to heaven, that had rendered my armies of immunity impotent against it?

It had begun to rain. There was the possibility of sheltering beneath what looked like some fairground props that leaned against one of the arches; they were like bits cut up from the representation of a tree. I thought – Poor old tree! Is this what happens to your branches? But then – Might this not be a memory that is telling me not to rest here; but to go on; which is what when we were with you we knew we had to do. I went past some old buses with small oval windows like the sort of transport in which people might once have crossed a desert; some portable toilet-cabins on trailers; an old police van without wheels. Behind me there was a noise as if of a riot starting; had the violent demonstrators that Connie had been watching on television reached the bridge? Or was it just rain beating down on some corrugated iron. The pressure in my head, the sickness in my guts, were now taking the form not so much of outside worlds forcing their way in as of my nerves or strands of cells or synapses or whatever bursting splayed outwards like the tentacles of some great squid; like rivulets forcing their way through barriers to form a landscape. And so, yes, they might be telling me not where to lie down, but where to go. Christina and Emily had turned up on that train out of the blue; Eva and I had stopped at the bridge out of the blue; Edward had come riding by on a bicycle with his message. So what should I be trusting? Were not these intimations blown like leaves from the tree?

There is a form of organism that lies scattered on the floor of the forest in bits and pieces, and when it needs new sustenance its bits come together and form a worm or slug; this sets off on a journey through the forest to find new nourishment. When it has discovered this it puts down a root and rears up as a mushroom, and after a time its head explodes and scatters in bits and pieces. And so on.

The message to me at Edward's house could indeed be from Julie. She had had the address. And after my meeting with Christina, and the news about the baby, might there not be the chance of a new dispensation with Julie? With bits and pieces exploding in my head, my guts, like slime mould, might Julie even be having a baby?

I had never before been to the house where Edward stayed when he was in London. Perhaps I needed a rest from seeing Edward during termtime; perhaps I had been keeping away from the gang of people I understood he was with – the group of hackers or crackers who thought they might be able to subvert (or save?) the social order by behaving like a cluster of cancer cells rebelling against what they saw as a body they were no part of. But the hackers became experts on the technology developed by that body; they thought that by this they could defeat it; however it was by this that they became like cancer cells; wittingly or unwittingly they would kill themselves along with the body they held in contempt. I had not known how serious Edward was about all this – I had not perhaps known how serious Edward was about anything – he sometimes seriously seemed to think that nothing should be taken seriously. I had had some sympathy with this with regard to the social world; but if I tried to talk with Edward about anything beyond this he had a way of closing his eyes as if one were being unseemly. He had once or twice got as far as explaining that the hackers or crackers he was involved with were concerned mainly with making jokes: they were part of the Carnival Against Capitalism but they wanted to cause disturbance amongst financial institutions and government departments not by direct attack but by way of teasing: the idea being that people could fight back effectively if attacked but might become disorientated if their lifeblood was made to seem just silly. That at least was how Edward put it. But during the summer there had been reports of injections of so-called viruses into computer networks that had incapacitated businesses for days; there were rumours again of military networks having been tampered with which even might explain how in the war against Serbia for instance so many bombs had gone astray. When I had questioned Edward about this he had said – Well you're the one who says that nowadays one can't tell what's reality and what's not. I had said – No I just think it's difficult to talk about it. And then when I had been running along the Embankment with Edward I had wondered if he might be having a change of heart about this.

The address that I had for the house that Edward stayed in was somewhere by Shepherd's Bush. After I had climbed out of the far end of the junkyard I thought I would walk; it would be three or four miles, but I thought that so long as I did not die, some daft exertion might help me to find new nourishment. Why else had the image of slime mould come into my head?

I had imagined that the place where Edward stayed would be in a rundown area. And when eventually I got there it turned out to be one of a row of small Victorian houses of such quietness and respectability that indeed if the setting had been in a film one might guess that there would be appalling goings on within. I knocked on the door and at once began to feel more ill. This time it was not so much sickness as the onset of fever.

The door was opened by a person, an apparition, that for a moment I thought might be Julie: it was dressed in white overalls which Julie sometimes wore. But it had its hair cropped close, which was like myself. I said 'Hullo.' The person said 'Hullo.' He had a masculine voice. I lost my nerve about thinking he might be Julie, and said 'Is Edward here?' The person said 'No.' I said 'Oh well never mind.' The person looked amused; he said 'Won't you come in?' I thought – These hackers or crackers might be able to make holograms of people? Then – But this isn't Julie; it's Peter: he's had his hair cut off.

The door led to a small passageway to one side of which was a room with sleeping bags on the floor and a stuffed figure lying propped as if it were stoned; this was like one of Julie's dummies in the cottage. The person with the cropped hair led the way through to a long back room where it seemed at least two houses must have been knocked into one; the windows at the back were boarded up, and on tables and shelves and most available surfaces there was electronic equipment – screens and keyboards and consoles – but these seemed to be in the process of being dismantled. There was only one other person in the room; he was sitting in front of a computer screen on which there was occurring a sequence of slightly flickering images; he was staring at these with such intensity that it was as if by this he might be controlling them. At least I knew who this was: it was Edward's friend Stanislaus. I said 'Edward hasn't got back yet?' Without turning he said 'But you got our message?' I said 'Yes.' He said 'Are you coming?'

The person who had let me in had gone to a bunk bed against a wall on which there were no mattresses but just more equipment; he was leaning against it smiling as if he were one of those amused figures on the walls of ruined churches. It had seemed too improbable that this person was Peter: but now – Peter might have had his head shaved because he was in hiding? This rebel hideout was the sort of place he might know about quite apart from having got the address from Julie? I said 'I didn't recognise you.' He said 'Well you've only seen me in rain or in the dark.' I said 'Did Julie get hold of you?' He said 'She wanted to tell you not to worry.'

On the screen that Stanislaus was watching there were ruins and piles of rubble next to high-rise buildings still standing. There was one large rectangular building knocked over on its side like a toy. Stanislaus said 'So you did see Edward.' I thought – Didn't I tell you?

There had appeared on the screen in front of Stanislaus the picture of a ruined tower in a desolate landscape; I thought – Oh yes, that's the tower they were building up to heaven. Stanislaus said 'That's our logo.' The outlines of rectangles appeared on the screen and Stanislaus clicked and there appeared in close-up the picture of a sternly staring saint with a shepherd's crook. I thought – Oh well, for God's sake, I suppose that's Gregory the Illuminator. I was not sure whether all this was happening because I was ill; I felt that I had to go and lie down on one of the bunk beds, but they were covered with computer equipment. Peter cleared a small space for me and I sat down on the edge. I thought – I really may be getting into a position in which I do not know what is reality or what is not.

Peter said 'You're not well.'

I said 'No.'

'Julie told me.'

'What.'

'But you got here.'

'Yes.'

Peter was looking at the screen in front of which Stanislaus was sitting. The images had changed. There were now scenes of people running through the streets and throwing stones and petrol bombs; a burning city.

Peter said 'Will it affect the baby?'

I said 'Oh no they don't think so.' I thought – What baby?

'Could it even be beneficial?'

'Oh no I don't think so.'

'Well it seems to have been for you.' Peter smiled.

I thought – I am going crazy.

Peter left me and went and stood with his hands on the back of Stanislaus's chair, watching the screen. Stanislaus said 'Edward says it's like a hole in the ozone layer through which either disasters or something useful might get through.'

I was trying to find a place to put my head down on the bunk, but the computer equipment on it was too hard and spiky. In the junkyard I had had the impression of forces, influences, that had hitherto naturally been kept out forcing their way into my brain; these included scenes from imaginary worlds which might or might not be useful in trying to make sense of things. Might not what was happening have something to do with the story of the bomb at Victoria Station: might not Peter or the people either with or against Peter have been involved with planting it or preventing it going off? In any case, the train had been stopped on the bridge short of the station, and Christina and Emily had been looking out of the window.

A new picture had come up on the screen. This was of a huge box-like structure half toppled over in rubble. Stanislaus said 'That's a bloody clever place to build a prison.'

Peter said 'They'll dig their way out?'

'It's possible.'

'And then what.'

'Oh well, there may be a plague.'

'Of frogs and locusts?'

'Of cholera. Wild honey.'

Peter left Stanislaus and came back to the bunk on which I was balancing as if on a fakir's bed of knives. Peter said 'You should lie down.'

'I am lying down.'

'Didn't you want Julie to look after a baby?'

'Oh that baby, yes.'

'You think Julie might be going to have a baby?'

I was beginning to shake. I had reached this stage in my illness once before and had had to be taken to hospital. There I had stayed about a month while they did tests and tried various drugs to deal with my fever without success. From time to time I had had hallucinations; from time to time I had wanted to die; but in hospital this had not seemed possible. Then I had had visions of myself looking down on myself quite peacefully from the ceiling: on the bed I was in the position of some javelin thrower in a frieze. Then after a time the fever had stopped of itself; and what had caused it was never established.

Stanislaus switched the computer off and came over to the bunk bed. He said 'Edward thinks his father might let us have the small plane to fly to Turkey.'

I said 'Where is everyone?'

'They've packed up. Gone. Edward wondered if you would come with us.'

I said to Peter 'When did you get here?'

Peter said to Stanislaus 'You'd better go. I'll stay with him.'

There was a banging from the direction of the front door. Then the voice of Edward shouting 'I haven't got a key!'

Stanislaus went to one of the boarded-up windows and seemed to be trying to open it. When he failed, he stood facing the passageway to the front door. There was more loud banging. Peter said 'We might have got this sickness.'

Stanislaus said 'I'll see you then.'

He went out of the room towards the front door. After a moment there was a crash as if the door were being broken down and two men came into the room of the kind that in films are bailiffs come to repossess your furniture. They were followed by Edward who was saying 'I told you there's no one here.'

Peter was crossing the room to a corner where there were some gas rings and a sink; he said 'Would anyone like some coffee?'

I said 'Yes please.'

Edward waved a hand round the room and said to the two men 'Take the lot. There's bugger all on it. There may be a bit of pornography.'

One of the men said 'Mixing business with pleasure eh?'

Edward said 'This was once a thriving business employing millions.'

I was trying to get into a more comfortable position on the computer equipment. It struck me that I might seem to be trying to cover something up or surreptitiously to wipe it out.

Peter said to the two men 'How do you like your coffee?'

The first man said 'Who are these two then?'

Edward said 'I don't know. He was passing by.'

'And that one?'

I was beginning to shake so much that the bunk was making a rattling noise. I thought – Yes, I might have been caught by that stuff that was going to be released into the atmosphere by the bomb at Victoria Station: perhaps its code name was Jerusalem artichokes.

The second man said 'What's wrong with him then?'

Edward said 'God knows.'

The first man had begun to disconnect and unplug various bits of equipment. He said to Peter 'Can you give us a hand with this then.'

Peter said 'No I'm not touching it!'

The man said 'What's that supposed to mean?'

Peter was coming across the room carrying a cup of coffee. He said 'Mind you don't drop it!'

The first man was leaving the room carrying equipment. The second man was watching me on the bed. Edward came over to me and said 'Are you all right?'

I said 'No I don't think so.'

'Should I get hold of your father or your mother?'

'No.'

'Should we get you to hospital?'

'I don't know.'

'I think you should lie down.'

'I am lying down.'

'There's a mattress in the next room.'

'I don't think it's contagious.' Then – 'I mean it might be. Oh yes of course it might be!'

Peter said 'Of course it might be.' He was propping me up and helping me to drink the coffee.

I had begun to have the sort of feeling that I had had when I had been with Christina and Emily by the river – that if this was a film, a work of art, it must not go on too long, it should be cut quite soon. If I was not going to die, perhaps I could become unconscious.

The second man, who was standing by me, said 'We'll want that stuff that's underneath him.'

Edward said 'Good, yes, you take that.'

Edward and Peter were helping me up and supporting me while we made our way to the front room. I was shaking badly now. My teeth would soon be making a rattling sound. I said 'I usually have some pills.' Edward said 'What for.' I said 'Oh to make me better!' I laughed. Edward said 'I think you're doing extraordinarily well.'

In the front room there were mattresses on the floor and

I was lowered on to one of them; it was like a wrinkled sea far below. Just above the surface there was what seemed to be a small aeroplane flying. I thought – That is either a fly, or Edward and Stanislaus are on their way to Turkey.

I was lying on one of the mattresses. Edward was standing over me. He was saying 'Now you stay here. I'll get an ambulance.'

I said 'It was Peter who was here?'

'Yes. You did want to see him?'

'Yes.'

'He's coming back. Stanislaus has gone.'

'Where's Stanislaus gone?'

'Peter will stay with you.'

There was some altercation in the street outside. I thought – People have come looking for Peter, but those two men like furniture removers were policeman, and they have shot them.

And Stanislaus had just been hiding behind the door when the furniture removers broke in?

The stuffed dummy that was propped up on another mattress at the far side of the room was like one of those in the cottage. I said – 'Hullo Julie.'

One of the men who had been carrying equipment came into the room. He said 'Where have they gone.'

I said 'Aren't they still here?'

'Is there a way out at the back?'

'I don't know.'

'God damn it!'

He went out again. There were noises of people arguing in the street outside.

I thought – Peter will be explaining how he was nowhere near Victoria Station. Two men were following him across a burning city. There had been an earthquake, and the walls of a prison had fallen down.

Peter came into the room. He said 'Have they gone?' I said 'I think so.' He sat down beside me and looked at the dummy across the room. He said 'How did that get here?' I said 'I don't know.'

He said 'Julie doesn't want to do that sort of thing any more.'

I said 'I know.'

'Do you know what she does want to do?'

'I think so.'

'I suppose she can hardly say so.'

'No. What happened in the street?'

'Nothing.'

'Nothing?'

'No. Julie just asked me to give you the message.'

'Not to worry —'

'Yes.'

'And that's why you're here.'

'Yes.'

'And that's all.'

'Yes.'

'I suppose there wasn't need for any more.'

'No.'

I thought — All right now; cut it.

XII

The idea that one lives in a world of potentialities amongst which one has the ability if not exactly to choose then at least to be aware of the possibility of choice – and by this to make available one thing rather than another – this was a fancy that it had seemed to me one might take note of like a beautiful stranger passed in the street: but what would it be to possess it, experience it, live with it as if it were normality? One would not presume to dictate to it; much of the time one might not quite even know what was going on; often it would be difficult to maintain belief in something so presumptuous. But it was trust in the long-term effectiveness of manipulation that seemed in general to be being carried away like computer equipment by repossession men; and if at the same time I happened to be being carried away on a stretcher – well, what might evolve from that; what might have been learned.

For part of that autumn I was in hospital with an intermittent fever while doctors tried and failed to pin down what was plaguing me: was it a virus, a bug (unlikely to be anything released by hostile forces into the atmosphere). There was something wrong with my immune system, yes; and I was no longer able to suppose that it might be something right – it was too alarming. There might be increased chances of change; but mainly of dying.

When my fever was not too high I tried to imagine more precisely what might make one potentiality rather than another actual: if not choice, then what? observation? consciousness? what scientists called measurement? But to scientists measurement seemed to imply not much more than a form of precise attentiveness. Would it not still make more sense to see the business of one thing happening rather than another as chance or simply luck –

– Or was there not a meaning of the word 'measure' that referred to an activity like a dance?

Then when my fever was high I had the experience of being experimented on by a ruthless but still not necessarily malignant God – how had the idea ever arisen that God should be kind? I had once visited with my father a biology laboratory where mice were experimented upon with the aim of finding out whether characteristics of a species could be altered or enhanced; the animals sometimes seemed to be in pain and sometimes not: I had thought – If humans can do this to animals why should we, who say we are made in God's image, be surprised if God does it to us?

The biologists had been trying to find a gene that might be responsible for intelligence, and to see if this could effectively be inserted into a presumably stupid mouse. There had been a number of failures: I wondered – Did the bones of those mice shake and their teeth rattle? Then one mouse had eventually found its way more quickly through a maze, and the biologists had felt something important had been discovered. I had thought – But it's just that we should have a different idea of God.

It was my mother who had got me into hospital. Edward had telephoned to her, and Peter had stayed with me till the ambulance arrived. There had been moments at the beginning of my fever when I had imagined once more that Peter was Julie, and this had seemed a happy superimposition of worlds. Then by the time I got to the hospital Peter had disappeared; and it seemed right that my mother was taking over.

In the hospital I was in a room on my own because of the unknown nature of my infection. My mother said 'Why didn't you tell me you were ill?' I said 'I didn't know. And anyway I like to think something's being worked out.'

'Worked out by your being ill?'

'Yes.'

'That's fairly mad.'

'For one thing, now I needn't go back to the university.'

'Oh yes you were talking about that.'

'It might have been difficult otherwise.'

My mother and father took turns to spend time with me. They seemed to be taking care not to be at the hospital at the same time. I thought – Well don't you think that between you two something is being worked out?

When I was with my mother she did seem to want to talk about what was intriguing me. She said 'What do you mean by being worked out?'

I said 'Well, like trying to do art. You try things out and this seems right rather than that. Otherwise, what's the point of calling it art?'

'An art work can be about evil.'

'But then you'd still be trying to work it out.'

I thought – She's thinking of that piece she wrote about herself and Connie.

My mother said 'People get killed.'

'You're thinking of that chauffeur.'

'What chauffeur?' Then – 'Oh Lennie, yes.'

'If it hadn't been for Lennie you might not have met my father. I might not be here.'

'But that's not cause and effect.'

'No.'

My mother blushed. She said 'Anyway, we don't know if Lennie was murdered.'

I said 'But for me I suppose that's not the point.'

'It would be for Lennie. And for me and Connie.'

'Yes. But what have you found out. What have you learned.'

My mother and I sat in silence for a time. I thought – Perhaps my parents may now be learning as much from me as I have learned from them: though I probably shouldn't be thinking this.

My mother said 'Anyway I am going to find out about Lennie. It's probably important for me, yes.'

'That's why you're seeing Connie?'

'Oh you're so bright! What did you do in Ireland? You found your girl?'

'We went and stayed on that island. You know, the one with the birds, where there used to be hermits.'

'You saw the people who've been using the cottage?'

'You heard about that?'

'What did they say?'

'Nothing much.'

'Really?'

'It's useful to them to go on using the cottage. They're running drugs now rather than guns.'

'And you think that's all right?'

'Well not exactly all right.'

'I thought your girl was using it.'

'Yes she was.'

'They didn't threaten you?'

'No, they offered to pay rent.'

I wondered – But how does my mother know about all this: she might herself have been back to Ireland?

– But not to see that man with curly hair!

I said 'I thought that was why you wanted me to read your story.'

'Why.'

'So I could learn.'

'From my mistakes?' My mother seemed to think about this. After a time she said 'Well, all right.' Then – 'But I didn't know you were going to Ireland.'

My mother seemed very young again, as she had done that day when we had gone bicycling over the hills.

She said 'And what else did you do in Ireland?'

I said 'Julie's a sculptor. Or rather she was, but she wants to see if one can make not objects but things come out right in life. I mean what is it that makes some things seem to come out right and others not: what is the feel we have of something being right?'

'Isn't it called love?'

'Well the word can mean almost anything now.'

'And you think Julie does this?'

'I think so. I'll find out.'

'But isn't that what's fashionable now – not to make objects, but to put ideas on show.'

'Not put on show. You see what happens.'

'And that's what she's doing with you now?'

'What?'

'By not being with you?'

I thought – That's clever, yes. Then – So cut the scene here.

– But what is it that I believe about this?

When people came to see me in my hospital room that was like a compartment in a laboratory they were supposed to put on a sterilised smock and gloves and a white cotton mask over their mouths. When my mother was with me she took off her mask, and I thought – Well that's

287

all right, she and I don't mind catching things from one another.

When I was on my own during these days I watched a certain amount of television. I liked to watch the news and current affairs programmes with the sound turned off: sound was like a bombardment, and if you were watching bombardments on the screen sound made it impossible to think. However there were continuing flashes of mysterious outbreaks of peace in the Balkans, in the Middle East; these were mentioned by commentators with an air of distrust and even embarrassment. The one place where it was reported with confidence that peace was continuing to break down was Ireland, where the stories were now of the beating up and mutilation of children.

My mother said she was going away for a time and my father would be coming to see me. I wondered if she was going to join Connie – in Paris? Hollywood? New York?

My father kept his mask on over his mouth when he was with me. I thought – Yes there has to be some protection, padding, I suppose, now between my father and me: might we be rivals?

He said 'I hear you had quite a morning with Eva.'

I said 'Are you really not going to make the film?'

'Oh I expect we'll make something. At this stage of proceedings it's all a bit of a game.'

I thought – A game between you and Eva?

– For me and Christina and Emily beneath that bridge it wasn't a game!

He said 'Is this Christina the girl that came up to us when I was with you in the pub?'

I said 'No that's her friend.'

'And they're going to look after the baby.'

'Yes.'

'Why didn't you tell us?'

'I didn't know.'

'And you don't want help.'

'Not at the moment. Thanks.'

I wondered – And how are things working out between you and Eva?

He said 'Connie said he was quite taken with some ideas you'd had about the film.'

'Oh yes, I think I said that if you were going to do it from a God's-eye view, then what God is interested in is how humans can change.'

'Not necessarily a supernatural God –'

'No –'

'You think it's to do with babies?'

'Well isn't it? And the teaching that one passes on. No not teaching. What one makes available. What one practises. From which they can learn.'

'You've read my script?'

I thought – My father thinks his script is the equivalent, for me, of my mother's story.

In my father's script there were the Arab boy and the Israeli girl who had become privy to secrets concerning a plot to blow up the Dome of the Rock. The Israeli girl came from a family of religious extremists; the Arab boy had been enrolled in a team at Beirut University working on the practicability of making the ethnically selective biological weapon. The questions at stake were – In such a situation, is it right to cling to traditional ideas of loyalty and betrayal, or can an individual see how he or she has the right to go his or her own way; according to some higher understanding of how the world works?

I said 'Wasn't that what you were saying? That an individual can believe that he or she might change the world?'

My father said 'There's a scientific theory now that this is in fact how things work. Individuals are like grains of sand in a pile. The movement, or addition, of just one grain – one grain being dropped on a hitherto stable pile – can cause an avalanche. You can't tell just what grain will cause the avalanche or when; nor just how events will fall out and resettle; there are too many millions of grains in the pile in their own critical state or equilibrium. But there it is – it's all worked out on computers – one grain dropped here or there can alter the structure, the nature, of a whole system. This seems to be the big scientific theory at the end of the twentieth century – The individual has power: though he doesn't know what power, nor what the effect will be.'

I said 'But haven't we always known that?'

'Oh yes, but now they've got it on computers.'

'But on computers people are playing games.'

'Oh yes, and they know that statistics are not reality.'

'So reality's the power that an individual has that can't be put on computers.'

My father pulled off his white cotton mask. He said 'And there's still the old theory about a bottleneck of genes; so you don't really have to wait even for the chance of genetic change; if you're ready, this may pop up.'

'Together with the avalanche.'

'Yes together with the avalanche.'

I lay in bed and wondered about the germs, the viruses, that were flying about the hospital like grains of sand: it did seem we often had the power to defeat them.

I said 'Yes, but if you accept this, and if you see that you are a peculiarly mobile grain of sand, then still, how do you find out, know, what is your power and what is not. How do you trust this.'

'Perhaps that's what my generation will have to hand over to you.'

'I sometimes think there's a bottleneck in my head.'

'Are you in pain?'

'Not always.'

'I suppose there have to be casualties. In states of mind, as well as in experience.'

I thought – You are thinking of yourself and my mother?

I said 'My friend Edward's got a friend whose family are under sentence of death in Turkey. They've welcomed the earthquake because the walls of the jails are falling down.'

'That happened to St Paul.'

'Did it?'

'Yes. And earthquakes are much the same as a pile of sand. One tiny geological fault can produce a catastrophe.'

My father's thoughts seemed to be wandering – towards how things would turn out between himself and Eva; between my mother and Connie?

I said 'I suppose you and Mum wanted to alter the world.'

He said 'And Connie. And perhaps Eva.'

'Mum's with Connie now?'

'She's coming back. She wants to be with you.'

'You're going to Jerusalem?'

'Connie still wants to make this film.'

'You'll be going with Eva?'

'It's in the contract. We need the contract. We'll see what happens then.'

I thought – There are too many old bottlenecks bunged up with earth in Jerusalem.

I imagined Julie and myself flying to Jerusalem, on our business of being two of the people for the sake of whom the world might be saved. But if one thought like this the plane might crash.

My father said 'Look, things will turn out all right between me and Mum, but one can't say too much about this, can one.'

There was a hiatus between my father going away and

my mother coming back. I sometimes had good days and sometimes bad: it seemed extraordinary that I should know less of what was going on inside my body than what I saw of the outside world on television. Bits and pieces of me were placed under microscopes or scans; indistinct images appeared on screens; once the whole of me was laid out and pushed into a tube like a coffin. On television it was being said that now that there was less large-scale violence, private violence was increasing. I wanted to learn about the aftermath of the earthquake in Turkey, but once the catastrophe itself was over, any aftermath or sorting out was not considered newsworthy. And I had no news of Julie or Peter. It sometimes seemed that the presence of Peter in Edward's house might after all have been a hallucination.

I tried to imagine my mother and Connie sitting in the elaborately candle-lit dining room of his house outside Paris, the wall of which had now been completed with its mechanisms which could call up any vision or representation one might desire. My mother was seated opposite Connie at the small round table on the daïs; she was saying 'Did you have Lennie killed?'

'Did I have Lennie killed? What a question!'

'I want to find out what matters.'

'I got rid of my newspaper, I stuck to making computers, I went into films.'

'Didn't you like what your newspaper was doing?'

'No.'

'You don't think films should just be giving people what they want?'

'No. Like Karl Marx, I wanted not just to describe history but to change it.'

'But you were being blackmailed —'

'Let's just say as they say in the movies — I didn't want Lennie dead.'

I had gathered from my father that Connie had had built on a rundown film lot outside Paris reduced-size replicas of the buildings on the Temple Mount in Jerusalem – the Dome of the Rock, the al-Aqsa Mosque, the Western Wall. There was even, incongruously huddled up, the Church of the Holy Sepulchre, though in reality this was half a mile away. When you walked inside this construction it could be seen to consist of no more than façades popped by struts and wires; it was when it was photographed at certain angles from outside that these appeared to be the Wall, the Church, the Dome, the Mosque. When my father had been taken to see this he had said – A psychologist once built a room like this to demonstrate how our minds construct so-called reality from unconnected bits and pieces. Connie had said – But it's in reality that these constructions are all much the same – the Wall, the Church, the Mosque.

My mother was saying to Connie 'So why did you want to see me again?'

'I wanted to make this film.'

'And you wanted a script.'

'Yes. And I wanted to see whether in any of our lives there is more than bits and pieces.'

'And is there?'

'Well here we are.'

'And what does that mean.'

'I'm told I'm dying. Perhaps it means – Will you keep an eye on Edward?'

'Dear Connie, yes. We always liked writing our scripts, didn't we.'

When my mother got back from France, and had come to see me in my hospital room, I said 'Well, did Connie have Lennie killed?'

'No, of course not.'

'And were there movies of you and Connie?'

'Well I didn't see any.'

'Edward thought there were.'

'Well he would wouldn't he.'

I thought – What I mean is, I would quite like to have seen them.

I said 'Does Edward know who his father is?'

'I suppose he thinks Connie is.'

'And he isn't?'

'Why not? Connie did things the way he wanted.'

'I thought you said –'

'What does it matter what I said.'

'Does Edward know who his mother is?'

'I sometimes think he likes to think I might be.'

'And you can't be?'

'Oh really!'

I thought – Well we're both of us trying to find out what's in our power to say or do: what does and doesn't matter.

– And in this cream-walled room, cork-lined noticeboard, bedside cupboard, table, chair; appliance for inserting fluids into a vein; a bed that can be adjusted to one's satisfaction like a torturer's or a masochist's rack – might not this represent a powerhouse, command post, nucleus, from which by imagining all possible worlds those which do not matter become exorcised, and those which do may come out right. I said to my mother 'I'd like to write about all this one day.'

'Then why don't you.'

'I won't know the outcome till I'm dead.'

'You never know an outcome. There's only what happens.'

'But I'll be making that?'

'You'll be doing what you do.'

I thought – For my children and my children's children I'll write a story. It will include your story. Like genes.

Then – But what on earth is Julie doing now?

I said to my mother 'Do you think Connie will leave you some of his money?'

'I don't know, do you?'

'I think Edward thinks he will.'

'Perhaps in trust for Edward.' Then – 'What sort of thing will you write? About your Irish girl? About why she's everything to you and she isn't with you?'

'That sort of thing, yes.'

'She's not the one who's having a baby?'

'No.'

'Why did you tell Eva and not me.'

'Eva asked.'

'And Eva makes films.'

'I suppose so. I was going to ask you to help look after the baby.'

'Which of course I would have done.'

'Thanks.'

'It's a bit late now.'

'There may be another one.'

'Really? You've got that all set up?'

'Not set up, no.'

'Another of your bizarre ideas about how biology works?'

'Well there needs to be two.'

'For what?'

'No. I didn't say that.'

'Look, I do seriously think you have to watch it.'

'All right.'

'Dad and I will sort things out.'

'You think so?'

'That sort of thing. Yes.'

When I was on my own again I tried to imagine my father and Eva on the reconnaissance trip to Jerusalem. Eva was a recently sought-after Hollywood producer to whom Connie had sent my father's script; she had felt puzzled and challenged; producers are said to be people who like to feel challenged until they remember that films are about what will make money; but in this case it was evident that the film would be backed by Connie's millions. And then Eva had met my father. I am not sure just when this was – before or after my father had gone back to the wildlife station to see whoever it was he wanted to see there; before or after Connie had decided to make contact again with my mother. But it is when everything seems to be happening all at once that there is the chance of changes.

But by the time my father and Eva got together the script was beginning to seem out of date. A new government had come into power in Israel and peace talks were under way between enemies that had hitherto seemed implacable. It was possible that the extremists on either side might yet be driven to a frenzied act at the prospect of peace, but a film about this would be about insanity rather than provide the warning that Connie wanted. And the hordes of Christians that it had been foretold would be converging on the Mount of Olives to await the Second Coming or indulge in mass suicide pacts, did not seem to be materialising. Commentators seemed somewhat baffled by this: was it possible that after all at the millennium nothing much would be happening? Eva said to my father – 'If you wanted a God's-eye view, God seems to have just got bored and to have got out of the kitchen.'

My father said 'Shall we go and find out?'

'You and me?'

'Of course there may be nothing cooking.'

'For God's sake we can do our own cooking!'

(I'm making these bits of dialogue up: but I feel my parents have passed on to me their way of talking.)

My father and Eva did go on their reconnaissance trip to Jerusalem. And there – after two nights or whatever in the

King David Hotel presumably doing what they had referred to as their cooking – on a grey cold day they climbed up the Mount of Olives having crossed the valley of Kidron into which it had once been thought the souls of the damned fell when they failed to make the tightrope crossing from the Holy City to the seat of Last Judgment. On the slopes there were a few squatters trying to shelter from the rain; they were crouching in hovels or small shelters built from the rocks; they were trying to keep warm but could find little to burn; might they thus have been nostalgic for the fires of hell? The police at one time had tried to move them on, but where could they go? They were like birds on ledges having lost the use of their wings. And now even the photographers and film crews had gone. My father and Eva stepped delicately round, over, recumbent or seated bodies. Eva said 'We've come all this way to discover that there's no film to be made?'

My father said 'We've come all this way to discover that if that sort of film can't be made, so what.'

'What sort of thing can we make a film about then?'

'I suppose a God's-eye view would be something we know about but can't see.'

'You think you can write a script about what you can't see?'

At the top of the slope the ground levelled out on to a stony plateau where there were a few concrete buildings like boxes on the floor of a modern art gallery. My father said 'You can write a script about the reality of wondering how things will turn out.'

Eva said 'That's what your son says.'

'I expect he got it from me. Or I got it from him.'

'Would you put that bit of dialogue in?'

There was a larger rectangular building at the top of the hill that might once have been a barracks or a school. There were lights on inside; on the hill it was already dusk, and the sky above the city across the valley was streaked with red like layers of lava from a volcano. My father went up to the outside wall of the building and found a concrete block on which he could stand. He looked through a small square window. Eva said 'What do you see?'

'It's a hospital.'

'What sort of hospital?'

'Casualties. Sickness.'

'Perhaps they have started killing themselves. Perhaps that weapon they all talk about has gone off.'

'No I don't think so, it's just ordinary.'

'What's ordinary.'

'People dying. People trying to do something about it. Come and see.'

My father made room for Eva to come up on to the stone beside him. She said 'No I don't want to.'

'Why not?'

'I thought you wanted to find out about what you can't see.'

'Yes.'

'All right then.'

They walked on over the hill. It seemed that they might be getting into a sort of no-man's-land where it would be dangerous or forbidden to move at night. My father said 'We can go back to the hotel.'

'I don't want to go back to the hotel.'

'Right.'

'You'll be going back home soon, won't you.'

'I suppose so. Yes.'

'Why can't one hang on to what's been good?'

'Because what's good is what one can go on from.'

'Go east, young man, go east! Walk away from the sunset!'

Towards the end of my time in hospital I began to get

298

out of bed and I was very wobbly. I walked with a stick. I thought – I am demonstrating all in one image the answer to the riddle of the sphinx. I still had heard no word from Julie. I still tried to believe there was something being tried, worked out, in my not hearing from Julie. Well did we or did we not believe this? I had a message from Edward saying that he and Stanislaus would come and visit me as soon as they got back. I wondered – Get back from where? Turkey?

I thought – What if they find there's not much happening in Turkey.

In England it was becoming a cold and wet time of year. And whatever excitement or ridicule there had been about plans to celebrate the millennium these seemed to be evaporating together with stories of collapse of communication systems due to the millennium bug. I said to my mother 'Perhaps there is something in the millennium business after all.'

'Such as what?'

'Nothing. Look, peace is even breaking out all over the shop in Ireland.'

'Don't you believe it.'

'Oh but I do! Of course people will have to go on saying something's happening.'

I wondered – Might Julie and I have started some sort of avalanche when we were on that island?

My mother said 'When you're well enough I think you should get away.'

'Where to?'

'Somewhere east. To the sun.'

'I might go to Turkey. Edward and Stanislaus are trying to set up some Garden of Eden in Turkey.'

'You can't possibly go to Turkey!'

'Why not?'

'It's freezing, and there are earthquakes, and of course it's nothing to do with the Garden of Eden or where the Ark came down.'

'Where is that then?'

'In your head, my darling.'

I could not remember my mother calling me her darling before.

She said 'You could go and join your father. He says he'd like that. He seems to have reached somewhere by the Red Sea.'

'Will you come too?'

'I don't know.'

'Is Eva still with him?'

'I don't think so. She left a message on her way back asking how you were.'

'I think Eva was rather keen on me.'

'Oh yes. And I expect your father thinks he'll find the origins or secrets of life when the waters have parted for him and revealed the bottom of the Red Sea.'

I practised walking along the corridors of the hospital. I thought – Well they had to keep fit, those people in the Ark, wherever it came down; and at least one goes diving, doesn't one, in the Red Sea?

– And perhaps Eva might one day make a film of us, of me and Julie and Emily and Christina, with one or two of us jumping off a bridge into the sea.

My mother said 'Look, you go and join your father. I'll come later.'

'Why not come now?'

'Connie's dying. He doesn't want Phyllis. I've rather said I'll take him on.'

'Don't you be decent and not let him leave you any money.'

'You worry about your Irish girl.'

'I do.'

'What about the other one.'

'Indeed.'

'I used to think it was wise to have some sort of back up.'

'And you did, didn't you.'

'And then the main thing may have a better chance of coming out all right.'

When I was on my own, in the middle of the night, I imagined Connie lying awake in his house outside Paris and wanting to perform some deed before he died that would seem like reality. He had lost interest in his film about Jerusalem: the world seemed to have moved on and left Jerusalem washed up in a desert. But what had he ever imagined it might stand for? Had not Jerusalem been where there had been destroyed those who might save the world? Connie got out of bed and found a dressing gown and went out of his house taking care to avoid the people who were supposed to be guarding him. They were not paying much attention to him now, because he was said to be dying. In the drive he found a small car that belonged to one of his bodyguards; he was not sure if he remembered how to drive; he managed to get to the gates and through them because the guard seemed to be watching television. Connie thought he would drive to the film set where he had built the replicas of the buildings in Jerusalem: the Dome and the Wall and the Mosque with the Church of the Holy Sepulchre nestling up against them. Connie thought he might go there like a beggar and sit outside the walls till he died; or perhaps even set fire to the whole structure like a gigantic funeral pyre. When he reached the film set there was a fence around it and a guardhouse with the sounds of more people watching television. Connie left the car and went along the fence supporting himself with his hands on the wire: he was an old soothsayer who had exiled himself from the Holy City; an old God who had thought himself omnipotent and now on his deathbed needed absolution. He came to a place in the fence where the bottom wire had been pulled up as if people before him had broken in; he got down on his hands and knees and crawled through. At the far side was a continuation of wasteland and then what looked like the outline of a walled city. This was the construction that he had built and had dreamed of knocking down like the Romans had done before him; or even God himself, in exasperation, with fire and brimstone. Connie had used to imagine himself a Roman; he had liked to give people what they wanted – circuses and destruction. Now he wanted to look inside and see how after all things had been kept going. When he got to the Wall he put out a hand and it swayed to his touch; he would have to be careful or indeed the whole structure might fall down. At intervals there were gaps in the wall where one section had been placed slightly behind another to make it possible for it to be propped. Connie went through one of the gaps, and then instead of a city there was an area open to the sky with a few people on the ground seated round a campfire. They seemed to have found fuel for this by hacking pieces off the props and façades. They were cooking. There were dogs prowling around but they did not seem to notice Connie. Connie went and sat by the fire with a group that consisted mainly of children. They regarded him gravely: they did not seem to be interested in why he had come or where he had come from. He estimated that it would be many years before they had used up all the wood in the structure for fuel. He was offered some food, for which he was grateful. From the props and wires that supported the façades there were hung bits of washing that drooped and occasionally fluttered in the gentle air like prayer flags.

XIII

My mother came to see me on to the plane. My father was to meet me at the other end of the journey. I was to travel business class because the fare was being paid by Connie's film company. There had been an arrangement for a wheelchair to get me round the airport, but when it came I said I didn't want it. My mother said 'Why not?' I said 'I want to feel free.' My mother said 'What, to disappear again?'

I repeated 'Why don't you come too?'

'I said I will. Later.'

'Connie can't just have disappeared.'

'Why not, it would be like him.'

In fact I wanted to be on my own because however much I hoped that my father and mother would be reconciled, I had the idea that Julie might still turn up at the airport. There had been a message to my mother ostensibly from Connie's office asking for details of my flight since they might have someone travelling out, they said, who would keep an eye on me. I had said this was the last thing I wanted; then I had imagined that the message might have come from Julie or from Peter, as the previous one had done that had reached me at Edward's house. And however much this could be thought mad, it had got me as far as the airport.

My mother said 'Tell your father I may be coming.'

After I had left my mother at the barrier I was still looking round for Julie: there was a moment when I imagined I saw her: I wondered if I would soon be hallucinating again. I was taken on an electric buggy to the business class waiting room where there were people burrowing into their laptops and strung up on their mobile phones. I wondered what form a message from Julie might take. The message I had had before through Peter had just told me not to worry.

We were still a week or two away from the millennium but there had been recurrent talk about the bug: it was also said that hackers or crackers were developing a bug of their own, so that if the inbuilt one was a myth there would still be businesses collapsing and planes falling out of the sky. I had thought – But this is not the sort of power that is supposed to be delegated to the individual!

Because I was still supposed to be frail I was amongst the first to be ushered on to the plane; in the cabin there was an empty seat beside me. I played the game of – Well, if no one comes to occupy this seat within the next five minutes then why should it not be for Julie? There's some value at least for hope in such games. A hostess leaned over me and said 'How are you feeling?' I said 'Fairly mad.' She laughed and flashed her eyes and said 'And a bit bad I hope!' I thought – That's what my mother meant by its being a help to have a back-up.

I got slightly drunk on the stuff that came with the late lunch; the hostess filled me up solicitously. I thought – They have been warned I may die on the plane, and they want me to go quietly? The seat beside me remained empty.

After lunch there was a film on the small screen at the back of the seat in front of me which gave the impression that I was looking into the back of someone's head. The film was a commonplace one about urban decay and violence; communications and law and order had broken down; gangs of humans and androids roamed the streets. I thought – There is not much need for a millennium bug when all these viruses have the run of our heads.

I was beginning to feel extremely depressed or even ill again. The feeling became localised, as it had done before, in a void between my head and my guts which nevertheless contained pain. In the hospital I had wondered whether one should not make a pre-emptive strike against sickness while one still had the chance; but in a hospital it is impossible to get oneself to die. Here, was it possible to smash a window and get oneself sucked out of a plane? I did not think so. It would be more feasible to wait and see if the plane fell out of the sky.

I must have dozed for a while because I had a half-conscious dream of that desolate landscape with the lake and the ruined tower; our plane was coming in to make an emergency landing; it bumped and clattered over stony ground. There was another small plane on the ground nearby with Edward and Stanislaus standing beside it; they were in First World War flying gear and carried pistols. Running towards them was a horde of figures in black – monks or assassins, one couldn't tell – and Edward and Stanislaus were facing them calmly. Behind them on the walls of the tower were one or two of those ironic saints and animals looking down. And within – I went groping after this to keep a hold on it while I woke – was Christina holding her baby and Emily was with them so that they were like the Virgin and Child with St Anne.

When I became properly awake there seemed to be a slight sense of unease in the business class cabin; it was as if whatever images or anxieties had been stirred by the film or by rumours of bugs were leaking out into the atmosphere from the backs of people's heads. Hostesses were hurrying up the aisle from the economy class cabin and squeezing into the pilot's compartment at the front; a steward stood at the door into this as if to guard it from a possible rush. I thought – They have had news of computer failure and the crew are preparing to bale out (can they do this?) and leave the passengers to their fate. Well this was a popular sort of film too. Or perhaps that hazardous biological weapon had gone off on the ground and we would be unable to land; we would go on flying like an albatross for ever or until the fuel ran out. Our hostess was being waylaid as she came back down the aisle; she was saying 'No problems, the captain will be making an announcement shortly.' I thought – So that does mean something serious is happening? And then of course my pre-emptive strike need not occur.

There was a slight commotion going on at the curtain separating the economy class and the business class cabins. I imagined – A man with a balaclava helmet and a gun; a hijacker who will force his way into the captain's cabin and persuade him to fly to – where? – to join Stanislaus's and Edward's revolutionaries in old Armenia? There I might join Christina and Emily in a beehive-dome construction and wait for Julie. And Peter might already have got there? Or if we were made to go to some grim alternative world such as, say, Afghanistan, then I could offer myself as the first hostage to be shot and thus become a martyr-hero because no one would know of my previous feebleness in wanting to die anyway.

Then I became aware that Julie was standing in the aisle by the empty seat beside me. This did not seem possible; but it seemed too exactly right not to be real. In this it was unlike the time before when Peter had opened the door for me in Edward's house and in bewilderment I had imagined he might be Julie. Julie was arguing with the hostess and was saying 'But I've got a ticket for this seat, I had two tickets, one for the economy and one for here, it's just that I haven't got the one for here with me at the moment.' The hostess said 'How did you come to have two tickets?' Julie said 'Someone's supposed to travel with him, he's been ill, then they couldn't come.' I was thinking – Julie, Julie I know you can do this, but it is not bearable, it is breaking through all probabilities, why haven't you come up here before? The hostess was being called up to the captain's cabin; Julie was settling down into the seat beside me. I said 'Julie, where have you been, why haven't you come up here before?' She said 'I wanted to be sure.' I said 'Sure about what?' 'That I could stay with you.' The hostess was coming back down the aisle and indeed she now went past Julie without paying any attention to her. Julie said 'Apparently there's trouble at wherever it is we were going to land.' I said 'How do you know that?' She said 'There was a man sitting beside me.'

Julie was wearing a white shirt and white trousers so that she was like Peter the last time I had last seen him except that her head was not shaved and indeed her hair seemed to be darker and more golden. She leaned forwards and rested her forehead against the blank screen on the back of the seat in front of her and said as if she were acting – 'Oh I know this is awful! I do want things to be normal! I don't want things always to be like this!' I thought – All right, Julie, all right: you don't really have to go through rituals like this.

Then she sat up and faced me and said 'I did look for you at the airport, but you were with your mother, and I didn't want to spoil things. Then I couldn't find you.'

'I was on my way up here.'

'Then I wanted to wait for a time when they wouldn't stop me coming up.'

She waited, watching me. Then she began half-acting again – 'Oh I know it's mostly luck, but we do have something to do with it!'

I said 'Yes, Julie.'

'All right it is just luck, but we do have to put up with it!'

'Yes, it's all right, Julie.'

Her eyes had filled with tears. Then she put her head against my shoulder and said 'It's sometimes so difficult.'

I put my arm round her and held her. I thought – It's when things that you've trusted have worked out right, they're almost unbearable. Then – She's making this bearable.

Then she sat up and smiled and looked at me and said 'But you did get my message?'

I said 'Yes.'

'Oh well that's all right.' She lay back and closed her eyes.

There was a scraping noise over the loudspeakers like that of an ancient gramophone being wound up with the needle already on the record. Then there was the hesitant, almost languid voice of the captain trying to reassure us. He was saying that information had been received that our flight might have to be diverted since conditions on the ground at our scheduled destination had become unsuitable for landing. It was not yet clear if this was due to climatic conditions – freak thunderstorms were not unusual at this time of year – but there was anyway no cause for alarm since he, the captain, and his crew, had everything under control, and they would pass on any further information as it came in.

I said 'But why didn't you visit me in hospital?'

She said 'I had to make things all right in Ireland.'

'And did you do that?'

'Yes. And you were being looked after by your mother.'

'Yes that was right.'

'And you wanted to find out about Christina and the baby.'

'Yes.'

'Well what happened?'

'Christina and Emily want to look after the baby.'

'They do?'

'Yes.'

'Oh that's wonderful!' She sat up. She stared straight in front of her as if she had seen a vision.

I said 'It was going to be difficult for you about the baby?'

She said 'Oh perhaps it was; but it wouldn't have been now anyway.'

I thought I might say – What do you mean, now?

I said 'But what did you mean, you wanted to be sure?'

She said 'I wanted to be sure I could stay with you, I mean not just when I came up here, but properly, so there would be no question.'

I watched her. I thought – You mean, there was some sort of grain of sand on that island causing an avalanche? I said 'And now you are sure?'

'Yes.'

'Julie!'

'Yes?'

'You can't know yet.'

'I can.'

'There hasn't been time.'

'There has.'

'What did you do in Ireland?'

'I stayed in the cottage. I wanted to get everything ready. Even if we never needed it. Even if something quite different happened.'

'As it has.'

'Yes.' She put her head on my shoulder again. She said 'Even if there's nowhere to land, do you think anything could possibly be better than this?'

The atmosphere in the cabin of the plane had become more

calm. People who had been trying to see what was happening outside were now lying back in their seats with their eyes closed, listening to earphones. We were travelling above and sometimes through clouds; and since we were heading east, these were becoming tinged with red from the setting sun.

Julie said 'I don't think I really knew until I had got the cottage ready. Then I realised that the cottage didn't matter. If I was having a baby, we'd have it with us wherever we were. So I set off to find you.'

'Does the man you were talking to think he knows where we might be going?'

'He thinks Cyprus. Or Turkey.'

'Did Peter tell you about my friends Edward and Stanislaus who are on their way to Turkey?'

'Yes, that's where Peter wanted to go.'

'You saw Peter?'

'Cyprus is where when Venus was born she came floating ashore in a shell.'

'It may be a boy.'

'Oh it may be anything! Everyone will be what they will!' She sat up excitedly. One or two people looked round.

The voice of the captain was coming over the speakers again now more wearily. He was saying that information had been received that we were going to be allowed to land, at least to refuel; and if necessary accommodation would be provided for us. But he still did not seem to be saying where.

I said 'If you could choose, where would you go?'

'I don't think that place where Christina was digging. That's in the past.'

'Then not Jerusalem.'

'No not Jerusalem!'

'My father's staying somewhere by the Red Sea.'

'Does this plane have parachutes!'

'Of course it doesn't have parachutes!'

'I don't know. I don't know about planes. What are those things they were saying were under the seats?'

'Those are life jackets for if we come down in the sea.'

'I think I'd rather come down like a seed on to land.'

'I think we've got past Cyprus and Turkey.'

I thought – Or perhaps we're like mythical birds that might stay in the air for ever.

After the captain's latest announcement people were sitting up and looking round the cabin and talking as if they might discover from one another where they were going. Outside, on the clouds, there was a giant shape swooping and coming close and then disappearing: this was our shadow cast by the setting sun. It seemed to be now here, now there, so it was difficult to tell in what direction we were heading.

Julie said 'You were going to write something.'

'Yes.'

'So how was it going to end?'

'It wasn't.'

'And I can illustrate it.'

'Yes. But I thought we weren't going to do that sort of thing.'

'Oh of course we'll do that sort of thing! Now there's some point to it.'

'So it can learn.'

'Yes.' She laughed. 'Oh all right, so they can learn!'

Outside the plane the clouds briefly separated and there was a view of the sea far below. And because the light from the setting sun was colouring the edges of clouds, it was as if these were waters that were red, and the sea's surface was like its depths far below. Just above this there was a small aeroplane flying; or it might have been our shadow, or a bird.

She said 'And why shouldn't it sometimes seem too good to be true? The fact that there's life at all is like a fairy story!'

I said 'Yes.'

'How did life begin? The chances against it were billions and billions to one.'

'Yes.'

'And how does life carry on? It's death that's likely.'

'Yes.'

'And we'll have survived because if we hadn't we couldn't have written and illustrated it.'

'They won't be there if we don't survive. At least not two of them.'

'And that's all they'll need.'

'So we can stop talking.'

'Yes. Here. Stop talking.'

Nicholas Mosley

HOPEFUL MONSTERS

Whitbread Book of the Year

'A gigantic achievement that glows and grows long after it is
put aside'
Independent on Sunday

Meeting at a confrontation between Nazi and communist
youth on the streets of Weimar Germany, Max and Eleanor
begin a love affair that takes them from Stalin's Russia to
Los Alamos on the eve of the atomic age.

'This is a major novel by any standard of measurement. Its
ambition is lofty, its intelligence startling, and its sympathy
profound. It is frequently funny, sometimes painful, sometimes moving...It is a novel which makes the greater part of
contemporary fiction seem pygmy in comparison'
Allan Massie, *The Scotsman*

'Quite simply, the best English novel to have been written
since the Second World War'
N. Wilson, *Evening Standard*

'Enormously ambitious and continuously fascinating'
Paul Binding, *New Statesman and Society*

VINTAGE